CRASH

CRASH

DREW JORDAN

Interior Formatted by

BOOKS BY
DREW JORDAN

Crash
Hide
Expose

PART
ONE

CHAPTER ONE

Yᴏᴜ'ᴅ ᴛʜɪɴᴋ ᴛʜᴀᴛ ᴛʜᴇ ɢʀᴇᴀᴛᴇsᴛ love stories would start with something tender, but they don't.

They start with blood.

Like Romeo and Juliet's.

Marc Anthony and Cleopatra's.

Lancelot and Guinevere's.

And mine.

I smelled it first. The tinny, sharp tangy odor of fresh blood. And I felt it. Warm, sticky. It forced my eyes open, dragged me back from oblivion, where I had landed on impact. The first thing I saw was not the pilot or the floor or my leg wedged under the seat, but him.

A stranger, in black nylon, hair and beard dusted in snow, knit hat on his head, a strip of fabric in his hands, smeared red with my blood as he wrapped it around my arm. Confusion gave way to pain; raging, angry, snorting, bull-charging-through-crowds pain that made me cry out. His head turned at the sound and what I saw there had me instinctively pulling back, away from him. His eyes were the palest blue I had ever seen, like a filter had been put on the sky, draining the color. They weren't warm or compassionate or sympathetic. They were intense. Efficient. Passionate. The kind of eyes that make you instantly uncomfortable, like their owner could reach inside your body and swipe your soul.

Or maybe that was just the pain.

The trauma.

The fear.

All causing me to think strange, random thoughts.

I was a hundred percent certain I wasn't unconscious. The pain was too overbearing, too rich. Invasive. It throbbed and prodded, owning my leg, my arm, my chest. I tried to move, to shift away from him, but he held my aching arm still and my leg was stuck, trapped under something. My head throbbed, but I swallowed the bile that rose and spoke, my breath coming out in a visible mist in front of me.

"Why is it so quiet?" I asked. "Where are the others?" The pilot and the other passenger on the plane with me. Had they been injured or was I the only one? Either way, the air around me felt too still.

The silence was brittle, overwhelming. All I could hear was the wind outside and the rustling of the fabric as he wound it around my arm, over and over. Why was it taking so long to wrap? It was a thousand rotations, a million miles of fabric. Something was dripping, a monotonous plink on metal. There was nothing but pain and blood and the absence of explanations.

It took only a heartbeat for him to answer but that second felt endless, a tremulous wave of uncertainty, and in that brief span, the guttural knowledge that this was bad rushed over me.

"They're dead."

His tone was flat. His words matter-of-fact. I blinked, stunned. Then I panicked.

I didn't know the pilot or the passenger. I had just met them in Fairbanks when I climbed on the plane. But that was only an hour ago, or at least an hour of flight time. I had no idea how long I'd been unconscious. And now they were dead? No longer breathing, never wake up, fully one hundred percent not alive? It freaked me the fuck out and I heard my cry, a weird, low keening cry that morphed into gulping sobs.

"You're fine," he said, his voice low and smooth. "Just a sprained ankle and a laceration. Most likely a concussion. Maybe a bruised rib."

Did he think I was crying for me? No. I was crying for them. For the two men- Jack and Al, who had introduced themselves cheerfully and shook my hand. Jack was a trapper returning home after the summer tour months and Al was a twenty-year bush pilot. That's what I knew. All I knew. And now they were dead.

When I started to shove at the man with the bullish eyes with my free hand for a reason even I didn't understand, hysteria crawling up my throat and threatening to cut off my air supply, he stared at me, calmly. "Stop it."

"No!" I didn't even know what I was protesting. Not him. Just… everything.

"I can't carry you out of here if you don't stop."

In my frantic flailing my hand hit his face. His head snapped back and he went still, eyes narrowing. I stopped instantly. Out of fear, though I wasn't sure why. Then behind the stranger as he shifted, I caught sight of the pilot slumped over the dash. I saw his eyes, open. Blank. The dripping was the wound from his head. Drip, drip, drip as it landed on the floor. A beautiful rich puddle of blood was oozing toward my leg. I started to yank my trapped foot. No, no, no. That river of death couldn't touch me. It couldn't. I looked at the stranger, unable to speak, desperate for help, tugging so hard it felt like my hip dislocated from the socket. I swore I heard a pop.

The stranger's bloody hand came over my face, pinching my nose, covering my mouth. I fought, hard, turning my head. Right. Left.

Then nothing.

CRASH

———◆———

When I woke up again, it was because of the bouncing. It was like dropping into potholes in a truck without shocks, at a speed of fifty miles an hour. Bam. Bam. Bam. With each slam of my body, my leg screamed in pain, my teeth rattled. Prying my eyes open I saw nothing but black and white. There was black right next to my face and beyond that, the blinding sparkling white of snow. I was being carried and the dizziness proved I was upside down. I was on the stranger's back, strapped to him like a caribou carcass. Fear of falling instantly rushed over me and I tried to grab his leg to steady myself, but I realized my hands were tied to his leg already. There was no way for me to wrap my palms around his calf. My feet were strapped down too when I tried to wiggle them.

The jarring I felt was every step he took through the heavy snow. I'd been told on the plane it was the first snowfall of the season and likely to melt, but right now it was causing the stranger to lift his knees higher than normal, bouncing me heavily. He was saving my life. I was aware of that on some level. Yet at the same time, the idea of being carried on his back, like a kill he'd landed after hours of patient stalking, unnerved me. My stomach protested the movement, the pain, the panic. I started to heave, coughing and choking as I splashed vomit across the snow in a wide arch. It went up my nose and burned and a second round came up, the heat of the bile hitting the cool air in a steamy, stinky mess.

The stranger eased down onto his knees, so that I rested closer to the ground. I sucked in a breath, determined not to repeat that a third time. My eyes were watering, a single tear dropping down onto the snow and disappearing.

"You okay?" he asked.

I couldn't really even see his legs or feet anymore. They were tucked under me. It was the strangest sensation, being upside down and blind to everything but the snow and the trail behind us of his footsteps.

Was I okay? No. No, I wasn't. But that wasn't going to fix or help the situation and not only was I in pain, I was cold. My fingers were burning and my nose felt like sharp needles were being shoved into it. I couldn't feel my ears. Even though it felt like I'd been wrapped in a blanket before being tied to him, it wasn't providing much protection. The less I said, the sooner he could carry me to safety and I could raise my head, right my world. Process what had happened.

"Yes," I managed, my voice raspy and foreign. "Thank you." It was an inane thing to say, but it felt necessary.

He just grunted in return and rose to his feet again. That was no small task, lifting my dead weight. The stranger was strong. As he walked and I bounced, I thought about the pain. I thought about the pilot and the passenger. I thought about Michael, waiting for me to arrive at the airstrip, wondering why I was so late. Had the plane radioed for help? The last minutes before the crash had been normal, nothing alarming. Then suddenly we were dropping and I was bracing my body and eating my heart in my throat. And then there was nothing.

Until the pain. And the blood. And him.

He had knocked me unconscious when I'd fought him. He had pinched my nose and covered my mouth so I would pass out. So he could help me. So he could tie me to him.

It was a disturbing thought and I wasn't sure why. He was saving my life. If he hadn't come along, I would have died of exposure in the wreckage before anyone found me. I was sure of that. We were in the middle of the Yukon. On the way to nothing, passing over even more of nothing. No roads. No towns. Just isolated homes by those willing to attempt survival in Alaska.

Really, it was damn near a miracle this man had found me, though a plane crash must make a lot of noise. It must have been terrible, a howling, screaming collision of metal and earth, machinery and trees. I shuddered, glad I didn't remember it. But in the background now, I could hear something. Barking. Or more like a careening howl of multiple animals. Wolves? Fear made me clench up from shoulders to thighs.

"Are those wolves?" I asked.

But he didn't hear me. The landscape snatched my words on the wind and flung them off in a swirl of blowing snow. Or that's what I assumed. Maybe he was ignoring me. Either way, his stride didn't change as the barking got louder and I started to think maybe it was dogs, not wolves. My head was pounding and the barking was increasing and the jarring was aching and the world was spinning.

I closed my eyes and prayed for oblivion.

It didn't come and by the time the man was climbing steps, the wood creaking beneath our mutual weight, I was afraid I was going to throw up again. My teeth were chattering and my body was shaking from the cold. The fevered pitch of the barking dogs made it clear they were only feet away and this man was their owner. They were excited to see him. The clink of chains cut through the cacophony but he ignored them and opened a door with a shove. When he stepped inside and shut it behind us, turning me about ninety degrees, I panted, trying to regain my breath, trying to quell the nausea in my stomach. Warm air rushed over me, prompting another shiver. The door closing muffled the wild symphony of the dogs barking.

My hands were untied. The rope belt he wore around us both was loosened quickly and I was sliding up and over his shoulder, down the length of his chest. The blood rushed to my head and my vision went spotty and black. I reached out and tried to grab his coat to hold myself up but my fingers were numb, ineffectual. The blanket caught under my feet and I would have crumpled to the floor if his strong arms hadn't grabbed me by the armpits and held me up.

"Don't put any weight on your foot," he ordered.

I learned that a second too late. Pain lapped at my leg,

radiating from my foot to my knee, protesting loudly when I tried to stand on it. The dancing spots receded and I focused on the zipper of the nylon coat in front of me. There was snow and ice on it. For a reason I couldn't explain, I stuck my tongue out and flicked it over the ice, maybe to taste that it was real. This was real. But my warm tongue stuck to his cold metal zipper and I let out a cry.

His grip shifted to my hair. My head jerked back from his less than gentle touch as he wrenched my tongue free. "What are you doing?" he asked.

"I don't know." I shifted my gaze to stare up at him. Those blue eyes met my gaze, coolly. Emotionless.

That's when I started to cry. Great, powerful sobs that wracked my chest and produced snot instantly, which seemed to freeze in a glazed streak above my lip on my still icy cold skin. It was an ugly cry, the humiliating guttural sound of a woman totally losing her shit. Oh, God, oh, God. I was hysterical and I was bleeding and I was puking and I really, really needed to pull myself together.

"I'm picking you up. Don't fight me."

I had no intention of fighting. There was no fight in me.

He lifted me off the ground and carried me a few feet. There he deposited me on a bed and the soft sink of fabric beneath my ass felt like a marshmallow. It was a down comforter. And warm. The puffy white cloud of fabric rose on either side of my thighs as I descended into its depths. My teeth chattered and for a wild minute when he started to peel the blanket off, I felt fear. Deep, intense, powerful fear. Instinctively I jerked back, wanting space, but as he yanked the blanket out from under me, I forced myself to still. To take stock. To try to calm down.

Bending over so he was eye to eye with me, he said in a low voice, "You need warm and dry clothes. I'm going to cut these off of you."

"Cut them off?" I asked, stupidly parroting him. Why couldn't we just take them off? "Why?"

CRASH

"Your leg is too swollen and I don't want to unwrap your arm. I could peel your clothes off but it would hurt like hell."

That scared me more than losing a pair of jeans and a cable knit sweater. "It hurts enough already."

"Then cutting it is." He stood up and yanked a hunting knife out of his boot.

Now that he was standing, I had an even greater sense of how muscular and commanding he was. He filled the space in front of me, and shrank the confines of the small cabin. That he was holding a knife was equally as intimidating. He was still wearing all his outdoor gear, so I didn't have a clear view of his build or his features, but he wasn't above thirty and he was neither skinny nor overweight. He looked fit and healthy and raw. Masculine.

His hands skimmed off my boot on my injured foot more gently than I would have imagined, but it still made me grimace in pain. "I'll get you some aspirin in a minute," he said. "First we need to warm you up. Your fingers are frozen."

He was right. A glance down showed they were a curious white color, like all the blood had been vacuumed out of them. "Do I have frostbite?"

"Just the beginning stage. Frostnip."

That unexplainably made me giggle. But it was a silly word. It just burbled out of me.

He glanced up at me, the knife in his hand, and the laughter died on my lips. My God, his eyes were so intense. He looked like he could raise the knife and slit my throat. After giving me an orgasm.

The thoughts were so contradictory, so strange, I felt my cheeks flush. "Where are we?" I asked.

"My house." He bent his head again and inserted the knife into my jeans and sliced.

I winced at the tear of the denim, though I wasn't sure why. It just sounded… harsh. "But where?"

"Yukon river. Forty miles from the nearest town." Once the jeans were cut open on my bad leg, he peeled my sock off gently.

Then he stood up and went to the other side of the room and rummaged around in a drawer. When he came back, he bound my ankle tightly with a bandage and slipped a warm wool sock on over my bare foot. "We'll elevate it in a minute."

He repeated the process of cutting my jeans on the other leg and replacing my damp, bloody sock with the other half of the wool pair. It felt odd to have a man I'd never met sliding socks onto my feet. It was intimate, a caregiver's role. A mother to child. Nurse to patient. A lover to a lover. But I felt a palpable relief when each sock was in place, my eyes focusing on the top of his head. The snow on his hat was melting a little and I felt sleepy, disconnected from my body.

"Lay down," he commanded me, moving up from the squat position he'd been in.

Suddenly it felt sexual, invasive, which was ridiculous. But I still asked, "Why?"

"So I can take your pants off." He stared at me, waiting.

I stared back, anxious.

"I'm not going to hurt you." His voice was low, rumbling, yet somehow smooth. He touched my knee. "Lie down, Laney."

A shiver crawled across my skin. "How do you know my name?" I whispered.

"Your purse was next to you on the floor. I looked inside to see who you are."

"Oh." It seemed logical and I lay back on the bed, sighing in relief to be on the soft mattress. The ceiling was exposed wood beams running across in a standard grid. Very Alaskan. Not that I knew Alaska. Not really. Only what Michael had told me and what I'd read online and in one sad travel guide. From the slew of TV shows on the Discovery Channel featuring it. Alaska was a ratings boost these days for whatever reason.

The pain in my ankle was a sharp throb, and my fingers were starting to itch and burn. It hit me again that I had almost died. That two other people had and yet here I was. Alive. It seemed surreal and yet so real it was agonizing and terrifying. I was four months past my twenty-fourth birthday. I wasn't supposed to die this young. Apparently fate had agreed and I was rattled, but really fucking grateful.

I wondered how long it would take my stepfather to worry, to figure out what had happened. To inform my mother where she sat in federal prison for tax evasion that I'd been in a plane crash. My eight year old sister would be scared. I'd have to ask… *the stranger* if I could borrow a phone.

"What's your name?" I asked.

"It's not important."

I frowned at the ceiling. "What do you mean? What am I supposed to call you?"

"Whatever you want."

"Who are you?" I half sat up, regretting my question instantly. What if he said, "Your worst nightmare?" I would have a heart attack. But that was ridiculous. My anxiety was on overdrive because of everything that had happened, and the pain was making me nauseated again.

His fingers were on my waist and I realized what he was doing a second too late. When he undid my snap and slid my zipper down I was stunned into silence.

"I'm the man who saved your life by accident. I didn't come to this part of Alaska to have a name, so just call me anything."

He had cut my jeans all the way up both sides so that when he undid the zipper, the front was just a flap that fell down between my thighs, leaving me from the waist down in nothing but my panties and shredded denim. His fingers brushed over the front of my panties as he gripped the remains of my jeans and pulled them away from my body. He tossed them on the floor. Goosebumps raced up my legs and spread out over my body. It seemed desperately important that I know his name.

"Are you hiding?" I asked. "Is that why you won't tell me your name?"

He paused, knife still in his left hand. His eyes narrowed, but then he gave me a smile, the corner of his mouth turning up and making him look younger, more approachable. "Everyone here is hiding from something. From their past, from people in general, or someone in particular. But I'm not wanted by the FBI, if that's what you're asking."

He flipped the corner of his comforter over my exposed lower body. The initial breeze it created was replaced by the soft warmth of the down. Between that and the socks, I was getting the shivering under control. But now I was fixating on him. "So then just tell me your name."

The man bent over me, and studied my face. His eyes swept upwards and downwards. "You're very beautiful," he said. "It's been a long time since I've seen a woman."

The scrutiny made me uncomfortable, aware of how isolated I was, how utterly alone I was with this man. His words sounded a little creepy, yet he didn't look dangerous. He was intense, with a presence that filled the room, his movements sure. But he didn't seem like he wanted to hurt me in any way. Though maybe that's just what I wanted to tell myself. What I had to tell myself.

"I can't even see you," I said. "You're bundled up. Like a mountain man."

"I guess I am a mountain man." Then he seemed to snap out of his musings and he went over to the dresser again. He came back with a flannel shirt and sweat pants. For me, I had to assume.

Despite the pain in my arm and the awkward binding, I probably could have removed my sweater and put on the warm and clean flannel. But for some reason I just lay there, on my back, and let him skim my sweater up over my breasts and carefully remove my arms from the sleeves. His hands were rough, callused, a workingman's hands, yet he was gentle. He'd put his knife between his teeth, and I focused on the shine of the blade, the sharp gleaming edge that had torn through thick denim like it was butter. My eyelids felt heavy, like I was being dragged under into anesthetic pre-surgery. A drugged sensation.

The man rolled me slightly onto my side and popped my

sweater off over my head. Then I felt his fingers on my back, fumbling with the clasp of my bra. "What are you doing?" I asked, trying to shift away.

"There's blood on you," he said. "But I can leave it if you prefer. Do you want me to leave it?"

It sounded so ridiculous when he said it like that. A glance down showed that blood had soaked through my sweater and was smeared on my stomach. My previously ivory colored bra was stained a rust color in two spots. It wasn't a lot of blood, but it did make my stomach flip because it reminded me of that dripping sound on the plane and the puddle that had been reaching for me on the floor. The man had a voice that made me feel deferential. Or maybe it was that he knew what he was doing, and I didn't. Either way, it felt childish and unnecessary to insist he leave my bra on. He wasn't hitting on me. He had saved my life. My modesty seemed conceited and insulting to him. Seduction wouldn't be on his mind. Helping me was.

"No. It's okay. Take it off." Then I added, "Thank you."

He popped my bra open and eased the straps down over my arms, taking care with the bandage. When I was bare-chested, nipples taut from the air and my still-chilled body, I felt the ache for a man out of instinct. For him to turn and cover my breast with his mouth and lave at my nipple. My sexual experience of late had been non-existent. Life had been too complicated for relationships and I'd never been one for going online or to a club in search of a hookup. But it was a ludicrous time to be aroused. I told myself it was because I had almost died. Because here I was alive, and his touch was kind, his aura very masculine. Besides, he was undressing me and by association that meant sex.

I hadn't been touched a lot. Not really. So my body was as confused as my thoughts. He didn't have the touch of a nurse. It was that of a man.

But the man didn't bend over and flick his hot tongue over my tight nipple. But he did let his eyes drift casually over my nudity. There was no reaction and I found myself disappointed, stupidly so. I wanted the comfort of a lover, not clinical efficiency. He got me into the flannel shirt the way you would with a baby, and buttoned me up.

"Sit up," he urged, "and get under the covers. I'm going to get some warm water for your fingers to unthaw them."

He pulled my good arm, and I sat up, the room spinning slightly. Then I did what he said, moving backwards until I reached the headboard, sliding beneath the comforter after he pulled it back for me. It felt good to be in the flannel, and under the covers. I didn't lie back down though, choosing instead to prop myself up with pillows, my fingers trembling and burning painfully. I'd never been so aware of all the pieces of my body. From my throbbing ankle, to my icy fingers and my stinging arm, the pain rolled in waves, sometimes crashing into each other. My nipples brushed against the flannel. I never went without a bra. It felt too decadent, too sexual. But now it felt freeing. I had the strangest feeling of comfort, my eyelids hooded, because I needed it and he was providing it, even if his manner was silent, efficient.

The man- he of no name- brought a bowl over to the nightstand and he took both my arms out from under the blanket and submerged them in the water. I winced. "That's too hot. It feels like it's burning."

"It will feel better in a few minutes. It's not hot water, it's just room temperature."

He walked away and finally started to peel off his own layers. First he took off his hat, exposing light brown and unruly hair, and hung it from a clothesline that ran from one corner to the other of the cabin. There were other random pieces of clothing on it already. He unzipped his jacket and hung it on a hook by the door. Then he sat down at the chair by the small table and unlaced his boots. He dropped them in front of the wood stove, which was burning. I could hear the crackling on the fire inside its belly.

I wondered how far from his cabin the plane had crashed.

CRASH

How long had he carried me? He must have heard the crash and gone to investigate. "Did you see the plane crash?" I asked, swallowing hard. I felt thirsty, my throat tight, and I briefly closed my eyes, not wanting to remember the way the dead men had looked.

"I saw it and heard it. We don't get a lot of plane traffic here. He was way off course."

"Oh. I don't know. We were going to Fort Yukon."

He had no comment. He just peeled off his sweatshirt and hung it on the line. Then he stripped off his Henley shirt and undershirt too. I could see the white fabric was damp with sweat. From carrying my weight. His chest was a powerful display of muscles. He had no tattoos, only a scar on his upper chest that was at least four inches in length. His skin was a golden tone- not from the sun, but just his natural color. His jeans hung low on his hips and I was staring. I couldn't help myself. I'd never seen a man honed with muscles from hard work. The beard scruff wasn't unusual. I was from Seattle, where lumbersexual really was a thing. Flannel had been a fashion statement since grunge and Nirvana, when I was still a baby. But this was different. This was flannel worn for its original purpose and a body carved from manual labor.

He was a woodsman. An Alaskan bush person. A man who survived because of his own strength and skill.

I was grateful that he'd found me, saved me. "What's your name?" I asked again. "Please tell me so I can properly thank you."

He finished hanging his shirts on the line then turned slowly to me. His expression evaporated the sense of safety I felt. "Don't ask me that again. It's not a fucking game or a coffee date."

It was so rude and unexpected I jerked, instinctively wincing.

It sounded harsher than maybe he meant it. Or maybe he did mean to be an asshole. Either way, it was like a slap in the face. I pulled my fingers out of the bowl and raised them to my eyes, tears threatening to spill that I didn't want him to see. I was just trying to be polite. Why was I being polite when he was being weird and I was the one who had almost died? Well, fuck him. I didn't need to make small talk, he was totally right about that.

I heard him swear. Something clanked when it fell but I refused to open my eyes. My wet hands cooled my cheeks, which felt wind-burned and chapped. Then the bed creaked as he sat down on it next to me.

"I'm sorry," he murmured.

The unexpected touch of his hand on mine forced me to jerk my eyes open. "What are you doing? Just leave me alone. Please."

"Let me see your face."

"No."

"I just need to see your face," he coaxed, his voice low, soothing.

Without meaning to, I dropped my hands down. How did he do that? Just a few commanding words and I listened. It was something about his confidence in my compliance and the seductive timber of his voice. Or maybe it was just my senses were numb, my reserve down from my trauma.

He was staring at me intently, his blue eyes cool. Was there remorse there? Was there fire, passion? Lust, curiosity? I didn't see anything. Or I couldn't interpret it. It was like he had mastered the art of shielding his thoughts from others, which seemed so unnecessary here. Alone.

Why did he hide?

"I don't spend much time with people anymore. My social skills are rusty. I didn't mean to upset you."

I wet my dry lips with my tongue.

His eyes dropped, following the movement. I hadn't meant to attract his attention. Yet when he noticed, I felt a shiver of pleasure that I had no business feeling. "It's okay. Can I have some water?"

"Of course you can." His thumb reached out and wiped dampness from my skin. "Are you hungry? You should eat before I give you some pain medication."

CRASH

"My stomach is upset."

"I'll make you soup."

"Okay." The pain in my ankle was growing. I wanted to close my eyes again, but when I did, the image of those men danced in front of my eyes like macabre marionettes. I popped them back open. He was still looking at me. "John?" I asked, because I needed to call him something, and he looked like a John.

The corner of his mouth turned up. "Yes?"

"I almost died." It was a totally obvious statement. What, like he didn't know that? But I just wanted some reassurance that I was alive or something. I wanted comfort.

"But you didn't." John, I was determined to think of him as John, gripped my chin gently. "And now you're here. With me. Safe."

I nodded, shivering. I was safe. With him.

His grip tightened, pinching my skin. "Just do what I say. Always. And everything will be fine."

CHAPTER TWO

FEAR RETURNED, DIFFERENT FROM WHEN I was on the plane. That had been the terror of the plane free-falling and knowing I was about to die. It was a quick fear, a brief spike that had quickly morphed into the pain and the unknown and the shock of survival. This was different, a slow rising fear, like warm yeast, growing and bubbling. The fear that came from the realization that you were in danger. Not the kind where you have no time to process before it's already over, but where the prickles on your skin rise and your breath goes shallow and you try to tell yourself you are overreacting.

But there is still the undeniable sensation that someone wants to harm you. The stranger wanted to hurt me.

"What do you mean?" I whispered, my heart rate increasing so rapidly I could have sworn I heard it beating in my ears. In the room. Everything in me was screaming to jerk my chin out of his hold, but I was afraid to anger him. It took all the control I had to force myself to not break my return stare.

"It's dangerous here. The cold, the animals, the guns. You need to listen to me or you might get hurt." He let my chin go.

CRASH

"And we don't want that." John pushed back off the bed and stood up.

My breath released in a huge sigh. My armpits were clammy. His back was as muscular as his chest, but now I saw that not as sensual, but as a threat. He was strong. But maybe he really just had meant it as a warning on the dangers of Alaska. It was rough terrain and I knew very little about it.

But he definitely wasn't a John. Johns were loyal, reliable, easy-going. They made you laugh, didn't make you anxious. The stranger was none of those things.

If my leg wasn't hurting so badly, I would have plucked the sweat pants off the bottom of the bed and wiggled into them. I wanted more of a barrier between us. "What kind of animals are there?" I had no idea why I focused on that, which was most likely the smallest danger to me.

"Bears. Caribou."

Those were definitely big creatures but I wasn't planning on going for a stroll in the woods. I pursed my lips. As he opened a cupboard and got out something, I looked around the small cabin. It was rustic, but warm, both in temperature and in color from all the natural exposed wood. It was cluttered, though tidy, the kitchen area just one bank of cabinets with exposed shelving above. There was a pantry cupboard, and by the door, a gun rack. One, two, three, four, five, I counted six different shotguns. I didn't know what differentiated one from the other. I was an assistant manager at a sustainable clothing store in Seattle with a sewing blog on the side. I didn't know anything about guns or knives or bears.

"You have sled dogs?" I asked, still hearing the occasional bark or complaining whine outside.

The can he'd been holding hit the countertop. Hard. It made me wince. I decided I needed to shut the fuck up. I was clearly irritating him. But the chatter was both from anxiety and from needing to have something, anything to grasp onto. I needed to know where I was, what to expect. Both what was outside and what was in here.

"Yes. I have dogs." He kept his back to me.

That bare back. Didn't he need a shirt? Maybe he didn't get cold like I did. My thirst was distracting me. My mouth felt like I'd swallowed sawdust. I eyed the bowl he'd set on the nightstand for my fingers. At home, I would have thought it disgusting to even consider drinking water my hands had been soaking in. It would be like drinking from the manicure bowl at the salon. But I was too thirsty to care. I carefully lifted the bowl with trembling hands and raised it to my lips.

I was taking a small sip when he turned and caught me. His eyebrows shot up. "You don't have to drink that. I'm getting you water."

My cheeks heated. I shrugged. "I'm causing you enough trouble."

"It's not any trouble. Honestly." He took down a cup and filled it from a water cooler. He brought it over to me.

I'd guiltily set the bowl down and I reached for the cup he was holding, but he raised it right to my lips and tipped it. The cool refreshing liquid filled my mouth. I swallowed and pulled away. Some dribbled onto my bottom lip and chin. "Thank you."

His thumb wiped the spill up from the base of my chin up to my lip and slipping just slightly into my mouth. It was unexpected, that warm, rough pad of skin inside my lip and I sucked in a breath. His smile was seductive, whether he intended it to be or not.

"There. Good to the last drop."

Maybe he was a JT. Joseph Thomas. Or Justin Timberlake. That made me smile. Why had that popped into my head?

"See? There's a smile." JT tucked my hair behind my ear. "Good to know you've got teeth."

I gave a rusty laugh. But right then I shifted on his bed and my ankle protested. A cry flew out of my mouth before I could stop it.

The smile fell off his face. "I'll go get you that soup so you can take the painkiller. Don't worry, it's not broken."

"Are you sure?" It felt pretty damn broken to me.

"You'd be in more pain."

Dear God, what would more pain feel like? "What happened to my arm?" I lifted it slightly off the bed, noting that I was already bleeding through the makeshift bandage he'd bound me with.

"Something cut it."

That was more than a little obvious, but I figured it wouldn't be a good idea to get snarky about it. I just sipped more water from the glass he'd set on the nightstand and watched him move around his small kitchen. Looking around, I wondered where the bathroom was. I needed to go, the pressure building rapidly with each passing minute. I decided to eat the soup first though in order not to anger him.

Though it occurred to me I shouldn't have to worry that he'd get mad at me for asking a simple question, I suspected he would. If you were used to living alone and then some woman who didn't know jack shit crashed your party you might find her incessant questions annoying. I got that. I didn't like it. But I got it. Sean- maybe he was a Sean?- had said his social skills were rusty. I must sound like nails on a chalkboard to him and he had to be tired from hauling my unconscious body. Irritated. On edge.

Or maybe that was me.

He did the same thing with the soup that he did with the water. He came to the bed, sat down next to me, and spooned its warmth into my mouth. It tasted delicious and after swallowing, I opened for another bite. I should have protested, should have told him I was able to feed myself, let him go about his chores so I didn't inconvenience him, but I didn't. I just leaned against the headboard and opened for him, half a dozen times. I watched, trying to gauge his mood, noting the length of his eyelashes and the squareness of his jaw. He looked at me from time to time, and I couldn't read anything in his expression. But mostly he kept his gaze trained on my lips and the spoon as it traveled from bowl to mouth.

Though when I licked my lip I could have sworn I saw lust buried there in those icy depths.

"I think that's enough for now," I whispered. It was a hearty vegetable soup and for whatever reason it filled me up quickly. "What time is it?"

He glanced toward the window. "About six o'clock."

I'd left Fairbanks at ten am. I wanted to calculate what that meant- how long Sean had carried me, but I was too exhausted. I sighed and sank down a little into the pillow. "Is there a... restroom I could use?"

"There is," he said. "But as it's outside, I'd suggest we put these pants on you first."

I discarded the Sean name. That was wrong, too. "Outside?" Oh, Lord. It was an outhouse. I should have figured that out but it was still a shock. How did he pee when it was forty below? "Right. Of course."

"So you're from Washington state, Laney? What do you do in the land of Starbucks and Microsoft?"

"I work in a store." I reached for the sweatpants he had grabbed from the bottom of the bed, but he ignored me.

The comforter was yanked back by him, exposing my legs and my panties. The cold air brought goose bumps to my skin and I blushed for some stupid reason. He'd undressed me already. It was ludicrous to be modest now. Maybe it was just a knee-jerk reaction to being exposed to a stranger. He shot me a curious look.

"What kind of store?"

"Clothes." I didn't feel like going into detail with him. He would think it was lame, I could already tell. Maybe I wouldn't have cared if it wasn't for the fact that I was only doing it because I didn't know what else to do with my life. I'd gone to college and gotten a degree in sociology and then had tried to find a job doing... sociology things. My stepfather had told me those jobs didn't exist and it turns out he was right. I was willing to admit that. But now after two years out of school I had no clue what I actually wanted to do. This guy made me feel frivolous for my indecisiveness. I bet he was never indecisive.

"I guess this isn't the fashion statement you'd like to make." He lifted my bad ankle and gently eased it into the pant leg.

"I don't give a shit about fashion," I said, and it came out more vehemently than I meant it to. "I almost died." That was the second time I'd said it since we'd gotten to his cabin. Maybe I wanted more of an acknowledgment of the trauma. I was still freaked out and he just wasn't.

"I know. But I guess here we face death more readily." He put my other foot in the pant leg and eased them up.

I lifted my ass up a little so he could finish the job.

He had them up to my waist, but he paused for a minute, his fingers pressing into my bare skin. "Do you trust me?" he asked, eyes intense.

"Yes." I nodded. What other answer could there be?

"Don't." He stepped back. "Never trust anyone in the bush until you know one hundred percent for sure you can."

I blinked, startled.

"Make me earn your trust. Push me. Test me. Then trust me."

Suddenly I needed to get away from him. He confused me, frightened me. Intrigued me. I couldn't help it. He aroused feelings in me that he shouldn't. "Take me to the outhouse," I demanded. I just wanted to go pee and then close my eyes and fall asleep and forget any of this had ever happened.

He smiled. "Yes, ma'am."

Was it sarcasm or had I actually earned his respect? I couldn't tell.

He went and put a shirt on then brought me a bottle of Advil. "Take four."

My fingers still weren't working right and I couldn't get the bottle open. I placed it on the nightstand, frustrated and in pain so deep and aching, I felt sick to my stomach again.

He came over, opened the bottle and shook out four pills. He dropped them in my hand without a word.

"Thank you." I popped two of them into my mouth and drank some water quickly, then repeated the process.

He was pulling his boots and jacket back on. I swung my legs over and tried to tentatively put my feet on the floor. I figured I could hop a little and he could let me rest on his arm. But he stood up and glared at me.

"What are you doing? I'll carry you."

Maybe his name was TJ for The Jerk. Why was he the cranky one? I guess because I was inconveniencing him. It's not like I was having fun. "What if I don't trust you to carry me?"

A grin split his face for the first time. "Good answer, Laney. Good answer." He came toward me, arms out in a peace offering. "Let me prove it to you. You can trust me."

It wasn't like I had a choice. If I wanted to use the outhouse, I needed his help. "And what happens if I start trusting you?" By then I'd be leaving. Someone would come for me, or the stranger would take me to town.

He swept me up into his arms easily. His shirt smelled like pine needles. I wrapped my hands around his neck.

"If you trust me you'll find it to be a very pleasant experience."

I didn't dare to look up at him. Instead I focused on the necklace he wore. It looked like a piece of bone on a leather strap. Glossy, white, pure. He set me down on the kitchen chair and got another jacket off the hook and a hat, which he crammed onto my head, sending my hair into my eyes. I swiped at it then put my arms through the jacket he held out for me.

When he picked me back up, the jostling bounced my bladder but it was nothing compared to my ankle. There was definitely no way I could walk. He opened the door and stepped outside, kicked it shut behind us. I blinked at the blinding whiteness of the sun on the snow. But I could see we were surrounded by trees, nothing but trees, and in front of the cabin were the dogs, each on its own chain, next to a little wood doghouse. There were random things covered in tarps around the property and unlike a front porch back home, there were no rocking chairs on this one. It was stacked floor to roof with wood on one side, and a chainsaw on the other, sitting on an overturned bucket.

Going down the steps, we jostled a little but he held me without effort. He wasn't even breathing hard. In the yard, if you could call it that, was an ax sticking out of a stump. Between several trees were a couple of logs about fifteen feet in the air and there were sacks swinging on rope from it. I wasn't sure what they were, but as we moved closer to it I realized it was animal carcasses strung up. The bags were patchy with dried blood. My stomach flipped. Then I realized the one on the end wasn't in a bag yet. It was a deer or a moose, I couldn't really tell from the angle of it hanging by hooves, and I honestly wasn't well versed in animal identification, but its blank eyes stared at me, and blood was dripping down into the muddy snow below. Drip, drip, drip.

Like the pilot on the plane.

I buried my head in the stranger's chest and smelled deeply, afraid I was going to throw up again.

"What's wrong?" he asked, stopping in front of a small wooden shed. His fingers stroked the back of my head in a way that I desperately needed.

"The blood. It just reminds me of the accident."

His lips brushed across my hair, like a father to a child. Or so I told myself. It wasn't sexual though, if it couldn't be classified as paternal either. But comforting. "It's okay," he said. "That's not death, that's dinner."

It didn't really make me feel any better. Nor did it please me when he tried to take me into the outhouse. "What are you doing?"

"Helping you." He had set me down on my good foot and he was starting to pull my pants down.

"I can do it." It was super embarrassing. This was no hospital and he was no male nurse. He was a man. I was not letting him take my panties down and stand there while I peed in a hole.

He hesitated but then he backed out of the outhouse. He gave me a hard look. "Let me know if you need me."

"Okay." Tottering on my good leg, trying not to show how much pain I was in, I went to pull my pants down and forgot about the laceration in my arm. Shooting daggers of pain went through my arm. "Shit," I murmured under my breath. I took my pants down one handed in an awkward tug and shove. Finally I was on the bench and doing my thing in total relief. How did anyone do this in the middle of the night? I guessed you held it.

Somehow I managed to get my pants mostly up, though my panties were rolled at the waist and half up my ass. When I pushed the door back open, I couldn't look him in the eye. He wasn't waiting at the outhouse though. He was in the yard, playing with one of the dogs, who was still chained up. He was rubbing the dog's head, murmuring to him, smiling, and playing a game of pull with the bone in the dog's mouth. It made him look so much more... normal. Just a guy and his dog, playing in the yard. Except this was the middle of nowhere in Alaska and he was if not a survivalist, certainly living what Michael had told me was a subsistence lifestyle. The stranger provided for himself, eating animals he shot, and heating his cabin with wood he chopped.

But I wasn't even sure that was what made him abnormal. It was something else. Something that seemed to simmer below the surface. It was all the things he wasn't saying, from his name to his plan for returning me to civilization, to his lack of questions about me. Maybe that wasn't crazy or weird at all. Maybe he was being polite, giving me space. Or maybe he was living in isolation for a reason that extended far beyond discomfort with social situations. Maybe he was insane.

Right now he didn't look even remotely insane and I wanted to believe that the only thing off was what he had said- his social skills were rusty. Because I'd already been afraid enough in those two minutes before the crash and the minutes after to exempt me from fear for a lifetime, in my opinion. I didn't deserve to be afraid of my rescuer, so I decided I wasn't going to be. Even if he was a little different.

A man who played with his dog couldn't be a crazed killer or anything.

I could almost hear my stepfather scoffing in my head.

"Bullshit," he'd say. "Everyone is capable of murder under the right circumstances."

I knew that wasn't true. Some people, like me, would never be able to purposefully take another human being's life. If murder was so easy, so natural to us, then why didn't more people kill? Because death was terrifying, our own or someone else's. Hopping forward a couple of steps, I let the outhouse door slam behind me to get his attention. I wanted to lie down. I wanted to cry. I wanted my mom. God, how long had it been since I wanted or needed a hug from my mother?

Forever. Since I was fourteen or fifteen most likely. Not that she would have given it to me, because she never did. But I had still wanted her to change, right up until around the time it was clear she was spending more money than my stepfather had and hanging around a lot with his best friend, my "Uncle Jim." Such a fucking cliché. So ridiculous. And in the end, she'd landed her own ass in federal prison and my baby sister Victoria was without a mom.

That's why I'd been on my way to Fort Yukon. To see if I could marry Michael and take Victoria in the summers and give her an escape and my stepfather a break. Or maybe I was running away. Escaping. Like other people who had moved here. I wondered again if anyone knew yet I was missing. Michael must be worried. Had he called my stepfather?

The stranger looked over at the noise. I was shivering, despite the jacket. I wasn't used to it being below freezing so early in the fall. I wanted to start walking toward the house, to be independent. But I was exhausted, physically and emotionally and I was no survivalist. The worst things I'd battled were traffic and my mom's selfishness turning our household upside down. I'd sucked in gym class in high school and in college the only ailment I'd ever suffered from was a hangover. The day had more than caught up with me and I just leaned on the door of the outhouse, humbly waiting for… Steve to come over and help me.

He could be a Steve. Steves had shaggy hair and that kind of bold, confident walk. Not a Stephen, definitely no, but maybe a Steve. Why wouldn't he tell me? It was infuriating. But truthfully, the least of my freaking worries.

Giving the dog a final pat, he came over immediately and held his hand out for me. "You okay?"

No. I wasn't even remotely okay. But I nodded. "Yes." I took his hand and gripped tightly, needing to transfer some of my weight to him. I hadn't wanted him to carry me. Now I didn't want him to not carry me. It was so much easier to let Steve take the burden. I limped a step forward and took a deep breath, bracing myself for the hobbling walk.

Without a word though he just bent over and scooped me up in his arms. I gave a cry of surprise more so than protest. But he must have thought I wanted to walk because he gave a grunt of disapproval.

"Just relax," he said. "Let me make things easier for you."

That would be nice. I leaned against his chest again and fought the urge to close my eyes. The motion would be too much if I did that. Instead I concentrated on breathing, on counting the steps he took, on smelling the crisp clean air. I listened to the wind, and the dogs whining, and the occasional exhalation from Steve as he carried me. Once in the cabin, he kicked his boots off while still holding me, then put me on the bed.

"Your socks are wet." He eased them off. "You should have let me help you."

"I'm sorry," I said. Because women say they're sorry. It's what we're taught to do. At least I had been. I had an apology problem. Funny how my mother never apologized for anything she did. She just barreled her way through life with a big eff off attitude. She'd always said no one had any right to judge her and I guess she was right. But I'd always been more of a people pleaser and she'd made me feel guilty for that- like it was a weakness to want everyone around me to be happy, content. I just wasn't wired the way she was, and yet I was trained to apologize for that. For everything. For me.

"It's not a big deal," the stranger said. "But I don't want you getting a chill." He rested his hands on my knees, and they were big hands. Strong hands. He looked up at me and his blue eyes were filled something I didn't understand. Was it desire? I wasn't sure.

"You don't know the bush," he said. "I do. You have to listen to me. Do what I say."

He wasn't a Steve. No Steve would have that kind of intensity. The kind that made me feel naked, exposed. Aroused. Yet slightly frightened. I nodded quickly. His commanding presence made me want to obey. "Yes. I will. I promise."

The smile that crossed his face looked so genuine, it felt like a reward for giving the right answer and I felt a frisson of pleasure. "Good girl," he said.

I smiled back, shyly. "I think the Advil is helping," I told him, and I wasn't sure why. To feel less of a burden? To let him know his help was appreciated? I don't know.

"Good. I'm guessing you're tired and I have some chores to do. Maybe you should try to sleep."

I sighed, bone weary. "I think that's a good idea." I tried to scoot myself up backwards on the bed, but down a leg and an arm, I wasn't having much luck.

He came around the side and hauled me by my armpits. It didn't seem to strain him in any way, but I guess for a guy who chopped wood and hauled kills and did who knew what else, I wasn't that big of a deal. Once I was up and under the covers, he refilled my water, and brought me clean socks, again flipping the comforter back to skim them over my feet. He left the sweat pants on me and I was glad. I sighed, lying back onto his pillow. The sheets smelled like lavender. It was a disparate scent in the woods, for a mountain man, but I guess scented soap is scented soap. There was no reason for him to wash his sheets with a bar of Old Spice. How did he wash his sheets? He seemed to have electricity. There was a light on over the kitchen sink and there was a stove. The wood stove seemed to be the only source of heat though and he opened it and fed more logs onto it.

Breathing deeply, I tried to relax, focusing on releasing tension in my shoulders, my back, my hips. I inhaled and exhaled to the throb of the pain in my ankle. It didn't really feel any better. It was still deep and driving, the tissue all swollen, twice its normal size. He moved around the cabin, but I didn't look to see what he was doing. He left at one point, a gust of cold air entering the room when he opened the door. He was gone for what felt like an hour, but likely it was much less, it just felt like forever as I ticked time by in pain and worry. My foot hurt too bad to sleep and that worried me maybe it was actually broken. Also, I wanted to recover so I could get to where I needed to be physically, so that I could make my way to Fort Yukon.

When he came back in the stove creaked as he opened the door again, the new wood snapping as he tossed it in. I thought about how much wood must be required to keep the stove burning, and it was only late September. January must be... terrifying. He cooked something then, the sizzle on the stove making my mouth water. It was meat of some kind, maybe with onions. I thought about living alone, in total solitude for maybe months on end, and it wasn't a pleasant thought. That was way too much time in my head. Way too routine, disciplined, every day leaving no allowance for slacking.

But I supposed my life was pretty routine too, work, family, friends. Oil changes, hair appointments to take my standard brown hair to a darker auburn hue. Life had a rhythm no matter where you lived and I clung to the memory of that ordinary life, praying I could get back to it sooner than later. I dozed off, but when the stranger climbed into bed beside me, I woke back up. I jerked a little, startled. I hadn't thought about where he would sleep but it was a small cabin and it was his bed. The floor was probably freezing.

CRASH

He settled in alongside me, punching his pillow. "Sorry I woke you up," he said, his voice whiskey smooth in the dark. He'd turned the kitchen light out and it was inky black in the cabin, the air still, the room surprisingly airtight.

"It's okay," I whispered. "I'm having a little trouble sleeping."

"Your ankle?"

"Yes." That, and a whole lot more. "And I'm cold."

"Come here." His warm arm snaked around my middle and he pulled me toward him, rolling on his side.

We were spooning before I could even think about it and I sucked in my breath. He didn't feel like he was wearing clothes. Just underwear. But I wasn't going to look or touch to see. I was dressed, so maybe he did have a shirt on, he was just exceptionally warm. But he felt like skin, and I could feel the bulge of his cock nestled up against my ass cheeks. It wasn't erect, which was good. Because for a minute I had the crazy thought that I wanted him to turn me over and give me a rough, hard fuck, so that I would feel alive, and distracted from the pain, the anxiety. I wanted to take him into me and forget what I'd seen on that plane.

His body was big, muscular, and I couldn't relax. Not when his breath was landing on my shoulder and I was waiting for him to get an erection. Then use it. My heart was racing and I knew that if he did, if we crossed that line so immediately, out of my distress from the crash and his isolation, I would be embarrassed the next day. Not to mention that it would be like cheating on Michael, even if so far our romantic relationship had been long distance. I still knew him, we'd grown up together. We had an understanding. I wasn't sure near-death experiences exempted me from the rules of relationship behavior.

None of which mattered, because the stranger sounded on the verge of sleep when he asked, "Better?"

"Yes. Thank you." I closed my eyes and tried to fall back asleep.

His thumb was stroking my waist, and he had found his way under the shirt he'd dressed me in, so he was touching my bare flesh. It was comforting, his touch, and when his lips rubbed across my hair, I liked it. I waited for him to do something else, make another move, kiss my ear, my cheek, stroke my breast, but he didn't. In a minute or two I realized he was asleep.

I was both relieved and disappointed.

Behind my tightly squeezed eyelids I saw him. And I saw blood. And I saw his eyes right in front of me as he cut off my air passage.

Yet I didn't shift away from him.

I curled in closer.

CHAPTER THREE

THIS TIME, WHEN THE PLANE went down, I braced myself, determined to stay awake. I heard yelling, the screech of metal, and the pilot turning back to me with a grin, blood dripping from the crown of his head down over his face, into his eyes, covering his lips. I added my screams to the wild assault of sound around me as the plane nosedived, impact inevitable.

I jerked awake and felt both fear and pain rock my body. Blinking rapidly, I breathed in and out. I was in the stranger's house. I was alive. I was on the floor. I could see straight under his bed to the plastic bins he had stored there. My fingers were trembling and my ankle was throbbing as I tried to steady myself. Just a dream.

The bed creaked and his head appeared. "You okay?"

"I had a nightmare," I whispered.

His legs swung over the side and he stepped down onto the floor next to me. "It sounded like a bolt of thunder when you fell. I thought a bear was crashing through the front door."

Glancing up I saw he was holding his rifle. Where the hell had that come from? "Just me," I murmured. "No bears." I sat up and tried to stand, wincing. Now my hip hurt on top of my other issues.

He reached for my hand and accidently brushed over my arm injury. "You're bleeding again. Let me change your bandage."

I felt sleepy and disoriented, freaked out by both my dream and the reality of where I was, what had happened. "I'm okay. We can do it in the morning."

He tugged me up and I used my good knee to climb onto the bed. We both settled back down, though this time he lay on his back, away from me. My side of the bed felt lonely, the room dark, the weight of the blanket not enough to stave off the chill. It was so dark. A dark I had never known. The total absence of city lights outside the windows. Where was the moon? It would have reassured me in some way. I wondered where my cell phone was. Still on the plane, in my bag, I imagined. That was adding to my sense of anxiety. I was so used to checking it, to having access to everyone instantly. It was a weird and uncomfortable feeling.

I was where no one knew that I was. If the stranger hadn't found me I would have woken up only to freeze to death. The thought made me shudder.

But I was so exhausted it wasn't long before my eyes were drifting closed and my breathing was slowing down to match his. I liked hearing us both take air in and out, a steady harmony between myself and another human being. Thank God I wasn't alone. I wouldn't have the first idea about how to survive if I were alone. Even if I did, I thought that I would go crazy without someone to talk to. I don't know how he did it- endless days of solitude. I turned on my side, face away from him, but I did shift my body slightly in his direction, wanting his warmth. His confidence. It allowed me to relax enough to slide back into sleep.

Only to wake up again on the floor. And this time, the impact was so jarring I came to consciousness already crying from the pain. I'd landed with my injured leg beneath me.

He was up and off the bed immediately, crouching down next to me, his hand stroking the hair off my forehead. "It's okay.

I'll get you more Advil."

He started to scoop me up in his arms under my ass, but I shook my head. "Just leave me on the floor. I don't want to roll off again." I couldn't even remember what I'd been dreaming about that time. I'd never fallen out of bed before, but now it was obvious that the plane crash was dominating my dreams, and I was free-falling figuratively and literally.

"You'll freeze to death on the floor. There's no way."

Even when I protested again through my tears, he continued to lift me up. "Please. It hurts too much, I don't want to fall again." I'd never be able to sleep, terrified I was going to roll off the bed. My leg was throbbing and I felt stiff and sore everywhere.

"I have a solution. It will be fine." He set me on the bed and I could see the whites of his eyes as he leaned over me. "Don't argue with me. You're not sleeping on the floor."

It was a tone that brooked no argument. I shut my mouth immediately. He disappeared and a small light shone over by the kitchen sink. I heard him rattle pills out of the bottle. He brought two over to me and helped me sit up so I could take them with water. I lay back down with a sigh. He didn't get into bed right away. He went over by the door and came back with something. With the light on, I could see what it was- rope.

"What's that for?" I asked, confused.

"I'm going to tie you to me. So if you start to roll, my weight will keep you on the bed." He wasn't looking at me, but at the length of rope in his hand, tying off a knot as he walked.

A shiver crept over me. The idea made sense but... he couldn't be serious. I couldn't spend the night tied to him. Like a captive. Or his submissive lover. Just the thought of that made my body flush with arousal. A wet trickle slowly soaked the front of my panties, startling me. What the hell was wrong with me? That shouldn't turn me on. Yet it did. There was no denying it. Maybe because I was afraid and in pain and I needed him to take charge, to be in control. To distract me. He climbed onto the bed, stalking toward me on his knees, rope in hand, and I felt my nipples harden, heard my breath catch. My earlier desire to have him take me, to plunge his cock into me, returned fast and furious. Only this time, that unexpected urge was for him to tie me to him, then roll me onto my stomach and take me from behind.

His expression didn't look like that's what he had in mind. He just looked sleepy, effortlessly sexy, but not sexual. Not predatory. He tossed the circle he'd created over my head, making me feel like a cattle that had been roped. Then he put it over his head. "Lay down, like we were before."

I did, heart racing. When I curled on my side, the rope was an uncomfortable lump, but I wasn't about to complain. Nor did I really want to sleep on the cold floor. So this was my best option, even if it was unorthodox and made me feel a little like his prisoner.

He tightened the rope snugly, and this time when his body aligned with mine, I felt the unmistakable press of a hard cock into my flesh. So he was turned on by using the rope too, by binding me to him. That made me fiercely pleased. I wanted him to feel the things I was feeling, because they were inexplicable and unexpected and maybe even inappropriate. Yet for some reason, still fighting through the tail end of the worst day of my life, it mattered that he not find me completely pathetic. That he saw me as a woman, not a victim, or a liability, or a burden. That he found me as attractive as I found him, on a fundamental, base level.

When his arm wrapped around me, and his palm splayed out on my belly, I sighed. But I wasn't sure what emotion it expressed. Maybe it was just bone weariness. Everything on my body hurt. My heart was heavy with worry. But the stranger served as a pleasant distraction from all of those. I could concentrate on the weight of his warm hand, and the hard press of his cock against me. His scent was that of sleep and outdoors. It was like the exterior air clung to his disheveled hair. I wanted to touch him as casually as he touched me so I placed my hand over top of his. I almost laced my fingers through his but I resisted the urge.

This time when I drifted into sleep my dreams were erotic. The stranger stroked and pinched my nipples first, in the exact position that we'd fallen asleep in. It was like my dream took up where reality left off. In my sleep he did what I had been shocked to contemplate awake. He worked my nipples to hard peaks, his breathing warm on my neck, before his hand slid down my belly and into the sweatpants. The pad of his thumb stroked over my panties, circling my clit until I was shifting restlessly and giving soft groans of approval.

When he finally sank into my moist heat, I was ready for his touch, welcoming it. I scissored my legs a little so his finger would sink deeper inside me and my hips started to rock.

Then he pinched my clit and I came.

I jerked awake, head rising off the pillow. My inner thighs ached with the last laps of an orgasm. It was almost painful in its intensity, nothing aiding the throbbing crests, easing my swollen clit. My skin was hot, my neck damp under my hair. Holy shit. I'd just come in my sleep from dreaming about him touching me. My hand had fallen off of his, but that touch was still where it had been before, on my belly. He was breathing evenly, asleep. I relaxed in relief that I hadn't woken him up.

Not that he had been able to read my thoughts. But I still would have been embarrassed, the humming aftershocks of my orgasm making me feel warm for the first time all day. I drifted back into sleep, into my sensual dreams of stroking fingers, and nibbling lips at my ear.

I woke up again to the feel of him trying to gingerly ease the rope over my head without waking me.

And the unmistakable scent of my own body on his fingertips.

It was instinctive to try to sit up and in doing so I caught the rope around my neck. My heart was hammering in my chest and

I tried to shake off the dream, tried to assess what my body was doing, still aware of my lingering arousal in a way I didn't want to be.

"I didn't mean to wake you," he murmured in my ear. "I need to go chop some wood."

Turning, I could see his face, so close to mine. It was strange to be so physically close to someone I didn't know at all. I knew nothing about him. Not even his name. Had he touched me while I was sleeping? Now as his fingers worked to slide the rope up over my mouth, nose, eyes, I couldn't smell anything but skin. Just warm, male skin. There was no scent of me on him and I wondered if I had imagined that. Had it all been part of the confusion of my dream spilling over into my first few waking seconds? I didn't know.

"It's okay," I said, swallowing hard, and lifting my head so he could finish skimming the rope off. "I was having a bad dream."

His eyebrows shot up. "Is that what it was?"

I wasn't sure what that meant. Had he heard me? Had I been moaning in ecstasy? God, I hoped not. So I just nodded. Then in an effort to change the subject, "Did my phone get left on the plane?"

His eyes flickered with an emotion I couldn't pin. "I brought it with us, but it won't work here, you know. There are no cell towers. I grabbed your wallet too."

That was a huge relief, though I wasn't sure why. Maybe because having those things proved I had a life back in Seattle. That I was Laney Turner, with people who would be missing me. That at some point, I could get somewhere and be able to reach out to the world with my phone. "Thank you. I appreciate it. I appreciate everything you've done. You saved my life."

Lying in bed next to someone was so intimate that it didn't feel strange when he reached out and touched my lip, dragging his thumb across the flesh. "You're welcome. I'm glad I found you."

"Me too." It seemed like he was going to kiss me. I wanted

him to. But he didn't. So I asked, "How long have you lived here?"

"Five years."

"Where are you from?"

"Anchorage." His hand shifted to cup my cheek. "And you're from Seattle. It doesn't mean anything. You don't need to ask me inane questions to make small talk."

That was just rude, and arrogant. Or maybe it was brilliant. I didn't know, but my response was negative, bristly. "Where we're from contributes to how we became who we are."

"Do you want to get to know me, Laney?" he murmured.

"Yes." I did. I was curious. I was grateful to him and attracted to him and all of my jumbled emotions were overwhelming me. The fear that niggled at the back of my consciousness begged to be soothed. I wanted to know that he was the decent man I wanted him to be. That there weren't literal skeletons in his closet.

"But you think it will make you feel better, and it won't. Just decide who I am- it's what most people do anyway."

I didn't know what to say to that. The rope was above my head on the pillow and his hand was still wrapped around it, his other hand sliding up my cheek and into my hair. I had the sudden sense, looking into his eyes, that he could snap my neck right now. He could just yank my hair back, slit my throat. Strangle me with the rope. Tear a piece of my face off with his teeth. The graphic thoughts startled me. I had never been one for macabre voyeurism. I didn't watch excessive crime TV and I didn't walk around sure everyone around me was determined to harm me. It was the plane crash. It was the eyes of death on the pilot. It was fucking with my head.

It was all the blood.

The isolation. The staring death in the face and surviving with nothing more than a sprained ankle and some cuts and bruises. Probably a minor concussion. Which might explain why I said the next thing I did.

"What if I decide you're the man who wants to kiss me right now?"

His eyes flicked down to my lips and his grip in my hair tightened. "I would say that I am that man already. But you almost died. You just want comfort. You don't want me. Not really."

I splayed my hand out on his bare chest. He frustrated me. "Yes, I do want comfort. But that's not it. I just think… it would feel good," I finished lamely.

"Good isn't good enough. There's no point unless it's going to be fucking amazing." He sat up rapidly, yanking the rope away from me. "I live my life with discipline and control. You're tempting, but I haven't decided yet if you can handle me."

Even as I knew there was probably some serious truth to his statement, I still balked. "I can handle you."

He smiled, a slow seductive smirk that turned my insides to melted chocolate. I could still feel the dampness of my inner thighs.

"You can handle your version of me. But in reality, I'm not so sure."

"Let me try." I explored his chest then touched his beard, wanting to feel if it was soft or scratchy.

He grabbed my hand. "Don't touch me. Not unless I give you permission."

Jerking my hand back like it had been scalded, I felt my cheeks heat up. I was sorry I had brought up kissing me. He made me feel foolish, desperate. "You don't ask my permission when you touch me," I said defensively. He'd made me feel stupid and I wanted to put up a fight, show him he was a hypocrite.

But he didn't protest. He just said, "That's why you can't handle me. I make the rules. You obey them. That's the way this will work if you want me to kiss you."

I blinked at him. I didn't know what to say because I wasn't sure what I felt. After a pause where we studied each other, he let go of my hair and pulled back.

"That's what I thought." He got out of bed, dropping the rope on the nightstand.

In nothing but his boxer briefs, he walked across the room,

and bent over to throw some wood on the stove. His ass was firm, tight. His legs were strong, with a sprinkling of light hair across them. His back had muscular definition everywhere it should or could. His biceps rippled. He was everything you would expect in a man who did manual labor all day, every day. Maybe he was right. Maybe I couldn't handle him. I wasn't exactly known as the seductress in my social circle. I was too sweet to be a vixen, a Taylor Swift blending into a world of florals and beanies. The nice girl. Who made safe albeit boring choices. I drifted through life, never taking risks.

Flying to Alaska had been the most adventurous thing I'd ever done. And look what that had gotten me.

"Can you take me to town today?" I asked, sitting up, and pushing my dark hair back off my face. If he didn't want me, I wanted away from him. I wanted that anyway. I wanted to go home. Forget any of this had ever happened.

"No." He didn't even turn around to look at me.

Just no.

I waited for an explanation but knew that was a waste of time. "Why not?"

"Because you can't walk. And I have other things to do than carry you on my back for forty miles. The river isn't frozen yet so I can't take the snow machine."

My whole body was stiff and when I swung my feet over the side of the bed, I knew he was right. My ankle was still hugely swollen and sore. I couldn't bend it. There was no way I could even walk twenty feet, let alone forty miles. Jesus. Forty miles. The sense of being trapped descended on me. "Don't you have a car?"

That had him turning around to look at me incredulously. "To drive on what? There's no road, Laney."

"Oh, right." City girl alert. I guess I'd known that, but it still just incomprehensible. We were cut off. Totally alone. "I'm sorry you're stuck with me. Is there a way you can radio for someone or... something?" I hesitated, afraid whatever I would say was totally wrong. It was intimidating not to understand anything about a way of life.

"No." He came toward me again.

I felt fragile, vulnerable. I needed him to say it was okay. That everything was okay. I needed him.

Whatever he was thinking was a mystery to me. But he bent over in front of me, his thighs brushing my knees, his palm cupping my cheek. "Hey. It's okay. I'll take care of you. And all you need to do is get better."

I nodded, and I felt five years old. I felt like a little girl seeking a father's approval and reassurance. It was an unpleasant need that swirled inside me, even at the same time I was grateful for his attention, comfort. I'd never thought of myself as needy, per se. I'd been single more than I'd had boyfriends, because I wasn't someone who sought out a guy the minute one relationship went south, because when I was in, I was all in. I was used to being alone emotionally.

But then I'd never been in a plane crash before. It was okay to be needy.

"Thanks, Devin." I don't even know why I called him Devin. It felt like a name of a nice guy. A guy who would be there for you. I wanted him to be a Devin.

He smiled. "Good. I like it when you do that."

"Do what?"

"Make me what you want."

After he moved away from me, he pulled on the jeans he'd been wearing the night before. They had just been tossed over a chair. Then he brought a few things over to me on the bed. "Your phone. You should turn it off. I didn't see the charger so it's going to run out of battery. Your wallet. And your birth control pills." He set everything on the nightstand.

"Thanks." I caressed my phone, checking for messages and notifications, even though I knew I wouldn't have any. It indicated I didn't have a signal, so I scrolled through the last few messages I'd gotten. Michael, telling me he'd be at the airstrip to meet me. Victoria, sounding petulant about my departure. My stepfather telling me to let him know when I got to Fairbanks, which I hadn't done. I felt guilty for blowing him off.

Then I busied myself looking at pictures I had in my camera roll. Me and my friends on my birthday, wearing Downton Abbey inspired hats. Then later in the night, dancing at a club, looking a little drunk, but happy. Our family dog. My baby sister. I wondered what everyone was thinking.

Devin had a flannel shirt on now and was sitting down, stuffing his feet into boots. "Do you want coffee?"

"Coffee would be great."

"I'll make some when I come back in."

"I can do it." I felt weird having him wait on me.

"In a day or two you can. Just rest today."

Except that wasn't what I did. After taking my pill, worrying about spotting and a lack of feminine hygiene products in a mountain man's cabin, I hobbled around the room, slowly, taking better stock of my surroundings. It was sparse, but it seemed to be well built. There were no whistling winds coming through cracks and the floor was even and well sanded. I could have walked barefoot without risk of getting a splinter. The possessions were utilitarian in nature. Iron pots. The gun rack. A whole row of hunting knives on a shelf. Three pairs of boots by the door. One lone rug in front of the wood stove, and as I got closer to it, I realized that dark textured shag I'd thought was flokati was actually a bearskin rug. He had a bearskin rug. Damn. It made me shudder for some reason.

The only drawers were in the dresser, and glancing out the kitchen window to see if I could visually spot Devin, I debated opening them. I wanted to see if I could find something with his name on it. I located him in the yard, feeding the dogs. He was scooping some chunky liquid with a ladle out into their bowls. Keeping him in my sight line, I carefully opened the top drawer. It was underwear, socks, and T-shirts. The second drawer was flannels shirts and jeans. The third was miscellaneous crap that most people would have in a junk drawer in their kitchen. A post it pad, some pens, a pair of scissors, duct tape. The bottom drawer had a present in it. A wrapped present, about the size of a book. Just tucked into the drawer next to a couple of sweatshirts.

Standing up I glanced out the window. He was chopping wood now. I could hear the dull thud of the ax as he swung. His strength was obvious. The wood split in two, the pieces flying. Feeling guilty for my nosiness, but unable to resist, I bent down again and lifted the gift box, shaking it a little. It didn't make any noise. The paper looked a little yellow, the edges soft. Underneath it was a newspaper clipping. An obituary. For one Chelsea Anne Newcomb, a pretty blonde who looked to be in her early to mid-twenties.

I did the math quickly. Twenty-four. My age. Her death had been five years earlier. Which was when the stranger said he had moved here. Was she his sister? His girlfriend. I quickly read the information listed. A nurse. Beloved daughter of Chad and Janice Newcomb. Survived by brother Jason and sister Kiki. No mention of how she had died, just where the funeral was and how to donate flowers. I crammed it back exactly the way I'd found and set the gift on top. After shutting the drawer, my palms sweaty from fear I'd get caught, I glanced out. Still chopping wood.

Was he Jason? Chelsea's brother. I should have studied her picture better to see if I could find any similarities in their features. Sister, lover, friend. No matter who she was she'd been important to him and I felt a wave of compassion for my stranger. He had loved this girl. Lost her. He'd retreated to isolation in the wilderness. That spoke more about him than the words I'd managed to wrest from him.

Crouching had made my foot hurt like hell and I was out of breath so I limped to the chair next to the table. I didn't want to climb back into bed. I had to use the outhouse, which gave me a choice. I could wait for him and who knew how long he'd be, and then have him grope at my pants again like he had the night before, or I could put on one of his coats and hop there myself.

CRASH

I hadn't been wearing my coat on the plane and it was lost now to the wreckage, along with my adorable Kate Spade handbag. I didn't care other than I would have liked a coat that fit me to better keep the warmth close to my body. His coats hanging on the hooks were huge. I chose a black puffer coat and sat back down to pull it on and zip it up. I knew it wasn't even that cold out there by Alaskan standards- he was chopping wood just in his flannel shirt- but I was chilled to the bone. I would have loved a hot bath, but I didn't even see anything that could qualify as a shower.

I also only had one boot. The other boot must have been abandoned on the plane when he pulled my foot out from under the crushed seat. So I gingerly put my foot into his huge boot and tested my balance. This was a stupid idea. It would have been awkward on a regular day, but with the inability to really bend my ankle, it was bordering on dangerous. Once I got to the door I would ask him for help. Jason. I would ask Jason for help. I tried the name on for size, but then I realized I couldn't call him Jason without him realizing what I had done. Damn. That sucked.

Besides, my gut told me Chelsea had been his girlfriend, not his sister. That feeling was based on absolutely nothing, but I still had it. I limped to the door then out onto the porch, pulling the door shut behind me. I had the immediate concern that I'd just locked us out of the house, so I tugged on it again to make sure it would reopen. Maybe he didn't even have locks, but it was just a natural reaction. To me. The child of the mini-mansion suburbs.

The dogs were howling again. I wasn't sure how he could stand that. They sounded so urgent, yanking on their chains. Then I heard him.

"What the hell are you doing?"

I turned around quickly and grabbed for the porch railing. I took the steps down carefully. He had put his ax down and was wiping his forehead.

"I have to use the outhouse."

Picking my way carefully across the snow, I realized that the sun was shining and it was actually starting to melt. The yard was showing patches of mud and grass. The outhouse was to the right of the cabin, buffered by a copse of trees.

"Laney. Stop moving," he commanded.

"I'm fine." It made me feel in control to be walking, taking care of my needs myself, even though my gait was uncertain in his oversized boots.

"Now! Fucking stop moving."

I froze and looked over at him.

All I saw was the barrel of his gun pointed directly at me. "Oh, Jesus," I managed, my hands going up automatically. "Please. Don't. I'll stop." Doing what I didn't know. But I would stop everything. Anything he wanted, I would cease and desist immediately. My heart was in my throat and I thought for a second I would faint.

Then the gun fired.

CHAPTER FOUR

CLOSED MY EYES IN PANIC, too terrified to duck or run, but my mouth opened on a scream. My voice was drowned out by the shot and the sound of the dogs barking ferociously. I waited for the pain, for oblivion, heart jumping in my chest. Death wanted me desperately, it seemed. I had survived the crash, but not the rescue. I hoped it would be over fast so I wouldn't have to see my own blood staining the snow.

But after a split second my eyes flew open and I saw that the stranger was running toward me, his gun up. "Get down, Laney!" he yelled at me.

I did, out of instinct, obedience. I turned to see what he was looking at and saw it then- a burly, thick furred bear, still moving, but down on the ground. "Oh, my God!" I tried to run and fell from the oversized boots and from my injury. I landed hard on my knees, a stupid girl who fell at the worst moment ever. Panicking, I started crawling, scrambling, away from the bear.

The second shot still scared me, causing me to jump, an involuntary yelp escaping before I could prevent it. The stranger had rescued me yet again. A frantic glance back showed he had a boot on the hide of the bear. He put the rifle to the animal's head and this third shot was muffled, less frightening. I lay on my hip, heart still thumping, throat dry from screaming. I just lay there, panting, waiting for him to tell me what to do. I was so rattled, I couldn't think. I had thought I was going to die. Twice in two days I had thought I was going to die.

Tears threatened, those same all-encompassing sobs I had humiliated myself with the day before and I bit my bottom lip hard to stop them, digging my fingernails into the snow and the muddy clay beneath it. I ground my fingers in, nails bending back, ripping off, my ankle throbbing as I dragged it out from under me. I couldn't give in. I couldn't. I needed to hold it together. Dirt and slushy snow covered my fingers as they sank, my skin splotchy and red above my wrists. I yanked them back out, watched the slide of moist earth down my arms, under my coat sleeves. The irrational action brought me back from the edge of hysteria.

The stranger's arm went under my chest and he hauled me to my feet. "You okay?"

I raised my gaze to his blue eyes and nodded rapidly. It was then that it occurred to me the reason I had fought so hard to keep the tears at bay was because I suspected he wouldn't have patience for them. I hadn't wanted to anger him. "I didn't know..." I said then clamped my lips shut again.

He didn't say anything else, but he was angry with me anyway, I could tell. His jaw was set. His eyes narrowed. I'd done what he had told me not to. But I wasn't sure if he was angry that I'd put myself at risk or just annoyed by my disobedience. It didn't matter, really. I just knew he was angry and I hated it.

"I'm sorry," I said simply. Over explaining wouldn't change anything. "Thank you for saving me. Again." A shudder rolled through me. I felt nausea rise in my throat but I fought it.

"Let's get you inside." He easily swung me up into his arms.

I wanted to wrap myself around his neck but my hands were

filthy so I let them dangle away from him so I wouldn't muddy his jacket.

"I have to take the bear down to the river and butcher him there," he said. "There's already too much blood. Any more and the predators will start coming in too close to the house."

That forced me to look back, at the bear still on the ground. The blood that splashed the snow was his, not mine. I breathed in and out, a sharp staccato, my breath a quick vapor that appeared only to disappear immediately in front of me, over and over. No words came out. I felt like this must be what a panic attack was-this inability to focus on anything other than my anxiety.

The stranger opened the door and brought me into the house. He set me on the chair. "Take the boots off," he said. "You're going to have to wait on coffee unless you get it yourself. I have to take care of this right now."

"Okay. That's fine." I bent over to undo laces but my hands were still caked in mud. They were ice cold from the snow and I debated what to do with them. There was no sink that just turned on and off but I didn't ask. I wasn't going to ask. I'd already made more work for him. I'd come into his world, an inconvenience and bother, disturbing his routine, offering him nothing but aggravation.

The weight of my situation rested on me, heavy, and anxiety melted into a deep, jarring depression. I didn't know what to do. About anything.

He left without another word, yanking the door shut. I wanted to stand up and watch him, so I went ahead and used my filthy hand on the laces. It hurt to pry the boots off, pain in my ankle and my scraped up raw fingers feeling stiff, uncooperative. I picked my way carefully across the room to the window above the sink. He was wrapping a chain around the bear, then winching it to the back of an ATV. His movements were strong, confident, but it was obviously a seriously heavy animal. Just moving a leg seemed to require a serious effort. Once it was attached to the ATV, he got in and drove, dragging the bear across the yard and down out of sight. The river. I wondered if I could hear it. I couldn't see it, not from the house.

I was aware of the fact that I still had to pee, but I wasn't going back out there. Fuck that.

Limping, I tried to figure out how to wash my hands and make coffee, but I couldn't seem to puzzle out how the pump on the sink worked. The drinking water in the cooler was obviously not for washing up so I didn't touch it. I just let the dirt dry on my hands slowly, moving a chair in front of the stove to accomplish it faster. Time ticked by with anemic, sluggish speed. It felt like he'd been gone a long time. My bladder hurt from fullness. My stomach growled. I felt the dizziness that came from lack of food and caffeine. After an indeterminate amount of time I got up again and foraged, drinking some water and finding some jerky in the cupboard. I tore into the salty meat with my teeth, saliva flooding my tongue.

There were things in his makeshift kitchen that I didn't know how to use. Didn't even know what they were. A glance out the window showed him coming back toward the house. My spirits lifted, but then I saw he was just covering the blood in the snow with something. Sawdust? I wasn't sure. Then he went back in the direction he had come from. When he turned, I saw it. The blood. On his jacket, his jeans.

That should have had me looking away, but I studied him. Jason. I studied Jason. The man who had lost his sister. Or the nameless man who'd lost his girlfriend. He moved with purpose, every stride powerful, planned. What brought a man to the middle of the wilderness? Who would want to live in a daily struggle for survival? Completely isolated.

I hated being alone. It didn't take an expensive therapist to pinpoint the how or the why. It came from all those nights when my mother put me to bed then went out. I assume she went out to bars or on dates, but I don't really know. We've never talked about it. Maybe she's convinced herself I don't remember or that I was never aware. But I was. I knew every single time. It was like the click of the front door ripped me out of sleep and then I would lie there on the bed, the darkness encroaching on me, smothering me. I heard every creak and groan of the walls and floors settling, every sound from the apartment upstairs. The toilet flush, the footsteps. I heard the wind outside, the windows rattle. I heard cars drive down our street and the occasional siren. If fear had a sound, I heard that too. It was the beat of my heart, the thump of my pulse in my veins, the shallow rhythm of my breathing, the scrape of my feet on the bottom of the bed, a weird self-soothing technique I picked up along the way.

One night I had to use the bathroom and eventually wet the bed rather than get up and go, too scared. In the morning, I changed my own sheets. I was six.

Then mom married Dean and everything got better. But being alone still scared me and I avoided it. I went from home to a dorm to roommates.

To Alaska.

The silence in the cabin crawled over my skin. It was alive, absence of sound creating a hum in my ears, the noise of anxiety, rising panic. It was like the plane after I woke up- the stillness obvious, unnatural.

He was gone a very long time. So long that I picked the dried flakes of mud off my fingers. So long that I found crackers and ate three of them. So long that I thought I would go insane. There were no books in his cabin. None. I thought about a meme a friend had sent me awhile ago that said "If he doesn't have books in his apartment, don't fuck him." That made laughter, irrational giggles, erupt from me. The need to go to the bathroom was so urgent, everything inside me hurt from the pressure. I was a jiggling leg, cramping gut, tense mess and I decided that if I couldn't go to the outhouse, I could still go. I put the boots back on and cautiously opened the front door, looking both ways. Then I scuttled out onto the porch, feeling self-conscious and criminal. I went to the very edge and sat down, easing my legs through the railings. Then I pulled my pants down and peed. I sighed in relief as it ran out, not even caring that it splashed my leg.

It wasn't until I stood, and I saw the stream in the snow below, and I yanked my pants back up, legs icy cold, that I felt the sting of humiliation. I wasn't sure why. It was just overwhelming. All of it. I felt a failure for surviving but not knowing how to be a survivalist.

Back in the cabin, I paced, dragging my bad ankle along behind me, welcoming the pain. As punishment. For living. For being so dependent. For having chosen the path of least resistance in my life. My response to a lonely, neglectful childhood? Pretend it hadn't happened. Play the role of dutiful daughter in a perfect-to-the-outsider family. But not so dutiful that I was successful. My rebellion had been underachievement. Never stress myself, never push myself, stay far, far away from the corporate world of Dean and Mom.

I pulled my cell phone back out and turned it on, unable to resist. I stared at pictures until my eyes filled with tears that I desperately wanted to shed. I turned it off. Put it in the drawer of the nightstand. There was a bottle of hand lotion in there. I pictured the stranger, naked, filling his hand with lotion and wrapping his fist around his cock. The image startled me. I wasn't the most highly sexual person, and I never walked around picturing guys jerking off. But all my senses, emotions, were heightened here. I felt more… alive. More aware of my body, every inch, every function. And it was terrifying. I didn't know what to do with all those feelings.

When the stranger finally returned, I was standing in the middle of the room, convulsively closing my fists and opening them again.

He stopped inside the door, reaching back to lock it behind him. His hands were covered in blood, as was his jacket. It looked like someone had taken a bucket of it and tossed it onto him. Or that he'd been elbow deep in a bear carcass. My stomach clenched. He stared at me without speaking as he removed his boots and his jacket, which he hung on the hook seemingly without concern for the state of it. He smelled sweet, tinny. Like the air around me on the plane. I fought the urge to panic. To run. Where the hell would I run to? On a bad ankle? And what was I running from? Reality?

"You hungry?" he asked, casually. He strode over and put more wood on the stove. It was down to embers.

I had noticed the cold, but it hadn't occurred to me to feed the stove. Useless. I nodded. "Yes. I didn't want to just dig around in your cupboards but I did eat some crackers."

"It's fine. You can eat whatever you want." He went over to the sink and did something that made water run.

His back blocked the movement so I couldn't tell what he'd done and I was too proud to ask. Or stupid.

"I'll cook you some protein. I'm sure you could use it. But let's clean up first." He put pots of water on the stove after he washed up his arms with a bar of soap. Then he stripped his outer flannel shirt off and tossed it over the back of the chair. I wondered how he did laundry. Nothing was the way I accustomed to doing it.

"Would you have killed that bear if I hadn't gone outside?" I asked, because it was bothering me. I was responsible for that animal dying. Because I hadn't listened to Jason.

He nailed me over his shoulder with his icy stare. "When a bear is sniffing around my property, I scare it off. If it comes back, I kill it. It's not your fault." Then he peeled his T-shirt off. He dipped his head under the running water and soaked his head. He lathered his hands with the bar of soap and washed his hair.

I wanted to offer to help, but why would he need my help? I studied his muscular back, the nape of his neck, the way the corded muscles rippled as he washed his hair quickly and roughly, movements jerky. "What did you do with the bear?" I asked.

He stood up, flipping his hair back, swiping at his eyes. Droplets ran down into his beard, down his back, over his shoulders. He made no move to grab a towel. If he had towels. "What did I do with it? I peeled its skin, like an orange, taking it off almost perfectly inside out, all intact. That takes time. Then I disposed of his organs so no other animals would come sniffing it around. I cut his flank off." He pointed to his hips. "Here. And here. Is that what you want to know?"

I nodded, chastened. "Let me cook dinner." I didn't want to be a burden any more than I already was.

"Sure. But lay on the bed first. Let's get you cleaned up." He pulled a towel out of a drawer and instead of using it on himself, brought it to the nightstand, along with one of the pots of water heating up on the stove.

I did what he said, climbing carefully on the bed, then lying down, heart racing. He took my shirt off, gentle hands at odds with his calluses, with his bear bone breaking skills, and his stern expression. He still hadn't dried his hair and it was starting to curl at the nape of his neck. The strands were still unruly but he smelled clean. Droplets landed on my chest when he bent over me, and I lowered my arms again docilely, no longer uncomfortable with my nudity in front of him. His gaze stroked over my breasts, but he gave no other indication that I was naked. His control was amazing. I could tell he was attracted to me, and he was a man who had been alone for an indeterminate amount of time. But he kept his touch appropriate, easing my pants down, leaving my panties in place.

Then he took the towel, dipped it in the water, rubbed the bar of soap over it, and started at my face, washing it the way you would a child. I closed my eyes briefly when he ran the softness over my lids, but otherwise, I watched him, sinking in to the intimacy of his touch. Human touch. It was immensely comforting to feel his hands skimming over me, the warm towel wiping away from dried tears, facial oil and dirt, the sour stench of sweat and fear. He glided over my neck, down my shoulder, dipping into the hollow of my clavicle bone. He lifted one arm over my head, and went down the whole length of it. I had a self-conscious moment about the downy hair now sprouting in my armpit, but he gripped me harder, not allowing me to clamp my arm down at my side.

He went back for fresh water, and the once again warm cloth went straight to my right breast. He rubbed, and his hand cupped the soft flesh, his thumb brushed over the nipple, fabric between his skin and mine. It made my breath catch, the sensation arousing me whether he intended it to or not. He went under the breast, not reacting to my rising chest, my hardening nipples, my shallow breathing. Then he went to the other side and repeated the process. Goose bumps rose on my skin, and I sighed, enjoying the way my nerve endings responded to his touch, firing up endorphins and easing me into relaxation. It felt good to get clean, to have the warm water heating my flesh ever so briefly, and leaving moist scented skin in its wake, instantly chilling.

When he moved down over my abdomen, I shivered when he dipped his finger into my belly button. It tickled and I squirmed a little. His hand landed heavy on my hip, stilling my movement. Then he spread my legs. He touched my inner thighs, and I couldn't help it, I gave a little moan. It was a tantalizing tease. But he ignored the sound and finished, down each leg, behind my knees, between my toes. I wanted to giggle at that, but I bit my lip to prevent it escaping. He had removed the bandage on my ankle and he rewound it now, tightly compressed. He put a new bandage on my arm. Then he went to the stove and got a new pot of hot water.

"What's that for?" I didn't have any parts left to wash, save one, and I was certain I couldn't lie still and let him take a cloth to me there, like he was a nurse, and I was an ancient patient, her sexuality and desirability long gone.

"Your hair. Come to the edge of the bed." He gave those instructions then he didn't wait for me. He pulled me by the armpits so that my head was just dangling over the side of the bed. The stranger got on his knees next to the bed and he carefully pulled all the dirty strands of my hair free of my neck and shoulders so they puddled over his fingers.

I fought the angle, not wanting to let my head fall back freely, but it was too uncomfortable. Plus his fingers wound tighter into my hair when I fought, so I gave up and let myself drop backward. I stared up at him upside down. I had a view of his chest and the underside of his chin. I counted the water droplets sluggishly making their way down his abdomen, to disappear in his jeans. I wanted to follow those rivulets with my tongue, to see what his skin would taste like. Blood?

In this position I imagined him peeling me like he had the bear. Like an orange, he'd said. Just tear from scalp to toes, turn me inside out until everything in me was exposed and he would hang me out to dry. I'd never shown the true inside of me to anyone.

He used his hand to cup some water and pour it over my hair repeatedly until it was damp in most places and the blood was rushing to behind my eyes. I closed them while he scrubbed the soap over my hair, without ever pulling the roots. It was pleasant, soothing, even when I grew lightheaded. After he rinsed, he dried it a little, squeezing the ends of my strands. Then he paused, doing nothing, still gripping those ends in the towel. I opened my eyes and looked up at him. "What?" I asked.

His expression was fierce, filled with lust. I felt a jolt of responding desire, immeasurably pleased that despite my inadequacies as a survivalist, he still wanted me. It would have been the final kick to my ego if he hadn't, if my appearance didn't at least tempt him, the man who lived alone in the woods.

"I'm thinking that you could have been anyone on that plane. Old, a kid, a man. And yet, you're you. A beautiful woman. I feel like you're an offering from the gods. One I want to accept."

I tried to sit up so I could turn my head, so I could tell him that he could have me. That I needed him to take me. That I had to feel alive, that I had to reconcile myself with the body that I primarily chose to ignore, never putting it through anything uncomfortable. I eased my body through every day with lattes and gentle bike rides, with hot showers and scented lotions, and a tangle free hairbrush. I never pushed it, I never felt pain or challenge or even the subtleties of hair raising on skin, or awareness of how my joints did their job constantly, without complaint. I wanted to sit up and see his eyes head on and see his appreciation.

But he curled his fingers around my hair, yanking my head back down, drawing at the roots for the first time, causing my eyes to fill with moisture.

"I didn't say you could sit up. Do you understand?"

I lay still, head caught, not mine to control. This was what he'd been telling me before. If I wanted him to cross that line and take us into sex, I had to be willing to agree to this. His dominance. I thought about it, my nipples hard, my inner thighs aching, wet with desire. For him. I was already under his control, technically. I couldn't do anything without his permission and I was vulnerable. The one who needed him for survival. It was in his power to drop me in the bush and let me die. But he wouldn't do that. I knew it. I could feel it deep inside. That whoever he was, whatever he had done, he wasn't a sociopath. He was asking permission to indulge his sexual preferences with me.

"How does this work?" I whispered.

He didn't pretend to misunderstand. "I already told you. You do what I say."

I was dizzy, spots dancing in front of my eyes, but it didn't occur to me to complain. I didn't mind. There was something erotic about the rush of my own blood, the steely grip of his large hands. The real world seemed far, far away. There was no escape from here, not anytime soon. I wanted his comfort, his touch. He wasn't going to give me a hug. But I wanted that connection to another human being. And what he was offering was something I never would have considered back in Seattle but seemed compelling, intriguing, here, in his bed, in nothing except for my panties. His hand in my hair after he had gently washed it.

"What if I don't like something?" I asked.

"Tell me. I'll stop."

Then he bent over and brushed his lips over mine. They were soft, and confident, caressing. My face was buried in his chest from the position, and I closed my eyes and breathed in the scent of him. Of skin, sweat, soap. He was inherently masculine, my mountain man, and I felt the very intrinsic feminine response of my body to him. I wanted to be possessed by him, invaded, dominated. I'd already handed over my life to him and now I wanted to matter to him. I wanted to be important. I didn't want him to regret that I had landed in his lap, an accident of fate. I wanted to be that gift from the gods.

My senses swam and I saw spots behind my eyes, as I kissed him back, gasping when he teased my lips open with his tongue. It was an exploratory kiss, kinder than I'd been expecting. It didn't last long. He pulled back. Then he raised my head using nothing but my hair and his arm strength. He tugged up, then pushed forward until I was in a sitting position on the bed, all the blood rushing out of my head. My mouth got hot and my vision blurred.

I couldn't see for a second.

But I heard him. In my ear. A rough murmur. Max. My soon-to-be lover. A man with a past sadder than my own. Who was strong enough to be alone with his thoughts. Something I could never do.

"We won't start with the ropes," he said. "But we'll finish with them."

CHAPTER FIVE

MY VISION CLEARED, THE BLACK spots dancing in front of my eyes receding as I sat up very still, in the position he had put me in.

It was a moment of total clarity. I wasn't strong enough to hike forty miles, or skin a bear, but I could take whatever he needed to dish out. In submission, I could find my strength. And I could satisfy him.

I wasn't sure anything would be sexier than satisfying Max.

"Do we need to talk about things? Have a safe word or share what we like?" I asked, my words sounding breathless and anxious, yet eager. Set limits. Establish fantasies. That seemed important, even if I wasn't totally sure what I liked. My sexual history was a flash of pleasant encounters, nothing more, nothing less. Soft rhythms, open thighs, warm skin. Like soaking in a bubble bath. Not the breathless thrill of a roller coaster.

What I wanted was for him to take me to the top slowly then shove me over the peak. Then before I could catch my breath, do it all over again.

Max lifted my hair off my shoulder and ran his hand across

my skin. "This isn't a club or some kind of formal arrangement. There is nothing official here. We're alone and I just want you and I assume you want me."

"I do want you." The way he stroked his fingers back and forth on my skin made goose bumps appear in a rapid trail behind his touch. I shivered. His presence was invasive and I liked that tension, that distraction. "But I'm afraid."

I didn't mean to say that. I wasn't afraid of him. Not all the time, anyway.

"What are you afraid of?"

Being hurt. Being inadequate. Being alone. The same things I had been afraid of since I was four years old.

I swallowed hard. "I don't know."

"You're so soft," he murmured, bending his head down, his lips brushing over my flesh. "So delicate. Don't be afraid, Laney. I'm not going to break my new toy."

I turned, wanting to see him. A drop of water ran down my forehead to my brow and I ignored it. The outline of his nose was inches from my eyes as he lifted his head from my skin. His gaze locked with mine. Fear didn't matter. Neither did the insistent underlying tension that I couldn't totally trust him. I moistened my bottom lip and said, "Tell me what to do."

The corner of his mouth turned up. "Lie down on your back and let me see you."

He'd already seen me. But I eased back without question, head on his pillow. My body was still weary, ankle aching. My muscles in my shoulders were tense and I took a deep breath, forcing myself to loosen up for him. My hands fell slack, my legs sank apart as he studied me, head to toe. Did he like what he saw? I couldn't tell. His eyes were shuttered, expression enigmatic. But he reached out and traced the contours of my face, my cheek, brushing over my lips. I turned into his touch, the cat in the sun spot, questing, relaxing, rubbing.

With one of his hands so gently stroking, my lips parted on a warm sigh, I wasn't expecting the sudden hard pinch of my nipple from his other hand and I gasped, startled. The sharp pain seemed to pull my focus away from my throbbing ankle. The pain drew from deep inside me, and both my breasts firmed, aching for attention. His hand fell away though to stroke across my waist, while his lips dropped down onto my neck.

I breathed deeply and I could have sworn I smelled the blood still clinging to him. The crack of his gun replayed in my head and I shivered, wanting to touch him, wanting comfort. But I didn't. I couldn't. Max caressed my skin, rushing his hands over me everywhere, his lips tracing a gentle path over my shoulder, the swell of my breast, my jaw, my earlobe. I hadn't expected him to be tender. It wasn't a hug, but it was better. It felt devotional. Like he was savoring the feel of my body, my skin.

The room was quickly darkening as dusk turned to night and I sighed, tears at the back of my eyes. I needed this. I needed him.

"You're so warm," he murmured, his beard scratching along my cheek. "Smooth. The only time I get to touch soft, warm things is when I'm tending the dogs. Or after I hunt. And they cool so quickly, it's not the same."

I stiffened involuntarily. My heartbeat kicked up a notch. He meant when he touched the corpses of dead animals. He meant I felt like creatures he killed. I started to shift away from him, unnerved. I had almost forgotten he was strange, my stranger. But that reminded me with crystal clarity that he lived in almost total isolation. His social skills weren't going to be impeccable. He didn't mean anything by it other than a sort of sideways compliment.

He stopped me from sliding out from under him by pressing his hands firmly onto my shoulders. "Where are you going?"

Before I could respond, he kissed me. At first, I hesitated, his physical weight oppressive. But his mouth teased and tasted mine, and my body responded without total consent from me. My arms wrapped around his back, feeling the smooth, hard muscles bulging beneath his flesh as my lips parted to give his tongue access. He kissed like he was in no hurry to get anywhere in particular, yet urgently enjoyed what he was doing. It was fervent and dominating, yet never rushed. I sighed, tangling my tongue with his, arching my back so our skin would touch, my breasts teasing against his chest.

"Where are you going?" he asked again.

Confused, as I wasn't trying to shift away, I murmured, "Nowhere."

"Exactly," he said, his voice satisfied.

In the dark, his head bent, shifting lower, and I swallowed my uneasiness, focusing on the tight desire coiling in my belly as he lowered his mouth over my nipple, sucking and teasing at it. Then he bit. I gave a soft cry. But he instantly returned to drawing the tip into his mouth, soft suckling. He switched to the other breast, and my desire grew, my grip on his back firmer. He pushed both of my breasts together so he could suck both nipples at the same time. I jerked a little, startled. No one had ever done that before. Why had no one even thought to do that before? I groaned, my head falling back. There was an element of pain, my breasts squeezed tightly, but mostly there was pleasure, each tug of the taut buds causing a matching tug of arousal in my inner thighs. I shifted, restless, anticipating the hot thrust of his cock inside me.

Would he take me hard? Or with a slow, steady rhythm. I couldn't predict him or his next move. But I found myself squeezing his back harder, rocking my hips upward.

Max shifted off me suddenly, leaving in his place nothing but cold, empty air. "What are you doing?" I whispered.

But I got my answer when he jerked my arms upward, over my head. I tried to see what he was doing, but I couldn't given the angle and the disappearing daylight. Then I felt the rough scratch of rope over my wrists, tightening, tightening. I sucked in a breath, shocked. Though not sure why I was shocked. Then turned on. My arms fell slack, then taut again as he tugged on the rope, securing a knot to the headboard. I was strung up. Like the animal carcasses in the yard. His fresh catch.

CRASH

His lips grazed my temple, then my earlobe, his tongue dipping inside with a soft little flick. His kisses across my cheek were gentle, feathery. He covered my mouth with his, but without domination. It was a beautiful, lovely kiss, intimate. Deep. I wanted to wrap my arms around him again but I couldn't. I tugged against the rope unintentionally, the shock of my restraint reoccurring every few seconds as I kept trying to touch him. Every time I realized I was being held back, tethered, I felt a hot rush of liquid between my thighs. It was exciting. Dangerous. He controlled everything, and I wanted him to.

No decisions to be made. He made them all for me, and it was a relief. A heady, arousing, terrifying relief.

Max sucked my nipples again, harder, more aggressively until I was groaning softly. He rested his hand on my mound, so it cupped me, a teasing reminder that he wasn't inside my panties, wasn't actually touching my aching clitoris, or delving into my body. It was delicious, languid. Yet I wanted more. He shifted away from me again and I opened my mouth to ask then shut it again before I spoke. There was a creak and I rolled a little on the mattress as he left the bed. He moved across the cabin in the dark.

"Close your eyes," he said. "I'm turning on a light."

I did. I waited a heartbeat. "Can I open them again?"

"Yes." He'd put on the lamp by the kitchen sink and it sent a soft glow around the cabin. "I want to see you."

He returned to the bed, but he didn't climb on with me. He stood beside the bed, his erection pushing against the fabric of his boxer briefs. His gaze drifted over me, settling on my panties. I fought the urge to squirm under his scrutiny or to lift my hips in invitation. I knew instinctively he wouldn't want me to do that. So I waited, my breath shallow, my chest rising and falling rapidly. My hair had soaked the pillow beneath my head and when I turned to see him, the cool damp of the cotton met my cheek. I had fisted my hands over my head in the rope. It wasn't an uncomfortable position. The only thing uncomfortable was the deep ache in me that demanded satisfaction.

Max took my panties by the waistband and pulled them down. He didn't remove them, but instead quickly wrapped them around my ankles, binding my feet together. I was confused, unsure what he was planning. But that was part of the excitement. He shoved my feet up a little so my legs scissored out and he leaned in, studying my sex, his breath tickling my inner thigh. I was tense, the struggle to hold myself still intense. He flicked his tongue across my clit, and I jerked a little at the sensation. Then when he laved slowly down, lower, then back up again, I gave a low moan.

But he lifted his head again and moved away from me. Frustrated and confused, I watched him go over to the kitchen cupboard and open it.

"What are you doing?" I asked, frowning.

"I'm hungry. I'm fixing us dinner."

"But…" I wasn't even sure what to say. I was naked, tied to his bed. He had started to eat me out, then had stopped, because what? One appetite was stronger than the other? "I want you."

I sounded petulant. Childish.

"I want you too," he said mildly. He turned and watched me. "But this isn't about instant gratification. Everything is better when you anticipate and savor it. When you work hard for it."

There was nothing in particular I worked hard for. It didn't take discipline to live my life. I understood his point, but it didn't make me any less frustrated. Or feel any less helpless. "This is sex, not building your own shelter or hunting your own food."

"Do you trust me, Laney?"

"Yes," I said automatically. But then I realized I didn't entirely and he had told me I shouldn't. "No." That sounded too harsh though. "Yes."

"That's why you have to wait." He turned his back to me. "That's why I have to wait."

"Wait how?"

"Stop asking me questions."

CRASH

I fell silent, knowing he wouldn't answer anything I asked at this point. He was done with the conversation. He was done with me, for now anyway. I lay there on the bed tied up, listening to my own breathing. Listening to him opening cans, turning on the stove with a click. He moved efficiently, calmly. His movements routine. It didn't seem that my presence altered his behavior in any way. He wasn't excited or upset or intrigued. I was there and he would deal with me, that was it.

He wasn't a Max. A Max would have slipped me his cock almost immediately. He would have pounded for five minutes, rolled over, grinned. I stared up at the ceiling, debating if this was a mistake. If I should demand he release me and put all my clothes on and sleep on the floor by the stove. If comfort and eventual satisfaction were worth this uneasiness.

I looked back at him again, watching his back. He was so strong. So masculine. Totally foreign to me. Rubbing my ankles together, testing the restriction of my panties binding me, I thought about the last time I'd had sex. It was with my friend Harrison after a party about six months earlier. We'd been drinking wine, because it felt mature, and because it was cheap. Four dollars a bottle. We'd bought a case of it and gotten a ten percent discount. There were eight of us there at mine and my roommate Sammy's apartment that night and we'd listened to indie rock and talked about a political rally that we all deluded ourselves we would attend the next day, but we wouldn't. We would be hungover or have to work or wouldn't have any money left to take the bus or would have to visit our parents. Any number of a thousand excuses and those would also fuel our procrastination for applying to grad schools, new jobs, doing our laundry, buying fresh food at the market. Instead we'd spend the next day in our respective beds for ten hours, watching YouTube videos and eating leftovers. Sammy and I would ignore the empty bottles and glasses strewn around the living room along with paper plates loaded with Chinese food.

Harrison would lie on the couch with me for a few hours,

snoring, while I wished he would leave, and Sammy's cat, Miss Priss, ate lo mein noodles off one of the abandoned plates and I wouldn't care enough to shoo her away. But before we would waste Saturday doing nothing that mattered in any way, that was totally unproductive, and completely insular, on Friday night we were twenty-somethings with big plans and big dreams. We were movers and shakers, excited, full of opinions and chatter and trivia, and sexual urges that could be met with friends because we were evolved enough to do that. We could dive in and out of bed with each other and it was all cool, man. We were cool.

What we were was fucking clueless.

What did we achieve from talking about everything we would do and never doing anything?

What had I gained from having vanilla sex with Harrison?

A mildly pleasant night. Entertainment. The illusion of being in control of my life, my choices.

Here, I wasn't in control at all. I was in the middle of the goddamn wilderness of Alaska, with a swollen ankle, and no means to communicate with anyone other than the man in front of me. And I was naked and tied up, arguably at my request. I was the one who had been obvious about wanting sex. He'd warned me off him and I had quested, reached out to him. This was where I was, and it was odd and terrifying that it was where I wanted to be.

But I did.

I had to finish this to the end. I had never pushed myself, seen how far I could take something. Since my mother had married Dean, I'd made it my life's work to never be uncomfortable. It was why I was a good girl, the one who never made waves and never took risks. But when I did take a risk, it was usually a massive one. A huge, burbling volcanic risk, like now. Like one or two times before.

I couldn't scuttle away from this. I had gotten on a plane to potentially go and marry a man I hadn't seen since I was twelve and that was bizarre. Risky. Yet all my friends had deemed it romantic- having an online relationship with a childhood friend. Winging off to the wilderness for a lovers' tryst, to see if the feelings were real or imagined. I'd done it with zero confidence and sleepless nights and the pervasive nag in the back of my mind that I was being desperate, seeking an answer to a question I hadn't even asked myself.

I had been desperate.

Like I had been since the crash.

This could change that dynamic. Put me in a place of quiet confidence, the woman who knows she pleases a man just by being her.

As I watched the stranger cook food on the stove, a meaty and spicy smell filling the cabin, his hair still damp on the nape of his neck, his skin softly illuminated from the kerosene lamp on the counter, I relaxed into my restraints. I moistened my bottom lip with the tip of my tongue, and assessed my nudity, my body. He had piled the wood stove high again so that I wasn't cold uncovered, and the bed was soft, his comforter I was resting on a squishy down. My ankle still ached. My nipples were still tight. My fingers tingled from being up over my head. I felt more free and sexual than I ever had, the position forcing me into total awareness of my vagina, my own damp desire.

So I said nothing. I waited, each minute that ticked by driving me further and further into arousal, a heightened sense of arousal and anticipation, never knowing when he might return to the bed. I shifted my legs restlessly so that I could feel my inner thighs rub together. I rolled side to side so the cool air would rush over the curve of my ass. I bent my knees for the same reason, to give my hot vagina some air, exposing my private desire to the stranger if he chose to look. But mostly to be aware of it myself. I felt sexy, in tune with my body.

Alive.

He had kept me alive and now he made me feel alive.

I bit my lip to enjoy the sting. I flicked my tongue over the salty flesh of my shoulder. I bent my injured ankle, up, down, to feel the pain wash over me. I dug my fingernails into my palms, and I lay there, open to him. Open to experience, to a thrill. A languid, slumberous arousal settled into my body, my eyes half closed, my thoughts unfocused. I felt a little stoned, on anticipation, on desire, on exposure.

More minutes went by, I lost track. Then he came over to me with a smile. It was a genuine smile of affection, like he was pleased I was there. With him. Pleased by my behavior. "You hungry?" he asked.

I nodded.

He untwisted the panties from my ankles. "You don't need these."

I thought he meant for the moment, but he actually turned and opened the stove and tossed them into the fire. I made a sound of protest. Those were my only panties. He hadn't recovered my luggage. But even as I felt a knee-jerk panic, the "I have to have those," my legs, now free, fell open for him. It was time. He was going to climb over me, push inside me.

But he didn't. He reached up and yanked the rope on my wrists free. His face came so close to mine I had to close my eyes so I wouldn't grow dizzy. His lips brushed over my eyelids, one then the other. It was tender. His fingers massaged my wrists where the restraints had been.

Then he was gone, standing up. "Come eat." He tossed me a T-shirt and sweats, casually.

Like I hadn't just been tied up. Like I wasn't wet and aching with need for him. I sat up, stiff, hair spilling over my shoulders. I couldn't think of anything to say. So I just swallowed the excess saliva in my mouth and put the shirt on. When the fabric brushed over my tight nipples, I was disappointed to cover up. Same with my pants. When I covered my sex, it only made me even more acutely aware of how unsatisfied I was. Maybe that was his intention.

I went over to the kitchen and moved in along side of him as he put stew in bowls. He was still only in his underwear but he was wearing socks. It felt intimate, like we were truly lovers. I wanted to wrap my arms around his waist from behind. Hug him. I needed to touch him. My heart and body ached with the need. With every need. I imagined leaning my head against his warm back, eyes closed, breathing in his scent. His strength.

Instead I crossed my arms over my chest, before asking, "Can I help?"

I couldn't. I knew I couldn't. I was useless here. I didn't know what anything was or how to use anything in his cabin.

He gave me another smile. It was small, mysterious, but it reached his pale eyes. "Just be you."

"That's not enough," I said before I could stop myself. I leaned against the counter, feeling too exposed. Which was insane. I was wearing oversized clothes now. Why did I feel more vulnerable than I had ten minutes earlier, tied to his bed naked?

"Of course it is. I don't need help doing any of my chores. I did them before you and I don't expect you to have to help with manual labor. But you're keeping me company." His hand brushed down the back of my hair. "I wasn't lonely but I'm glad you're here."

"Really?" That made me ridiculously pleased. He was being very sweet.

"Really." His fingers twisted in my hair and he pulled so my head turned. "Let me see your face."

I gazed up at him, the position awkward. "What?"

"Lovely Laney," he murmured, gaze raking over me, caressing me. "I just want to look at you."

That felt more real than any flattery I'd ever received before. Michael's compliments always managed to sound mechanical. Rote. "What's your name?" I asked, because he seemed tender. Open. I thought he would tell me.

He laughed softly. Even as his grip tightened on my hair, firmer and firmer until there were tears in my eyes. He jerked me upright. "Call me Sam."

I knew immediately that wasn't his name. "Why would I do

that if it's not your name?"

He let me go and I stumbled back a few inches.

"Eat your food, Laney. And tell me what brings you to Alaska."

I fell silent, staring at him. I couldn't tell him about Michael. I could say I was visiting a friend, but was that believable?

The silence drew out too long.

"Exactly. You don't want to tell me any more than I want to tell you." His hand came out, slid under my shirt. "Forget the past. It doesn't exist. All that matters is here. Now. You. Me."

CHAPTER SIX

ORGET THE PAST? IT WAS enticing, seductive. "Who am I then?" I whispered.

"You're mine."

I dropped my gaze, unsure. "I'm keeping you from eating. I'm sorry." I reached around him, picked up both bowls he had placed on the counter, and started to carry them over to the table.

"I can get these. They're hot and your arm isn't healed. And put some socks on, doll. The floor is cold." He took the bowls from me.

"Thanks." His concern, such as it was, made me warm inside. It wasn't a hug, but it was more than I'd been expecting and I liked it. "Can I get you a drink, Sam?"

He sat down and looked up. He rubbed his beard scruff and smiled. "Sure. Water, thanks."

I found the glasses and filled them from the water cooler. I set them both on the table then went to his dresser. I felt strange digging through his drawers but he didn't object. I fished out a pair of socks and sat on the bed, pulling them on. He was already eating. My ankle was stiff, but improving. I was hungry, and when I joined him, I plowed through the stew quickly for a half dozen spoonfuls.

"I have to cut down a tree tomorrow," he said. "It's dead and I think it might fall if I don't. It's too close to the cabin to leave it. It might take me awhile."

"Okay. Is there anything you want me to do while you're gone?"

His eyes lit up with curiosity. "Do you know how to make cookies? I always say I'm going to but I never have time. I wouldn't mind a good chocolate chip cookie."

So he liked cookies. Even the Alaskan man could be softened with sugar, apparently. I didn't entirely trust my memory but I figured I could experiment and get pretty close. "Sure. Do you have the chips?"

"Yes. It was me being optimistic last time I went to town."

It was a seemingly normal conversation. One that any couple would have any night of the week. It struck me as amusing. Isolated in the bush with the stranger, the dynamic was still so... domestic. Even with me not knowing his name and my panties in the fire. I wondered what he thought about all day, every day. When strange girls weren't crashing into the trees and becoming dependent on him. Was his brain just a checklist of survival tasks?

There was no way to know. But right then, he seemed like any other man. Relaxed in his own home. Hungry. Younger. Not the dominant alpha male he'd shown me on multiple occasions. So who was the real Sam? Neither, since he clearly wasn't a Sam. Maybe he was both. Because whatever he was, he wasn't dishonest and he wasn't interested in being polite because society demanded it.

"How do you figure things out?" I asked. "I mean, if I want a recipe I look it up online. I order makeup and perfume and all kinds of stuff online. What do you do?"

"I don't wear makeup," he deadpanned. Then he winked.

I laughed, startled. "Then you're lucky, because it's an

expensive hobby."

"I do order stuff online when I'm in town. Then I pick it up the next time I'm in town. There is a store there for basics. But I have about five shirts and I wear them until they disintegrate."

"What do you do for fun?" I took another bite of the stew. It was warm and heavy on sriracha, which surprised me. It wasn't a traditional stew spice. My belly already felt full. My stomach had shrunk in two days.

"I don't watch reality TV." He took a long swallow of his water and watched me over the rim of his glass.

Did he think I was insulting him? Calling him boring? "Then you're not losing brain cells. Though I can't say anything. It's a guilty pleasure of mine."

"I never feel guilty about any pleasure I take."

That I believed. I glanced around the room. "Did you build this place?"

"Yes."

"That's amazing." I wanted to say he was amazing, but he would scoff. Laugh at me. "Do you race the dogs?" I asked. Even now, I could hear them on and off in the yard. They were an integral part of the background noise of the cabin, given that the area was devoid of city sounds like planes and trains and taxis.

"No. They're for practical reasons. Getting into town. Hauling wood. Plus they are good company."

"Because they're loyal and happy to see you?"

"Because they don't talk," he said shortly.

Sometimes, he was seriously an asshole. This was one of those times. "Is that a hint?"

"It's a truth. That's all."

I dropped my spoon. "I'm finished. It was good, thank you." My voice was tight. What was wrong with trying to have a little conversation? I stood up and went to the sink. I studied it for a minute, trying to figure out how he made the pump work. There was dish soap sitting on the counter and I squirted some in my bowl.

"You don't have to do that."

"I can do it." But I couldn't. Not really. I lifted the nozzle and nothing happened. I searched for some kind of button but didn't see any.

"Laney." His chair scraped as he pushed it back and stood up. "Don't be upset."

"I'm not upset." My lip quivered and tears rose in my eyes. I couldn't figure the pump out. I let my shoulders drop. "Do you think anyone has found the plane yet? Or are those men just in there, dead? Will… animals get them?" I looked back at Sam. I knew it was stupid to ask him. Getting sympathy from him was like hugging a cactus and being startled when you got jabbed with a needle.

"I'm sure they've found the plane by now. They must have known immediately that it went off course." He came over to me and brushed my hair off my cheek. "You're safe, you know that, right? I will keep you safe."

"I know." I did. That was something I was sure of.

"Then why don't you go use the outhouse and then go to bed? You'll feel better tomorrow."

In other words, he didn't know how to deal with me or my emotions. So he wanted me to go to bed. Weary, and not having any clue what else to do, I nodded. "Okay."

As I sat down to pull on boots, he started to get dressed. "Are you coming with me?" I asked, torn between wanting to be alone for a minute to pull myself together emotionally and wanting him to guide me across the dark yard.

"Yes. It's too late for you to go alone. If there is one bear, there might be two."

I shivered. He handed me a jacket. I slid my arms in and zipped it up. He just shrugged into a flannel and didn't bother with anything else. He pulled his rifle off the wall. I wondered what it would feel like to hold it. I'd never touched a gun. What did that power feel like? Knowing with one small movement of just one finger, you could kill?

CRASH

He was right. It was dark. It was damn near impossible to see anything. The dogs whined, an eerie low keening howl that was caught up by the wind and tossed around and around us. It was like the Irish banshee from my childhood stories. My mother thought it was funny when I got scared. "Look, she's really scared," she'd say in amazement to her boyfriend of the week, and laugh hysterically. The day I knew that Dean was different, a keeper, was when she purposefully scared me with the 'banshee under my bed' fear tactic to get me to stay in my room, and Dean told her she was being a bitch. He'd said, "What the hell is wrong with you? Can't you see that she's terrified? Knock it off, Christine."

He'd lifted me off the bed and cuddled me close, taking me in to the kitchen for a glass of milk.

"Sometimes I think you like my brat more than you like me," she had yelled after us.

"I do," he had yelled back. He'd given me a wink and jiggled me in his arms.

I'd known then that he was going to stay. And he was going to be my father.

As I walked across the porch and down the steps I had a lump in my throat thinking about my stepfather. He was probably worried sick. He probably thought I was dead. I stumbled in the dark, not seeing the rock or branch in my path.

A firm hand reached out and steadied me. The stranger was like my stepfather- he was going to take care of me. Keep me safe. I could feel his presence behind me, hear his sure footing. A glance back gave me a view of his hulking shadow. He had a flashlight, but it barely cut through the oppressive blanket of night sky. But I paused and looked up, wanting to see what was up there. Even the stars couldn't penetrate the dark of an Alaskan night. I'd lost all sense of time. I knew days were longer here in the summer, but what about fall? I had no idea, and it could have been ten pm or two in the morning. I hadn't done any research. I'd just stepped onto a plane like an idiot.

"What's wrong?" he asked. His arm came around the front of

me and pulled me protectively back as he eased his body in front of me. I sensed him raise his arm and the gun.

"Nothing, I just wanted to look at the sky. I was thinking about my stepfather and how worried he must be about me."

"What about your mom?" he murmured. His arm went back down, but the other stayed around me.

It felt nice. Right. I could see my breath rising up as I tilted my head back and let the cold caress me. Why was it heat made you languid, lazy, yet cold made you feel alive? Like delineated edges against the air. Ice slamming into fire, an epic clash that jolted you to your highest state of being awake. "She's in prison for tax evasion. It will be awhile before she finds out because my stepfather will shield her from the fact that I'm missing until he can't anymore."

"At least you're missed."

I glanced back at him. "No one misses you?"

"I didn't mean anything by that. Just use the outhouse, Laney." He kissed the back of my head.

It struck me again, how surreal this was. Four days earlier I had been at the shop, saying goodbye to my co-workers. My trip was supposed to be ten days long, adequate time to determine if my relationship with Michael was real or imagined. It was unpaid vacation I was taking, and I was leaving everyone stuck covering my shifts. Now here I was, in the cold night, nestled in the dark wilderness, with a stranger I was actually starting to care about. He was my lifeline. Literally. But beyond that, he was a man, and he made me feel more like a woman.

"What's that sound?" I asked him. There was a pervasive hum in the distance. My city girl brain had interpreted it as traffic. Like a highway running through a suburb. But it had occurred to me that couldn't possibly be what it was.

"What sound?"

"It's like a hum. A whoosh."

"It's the river. The Yukon."

"Oh. It's very peaceful here." I felt like I was dreaming, yet, as intensely in a moment as one could possibly be. It was an oxymoron that I couldn't reconcile. In the absence of the noise of life, I could hear everything. Feel everything.

I expected him to be impatient, but he wasn't. He just stood there with me, waiting. Maybe he'd gotten used to the sound of my voice, like I'd gotten used to his already.

But after a few seconds, I started on to the outhouse, not wanting to ruin the moment with a reprimand that would come eventually.

He followed behind me, my persistent shadow. My protector. Savior.

Back in the cozy cabin, I yawned. I eyed the bed, yanking my boots off. My heart rate kicked up a notch as I contemplated what I must have looked like earlier, trussed up, naked, waiting for him. I was torn between wanting to just nestle into bed fully clothed, or stripping down for him. I hesitated, not sure what he wanted. I knew what I wanted. We hadn't finished what had been started and I knew I'd sleep better if he settled this ache.

Not wanting to be rejected, I opted to climb into bed in the t-shirt and sweatpants, pulling the comforter back. He peeled his shirt off before going to the sink and brushing his teeth. My tongue ran over my own teeth. I needed to brush them desperately. Would he give me a spare toothbrush? Apparently he didn't have one because he turned and offered me his.

"Want to brush?"

"Sure." I climbed back out of bed. Sharing had never bothered me. I would taste a friend's drink, use her fork. But a toothbrush was different for some reason. It only added to the sense of intimacy, of coupling. If the person who had found me was a seventy-year-old man with a massive pot belly and ear hairs would I have accepted his offer? No. I definitely wouldn't have.

He stood next to me while I brushed, his hand slipping under the shirt I was wearing. The other one followed until he was behind me, his body bumping my backside, hands shifting upward to cup my breasts. I shivered, pausing in my scrubbing.

"If I pulled your pants down and took you right now, would you stop me?" he asked.

"No." His words instantly aroused me. I shifted my hips, arched my back, seeking him with my ass to encourage.

"Good." He let go of me and stepped back. "Spit and then get in bed. Put yourself in the ropes."

I was both disappointed and intrigued. "Which ones? My hands or the one that ties me to you?" Maybe he just wanted to go to sleep, bound together, again.

He shifted my hair off my neck and kissed the nape, his lips warm on my cool skin. "I like that you asked. I want you tied to me. I want to hold you close to me all night."

"I want that too," I murmured. I wanted more than that. I wanted him to dominate, distract me, to erase all thought, all worry from my head. To make my gentle body feel powerful, like I could take it. Take him.

Without warning, his hand smacked my ass. "Then go."

I jumped at the unexpected contact. It didn't hurt. Just a mild sting. But I hadn't been expecting it. Without a word, I turned, searching his face for an explanation for who and what he was. But I saw nothing but lust.

"Clothes on or off?" I asked softly. I needed his direction. I craved it. I was already moving toward the bed because I wanted to show him I was obedient.

"Off." He was unbuttoning his jeans and taking the zipper down.

That sound made my mouth thick. I ditched the shirt quickly and skimmed his pants down over my hips. I got back into bed, this time undoing the knot tying the rope to the headboard and wrapping it around my bare waist. It scratched my skin, but I didn't care.

Maybe he was a Matthew. No. An Austin. An Austin would look at me the way he was right now, like he wanted to swallow me whole. Or Luke. Because an Austin would be too much of a jokester. He wasn't a comedian that was for sure.

CRASH

I watched him, not sure what he was going to do. Part of me wanted to close my eyes, to just feel, to let it happen as it happened. But I didn't want to miss the expression on his face. I wanted the chance to gauge his emotion. His jaw was tense, his eyes boring into me. He reached out and ran his fingers through my hair as he came up behind me, on his knees. His touch was gentle, questing.

He skimmed his briefs off and I watched over my shoulder, trying to get a better view as he moved in behind me. I hadn't seen him fully naked yet. I hadn't seen his cock, only felt it pressing against me. I only caught a glimpse of smooth skin and strong thighs before he blocked my view with a punishing kiss. I was disappointed not to have the full monty, but at the same time, I was swept away by the intensity of his kiss. Just when I settled into it, my mouth opening so he could sweep his tongue inside, he abandoned the embrace.

With a few swift movements, he had the rope cinched and secured, so we were perfectly aligned. Two spoons.

I wondered if it was calculated on his part that we weren't facing each other. Was there a reason he didn't want to look me in the eye? I didn't mind. I honestly wasn't sure I could look at him right then without exposing too much of myself. I didn't want him to see the parts of myself I had tried so hard to both hide and ignore. Given how vulnerable I felt, I wasn't sure I could keep any of that in. It would ooze out of me, an emotional mess.

He moved his hands flat over my breasts, so that his palms brushed my nipples, while his breath was warm on my temple. The rope rubbed, drawing my attention to where it chafed my skin, distracting me. I wanted to close my eyes, relax into his touch, but my eyes remained wide open, my shoulders tense. I stared at the wall that was a few feet away from the bed, focusing on a knot in the wood until my vision blurred.

The soft brush over my breasts continued so long it felt indefinite. I wanted to shove his hand lower or just swat him away. The whisper of a touch was not enough, driving me crazy, becoming both an irritant and an intense arouser. I wanted to turn. To scream. To come. It went on and on and my thoughts crawled around in my head, threatening to burst out of my mouth. I couldn't do this. I couldn't handle another hour like when he'd been fixing dinner for us and I lay there naked.

But then I realized I already was.

And that was the game.

He wanted to know how much I could take. How in control of myself I was.

One of his hands eased down past the rope to my inner thighs and teased at my curls. I had given up shaving everything bare about a year earlier in a moment of feminist defiance, and I was grateful that I wasn't dealing with itchy, stubbly new growth. I shifted, wanting to open for him, wanting him to press his finger down into my wet body, but he ignored the offer.

His hard cock still pressed against my ass and I didn't understand how he could have that kind of control. Discipline. But then again, no one could survive life in Alaska without discipline. You couldn't choose to take a day off and spend it in bed watching TV or you'd freeze to death.

Then finally, when I thought I'd go insane, his thumb raked over my clitoris and filled me, easing into my pussy. I moaned.

He pulled it out again.

I gave a cry of dismay.

His touch dragged lower, taking the moisture with it, and before I realized what he was intending to do, he was teasing at my ass then sliding in. I stiffened slightly, then relaxed, enjoying the in and out stroke. His other hand hovered over my mound, but didn't touch. Just when I was starting to pant heavily, and get into the rhythm, my ass rocking towards him, he pulled his thumb out. His other hand shifted, his finger slipping into my vagina. I sighed in initial satisfaction, but he did the same thing. Got me going, then disappeared, trading out front for back. He was taking turns finger fucking me, never letting me orgasm.

"I'd almost forgotten what a woman smells like," he murmured in my ear, as he slipped his thumb back into my ass.

I didn't clench up this time. I was relaxed, open, eager for his invasion. I craved his fingers, but I also craved more. I wanted him, but instead I concentrated on my breathing, on my body, on the tight sensation in my womb of a rubberband being drawn taut.

"You smell so sweet, so wet."

"I am wet," I whispered. "You make me so wet."

"I know. I can smell it from here without even bending over, and I love the way it feels."

I wanted to roll onto my stomach, taking him with me, so that he could plunge inside me. Either angle, I didn't care. I just wanted him to fill me. I was bucking against the rope without realizing it, losing track of time. Losing track of myself. I had been turned on before, but never like this. I'd never had a man intentionally draw out my pleasure so indefinitely, make me go to a different physical and mental space than I'd ever been.

"I want to fuck you, but I'm not going to."

"Why not?" I wiggled, wanting to see his face.

He took his finger away and said, "Stop that. You're going to tear up your skin on the rope if you move too much."

"I can't help it." I wanted to beg, but I didn't think he would like that. I didn't think it would give me the result I wanted. Either from him or from myself. So I forced myself to still, to exercise rigid control over my body.

"That's it, doll. And don't worry, I'll fuck you when I'm sure you can handle it."

I felt deflated. I didn't want to be his doll. A doll was useless. Only good for sitting on the shelf to be admired. To pet and stare at. Change her clothes. I wanted to be important, relevant. I wanted a purpose. I'd ripped myself out of my comfortable life by coming to Alaska, and the plane crash had done the rest. I wanted him to play with me. Not treat me like I was delicate. Fragile.

But I wasn't ready. I'd structured my life so that I was

surrounded by a glass display case, not taking any risks. Even coming to Alaska hadn't been about taking a risk really. I'd been seeking an answer. Running away. The easy route. Find a childhood friend. Marry him. Have him tell me what to do.

How long did I have with the stranger? A week? Two, tops? Before the snow fell hard and he could drive me into town on his snow machine. It wasn't much time to push myself. To see what I could do, learn. What I could endure physically. I wanted to earn the title of survivor, and by doing more than baking him cookies.

"I want to handle it."

"You will." He casually started stroking across my clitoris. "But if you want a fire in the stove, you have to chop the wood, and before you chop it, you have to find a log. One step at a time, Laney."

I closed my eyes because I couldn't see him anyway and I wanted to concentrate on his touch. He thought I was impatient. I wanted instant gratification. He was right. I didn't see why it was a flaw to want something when you wanted it. Why he thought it was more glorified to have to bust your ass first to get it. That seemed like an unnecessary hardship. But at the same time, I was understanding the appeal of pushing yourself, of seeing what you were capable of as a person. So I didn't protest, or argue, or beg.

I submitted, determined to find my strength.

"Do you want to come?" he asked.

I nodded.

He slid two fingers inside me in response, stroking steadily.

But then I thought about what he had said. I thought about the thrill of denial. Of waiting until I couldn't wait any more. "Actually, no, I don't," I told him. "Not yet."

Even as I spoke, I moved my hips, taking him deeper into me, to further arouse and torture myself.

"When?"

"When you tell me."

"Perfect." He slowed his rhythm then increased it. Slowed it again.

Then he loosened the rope, eased me onto my back, and bent his head down to me. His tongue worked over my clit, and I cried out. I wasn't going to be able to control myself and I clenched my thighs tightly, pushing at his shoulders. "Stop, please. I'm going to come."

"No, you're not. I didn't tell you that you could. Trust yourself," he murmured, raising his head to look up at me. "Control your body. I know you can do it."

I breathed in and out, hard, fighting the convulsions that seemed to have already started. I squeezed my vaginal muscles, I locked eyes with him, and I bit my lip, tearing into the tender flesh with my teeth to give myself a diversion, a new focus. After a few perilous seconds, I knew I'd been successful. Even while my body was tight, my inner thighs throbbing with the need for release, I felt a flush of triumph. I could actually feel the heat blooming in my cheeks, in my neck, a smile tugging at the corners of my mouth.

It gave me exactly what I'd been craving- the feeling of being well and truly alive. Like I had standing in the yard, the cold air stinging my face, the night sky opening up over my head.

He smiled up at me, and while it had a hint of a smirk, I sensed more pride and deep, male satisfaction than anything else. "Good girl," he murmured. "I knew you could do it."

I could. I could do anything.

He pulled me into his embrace, lifting my leg over his. The sweet slick moisture from my inner thighs dampened his hip, and his erection. I could feel him there, aligned with me, but not in position to enter me. It was a titillating, heart racing tease, and as he kissed my forehead, I felt a wave of possessiveness. He was mine. For now, for this moment, in this cabin, he was mine.

"Goodnight, Laney."

I studied his face, running my hand down his cheek, over his beard, across his jawline. "Good night, Sir Stranger."

He laughed softly. When he rolled over and turned the light off, I was left half on him and half off, legs drawn wide, body tingling and taut with desire.

Long after he fell into sleep, I lay there, listening to him breathe, enjoying the feel of my skin over his even if it was just my calf. He was at least letting me touch him. He had pulled all the blankets firmly up over us and made sure I was still secure in his rope.

I felt content. I shouldn't, given the dead bodies on that plane, and the fact that my family and friends must be worried sick.

But I hadn't felt this close to someone since Trent. Before it had all gone wrong. Before the restraining order.

I didn't dream at all that night.

CHAPTER SEVEN

"CHANGE OF PLANS," HE TOLD me first thing in the morning, when I was still groggy and taking a sip of the coffee he'd handed me.

"What do you mean?"

"The snow melted."

I glanced out the window, dismayed. Then I wasn't sure if I was dismayed because he couldn't take me to town, or because he could. I bit my tongue and waited for him to finish, my thoughts scaring me.

"But we're due a big storm in three days, so I need to bring in some fish today for the dogs."

"Oh. Okay." So it had nothing to do with a trip to town. Not everything was about me. I sipped the coffee. No cream. I wanted to ask for sugar, but I didn't want to be demanding. The thought made me smile. "Is there anything I can do to help?"

It was a stupid question. I would be more of a hindrance than a help.

"Do you know how to clean a fish?" He wasn't sitting down at the table with me. He was already moving around getting dressed.

I watched him pulling on his pants. His body really was beautiful, all ridges and planes and smooth, hard skin. He turned and caught me staring. His eyebrows went up as he reached for his flannel shirt.

"No," I said. "I don't. But I can learn."

"I'm hoping to put up a hundred silver salmon by tomorrow. This is the last run for the year."

My eyes widened. That was a lot of fish. "The dogs eat that much fish? They must have really silky coats."

He gave me a look of confusion. "It's a long winter."

"Fish oil is good for hair and skin," I added, in case he didn't understand.

But he didn't respond to that. "You can pull the fish from the boat so I can cut them. If I don't have to keep bending over it will go faster for me."

"Okay, I can do that." I didn't want to, but it was the least I could do considering he was feeding and clothing me. Or unclothing me. I sat there drinking my coffee and watched his skin disappear under layers of cotton. He didn't seem remotely affected by what had gone down between us the night before. I was acutely aware of my body, of the constantly present arousal he had created, that simmered low, like an electrical current under my skin. It hummed and when he was near, it rose in intensity, a high-pitched whine demanding attention.

His indifference and nonchalance was maddening. I wanted him to want the way I did.

"Get dressed then," was his only response. "I'd appreciate the help."

I did and after eating some dry cereal with the remains of my coffee we headed out into the sunshine. It was warmer, the snow definitely gone, the landscape soggy, the summer foliage looking like someone had dumped a bucket of muddy water on it. I squinted, wishing I had my sunglasses. The red pair. They were really cute. I liked to wear them with floral dresses and striped ballet flats. Mixing patterns with abandon was a signature style of mine. It seemed so irrelevant now, here, but I was swimming in the stranger's pants and shirt. I'd rinsed out my bra and was wearing it again. There were just things that couldn't be done without a bra and manual labor was one of them. But I'd never worn a bra without panties and it felt odd, decadent, the goal clearly to make me constantly aware of my vagina. Of sex. It was succeeding.

I didn't feel like me entirely. I felt disheveled and earthy. Sloppy. Yet I felt highly sexual. Sexy.

As we moved down the porch, the dogs jumped and whined and he turned and held his hand out for me. "Be careful. The ground is soft. I don't want you turning your ankle."

How pathetic that such a simple gesture was received by me like it was gold. I had a tendency to do that. I knew I did. I saw men as saviors. It was why I chose to stay single for long stretches of time. I had to be careful who I gave devotion to and I didn't always trust my judgment. My track record wasn't the best. But here I could trust the stranger and create an environment that was pleasurable and satisfying while I was there, or I could distrust him and create an atmosphere between us that was suspicious and volatile. I would much rather have this- his care and concern and me believing in the sincerity of it.

"Thanks," I said and gave him a flirty smile, squeezing his hand.

His head tilted. He dropped my hand.

I was disappointed. I had wanted him to kiss me. He noticed my face fall.

"Later, Laney. I promise I'll give you what I want. But life in Alaska requires discipline. We only have ten days of fall in total before winter hits. I need to fish and hunt or winter will mean starvation along with snow." He tweaked my nose. "So don't pout. It's not attractive."

"I wasn't pouting." Much. Annoyed, I followed him. Asking for a little smile here and there from him wasn't being petulant.

"It's not like I asked you to spend the whole day in bed with me. I understand you live a subsistence lifestyle. I'm not stupid."

"Feisty. I like it," he murmured.

But that was all he said and I could either go back to the cabin and pout and confirm for him that I was useless or I could suck it up and continue on to the river with him. I chose to follow. I also chose to believe that he was flirting. He didn't really think I was feisty, and I doubted if he would like it if I was full of sass. He liked to be in control and he didn't like unnecessary words. So I wouldn't give him any.

The river was loud. I heard it before we saw it. It was wide and clear and beautiful. I hadn't really given much thought to the beauty of Alaska, I had merely been concerned with packing warm clothes, not studying up on the area. I regretted that now, of course. There was no Google on my phone. There were only my own eyes and the stranger, and his lessons seemed to be done for the day. He had fallen into a brooding silence. He helped me into a small motorboat. Then we went down the river for about ten minutes. I wondered how far we had gone. Could we go forty miles to town in a motorboat? It seemed possible. But I didn't ask. Instead, I just wished I had a hair tie, because I was trying to take in the scenery but constantly getting hit in the eyes by my own hair. A hairbrush would be nice too.

He slowed the engine as we came up on a small wheel and basket type of thing and reached out for a rope to pull the boat in line with the side. I could see a whole pile of fish flipping around in a box on the end. The wheel turned, the basket scooped fish. It was pretty cool actually, though that was definitely a lot of fish. The dogs would be happy.

"Take this like this. Grab and flip." He demonstrated hooking a fish and tossing it into the boat.

I jumped a little as the fish slid towards me. He gave me a second hook. I took it tentatively. It was lethal looking. I hadn't dressed warmly enough for the windy boat ride and I attributed my shiver to that. In the sun with the boat idle, I guessed the temperature was in the fifties. Testing the weight of the hook I scooted down the bench while he started tossing fish rapidly. I leaned over and arched my arm, feeling the hook sink into the flesh of the fish. It was unnerving. I lifted and it dangled in the air as I studied it. The fish was staring at me.

"What is this again?"

"A silver salmon." He worked rapidly, the fish a blur as he transferred them quickly from box to boat. "The chum run is next week then that's it until spring."

I tried to shake the fish off the hook but it stuck. "How do I get it off?"

"Like this. Flick your wrist." He demonstrated.

This time, the fish plopped onto the floor. "Bye, fishie."

He made a sound of amusement. He had already moved about twenty fish, so I decided I needed to stop reflecting and start working. I snagged another fish, this time kind of enjoying the silver arch of the hook in the air. I could see why Freddy Krueger was into it. There was power behind it, and it tore through flesh with ease. I shivered again, at the oddity of my own thoughts.

"Do you think they feel pain?" I asked.

"Of course they feel pain," he said. "What living creature doesn't? We all have nerve endings. Imagine how dull life would be if we didn't. If we never felt the softness of cotton or the tingle of a sponge scrubbing our skin." He glanced over at me. "Or the sweet pain of an orgasm."

My mouth flooded with saliva. "I wouldn't know," I said, and my voice was petulant again. I hated that.

"You've never had an orgasm?"

"You know what I mean." I wasn't going to say it. It was too close to begging for my comfort.

"Do you want me to fuck you?" he asked, and his voice was low, hypnotic. "Is that what you want?"

"You know it is."

"You don't get your reward unless you do your work."

I hooked another fish, swinging hard, making it bounce with the violence of my arch. He liked taunting me. It was starting to make me angry.

Then I realized I hadn't given a single thought to the fish. My frustration made me uncaring. I shook the fish off quickly, disgusted with myself. I wanted to go home desperately, acutely. I wanted to lie in my soft bed alone, my greatest concern going to the store for more iced tea, the kind that comes in powder form and you mix it with water until it's goopy and cloudy, but tastes like chemical heaven. Cool and refreshing. I wanted to be on solid ground, understanding who and what I was, not rocking back and forth in this boat, the wind chafing my cheeks.

The stranger finding me lacking.

I found a rhythm, bend, hook, stand, flick. One fish after the other, the pile in the boat growing higher, fish sliding down off the growing mound, covering my feet. They wiggled and stared and bled and I tried not to cry, tried not to feel sorry for them. For the men on the plane. For me.

When the last fish was on the boat, I sat back down on the bench, cheeks warm from exertion, arms aching, fingers a little numb. I couldn't look at him. I was afraid I would break down. He moved in beside me, and I fought the urge to shift away. He touched my cheek and I shivered. His fingers were wet and the scent of salmon wafted up from the pile of fish next to us. It wasn't a sexy or romantic setting in any way, yet I still felt instantly aroused by his touch.

He kissed my ear lobe, drawing goose bumps from me everywhere. "I want to fuck you so hard and so deep that I knock all the air out of you. But I don't have any condoms and you haven't been taking your pill correctly, have you?"

I shook my head. My shoulders sank in disappointment. He was right. I had been off schedule for three days now and it was probable I was ovulating or would be soon. I couldn't get pregnant, obviously. Which meant he couldn't come inside me, or even really enter me the way we both wanted him too. I appreciated his restraint, his respect for me. He had been celibate for who knew how long and I knew he wanted me. Yet he was maintaining control for more than one reason and that made me both frustrated and grateful.

"What should we do about it?" he asked, and I knew it wasn't a question. It was a test of some kind.

"I don't know," I whispered. "I could..." For some reason I couldn't say it out loud. I couldn't say that we could give each other oral sex and find satisfaction that way. For all the naughty he drew out of me, I also found myself reverting back into shyness. I felt sixteen with him, a novice. In need of guidance, instruction. A sexual awakening.

"You could what?"

I shrugged again, turning a little. His light blue eyes pierced me. He looked feverish, excited. I pulled back, away, unnerved. "Whatever."

"You could whatever? That doesn't sound all that exciting." He sat up and reached back, yanking the cord on the motor. It started up, drowning out further conversation.

We rode in silence, and I looked out at the trees. When we docked back at his place, he cut the motor. "How about I whatever you?" he asked.

I just shrugged, hugging my arms over my chest. I felt tired and overwhelmed. The urge to go home, not to my apartment but to my real home, was so strong it was like I could feel myself in my parents' house. Smell the astringent cleaner the housekeeper used. Hear the music of my little sister's constant video games. Feel Dean's arm around me.

The stranger leaned over and kissed me. It was a light, teasing, loving kiss. I sighed, melting into his embrace. How did he always seem to know what I needed? What I wanted? I wanted his tenderness right now.

"You're so sweet," he murmured. "You're like a little box of sugar candy I've been given. Come inside and let me taste you."

I arched toward him, a flower toward the sun. I felt the

warmth of his approval, affection, and I thrived on it.

It was the trauma. The loneliness. I was used to being surrounded by people but here, he was it. I felt small, stupid for having undertaken this trip without knowledge of what the hell I was doing, and I needed him not to chastise me. I needed him like this, semi-smiling, looking happy to have me there.

I would have gone inside and let him do anything he wanted at that point. I would have got off from pleasing him alone.

But before we could go in, the fish had to be unloaded from the boat onto a sled. The dogs could be heard whining and howling. They must have been able to smell the haul.

"Keep unloading," he told me. "I'll bring a couple of dogs down to pull it."

"Okay." I moved fish methodically, better at it this time, my arm sore though. I liked that pain, the satisfaction that came from knowing I'd used my muscles. I was helping to feed the dogs, myself, him. I tried to put a name on him again, but I couldn't. He seemed too rough for classic male names. Yet a hippie name didn't seem like it would suit him either. He wasn't trendy. Or Greek. Definitely nothing Russian or exotic. I didn't know.

I wondered if my name was a good fit for me. Probably. It was a babydoll name. The name of someone you didn't particularly take seriously, though you were fond of her. And didn't he call me doll? Maybe he was right.

When he came back with four dogs on harnesses they ran right up to me. "Can I pet them?" I asked, already reaching my hand out.

"Sure. This is Royce, Colonel, Zeke, and Bourbon." He pointed them out one by one, but I couldn't tell who was who as they were all tumbling over each other to greet me, licking my face and panting.

I laughed, freely, rubbing fur and heads, enjoying their enthusiasm. "Hi, guys, it's so nice to meet you."

"I think they're confused. They've never smelled a woman before."

"They can't possibly smell anything but fish." The whole air stunk like salmon.

"I can smell you."

My head snapped up. "What do you mean?" I couldn't smell good. I hadn't had a shower in three days.

His hair fell over his face as he leaned forward to jerk the dogs back, firmly but gently. "I mean, I can smell you. Your skin. Your hair."

If he had stopped there, I would have been pleased, aroused. But he didn't. He didn't ever seem to stop when I thought that he would.

"Your pussy."

At moments like that, I couldn't decide if he was sexy or disturbing. My body had already made its decision. My head wasn't so sure.

"I'm not sure that's a compliment," I said.

"I'm not sure it was meant to be one." He tucked my hair behind my ear. "You should have worn a hat. Your ears are cold."

"You're right."

"Wait here and I'll come back for you."

I grabbed his arm as he went to turn away. "You will, won't you?" My heart pounded at the thought of being abandoned, left outside for an undetermined amount of time. I could walk back to the cabin if I really had to. It wasn't that far. But I was afraid even with that short of a distance, I'd get lost. Or stumble across a bear.

"I'll come back for you. I wouldn't save you to let you be left behind now, would I?"

"That doesn't mean anything," I murmured. "People change their minds all the time. They care. Then they don't."

I was thinking about my mother. About Eric. About my best friend in grade school who decided I could no longer sit at the table in the cafeteria with her because I wasn't cool enough and boys didn't like me.

All those hurts, slights, rejections we experience in a

lifetime, amassed over time that scrape away at innocence, trust, confidence. Like an ice scraper on a windshield, they chipped away until we were clear, smooth glass and emotion skated across the surface, no one able to get in, us not able to get out.

"I don't change my mind," he said. "And I finish everything I start."

It wasn't what I wanted, not exactly. But I sat there, watching him head toward the cabin on the sled, his voice occasionally calling out to the dogs. I sat on the boat, cold, hunched over, and waited.

What was I waiting for?

Him to tell me what to do.

Finish what he had started.

He wasn't gone long, not even long enough for my fingers to go totally numb, but it felt like forever. I said nothing, stupidly glad to see him as he rode up to me, his grip on the sled steady, his hair being kicked around by a breeze. He said nothing. Just put me into the sled, setting me where the fish had been, and I held the sides as we bumped and flew up the bank back to the yard. The dogs seemed to love the exercise and I loved watching them. For the first time, I could actually see the appeal of this lifestyle. Of being isolated from the noisy world of consumerism, electronics, social media. The world news.

The stranger was a man alone in his world with nothing but his dogs and there was something very peaceful about it, even if nature was actually in and of itself very violent. I stared down at the remains of the fish haul, a watery, reddish, slimy sheen across the bottom of the sled. I remembered the weight of the hook in my hand. The way it sank into the fish flesh. I heard the boom of the shotgun as he pulled the trigger. The bear's heavy body, down on the snow.

The flanks and carcasses dangling in the air from his

platform, like macabre piñatas.

No. Not peaceful at all.

In the cabin, we kicked off boots and I moved toward the stove. The fire was down to almost nothing. I opened the door to feed it, but he came up behind me.

"It's fifty degrees outside. I don't think we need a roaring fire just yet. Wait until dark." He pulled my hair off my shoulder and kissed my neck. "I'll keep you warm."

"With stew? Coffee?" I asked then wondered why I played the innocent. Was that really appealing to men? That coy flirt? When we both knew that I knew exactly what he was talking about. The innocence was bullshit, a con veiled as flirtation. I had the doe-eyed look, and back home, I dressed like a child, but I was a woman. I knew things. I knew what he meant and I wasn't sure how or why or who had trained me to pretend otherwise.

Or if it mattered one way or the other.

It was the game. The dance. I followed his lead. Hand out, I took it. This was our tango, him in control, planning the choreography. Me, his partner.

"Take your clothes off," he told me. "Let me look at you."

I did, without hesitation. Not quickly, but not strip tease style either. I just took my shirt off first then skimmed my pants down over my hips. It left me in just my bra which I saved for last, sliding it down my shoulders before standing in front of him naked. My ankle was bothering me and I focused on the throb deep in the tissue where foot met leg and let it ground me in the moment as I watched him. Waited.

The air caused the soft blond hairs on my arms to lift, my nipples to harden. Despite what he said, it was chilly. His eyes raked over me, his lips parted. His gaze was hungry. I dropped mine to his jeans. I could see the outline of his cock and I wanted to take charge, to drop to my knees, to pull the length of him out and into my mouth. It was how I always felt in control. I had never understood how that was considered such a subservient position for a woman. For me, it was when I felt powerful. But this was a different type of power. It required me to totally let go, to trust, in order to find out what I was capable of. So I stood still, my breathing slow, controlled. I didn't feel like he would draw out my wait and I was right.

"Back up until you hit the wall and raise your arms."

Glancing behind me to make sure I didn't stumble on the floorboards, I did as he said, stopping short of the rough-hewn log walls. I didn't relish the idea of my tender skin on splintery boards.

But he wasn't having it. "All the way back." He hadn't moved. He was still by the stove, still fully dressed.

I took the final step backwards, recoiling a little at the sensation of cool wood, though it was smoother than I expected. Belatedly I realized I was supposed to raise my arms. I had them half up when he bent down, picking up some rope and tying an intricate knot. I paused to watch him throw it up over the beam that crossed the ceiling. Understanding dawned.

Quickly, I dropped my hands. "I don't want to be tied standing up," I said, though I wasn't even sure why. It just sounded uncomfortable. The bed was one thing, the wall another.

"Do you have a choice?" he asked.

I did. Of course I did. "I don't think I can," I said, already hedging.

I wasn't even sure why the concept bothered me. It hadn't been upsetting to be left on his bed for an hour. But something felt… off. More intense. The coolness in his eyes had been replaced by a fiery excitement. For the first time I questioned if he were fully in control of himself.

He slid his hands down my arms, his mouth nuzzling into my neck tenderly. "Your skin is so soft. I could touch you forever."

I stood still, confused by how quickly he'd shifted gears. I wasn't sure what he wanted from me. But that was a stupid thought because he wanted whatever he wanted. That was all. Yet it still puzzled me why he didn't just take me. I was in the perfect position for him to just thrust into me against the wall, and I wanted that. I understood that. This, I didn't. His hands skimmed over my body, teasing my nipples, a finger sinking into my damp inner thighs. I spread my legs a little for him, rocking my hips. My eyes drifted closed as I allowed my body to awaken, respond to him. I wanted to come desperately. It would make this edgy confusion go away.

Just as I started to relax, his lips soft, his touch reassuring, worshipful, he yanked my arms up without warning.

"I want to string you up," he said. "Let you hang in the ropes for me, so I can take a piece of you whenever I want like my other catches. I want to keep you safe, where no one else can touch you but me."

The words penetrated slowly. "String me up…" I stiffened. "You want to lift me off the ground? No."

But he already was. He had the ropes around the wrists firmly. Then he pulled the other end, wrapping it around his own wrist. My arms strained, drawing upwards in a way that wasn't comfortable. My feet didn't leave the floor, but I was on tiptoes. If he had a name, I could have used it sharply then, protested that I'd passed my comfort zone. But I didn't know his name.

"I can do whatever I want, you know. You're my kill."

That made me panic. I started to jerk against the ropes, totally freaked out by his words. I hoped he just meant I was like the animals hanging in the yard, owned by him to taste when he wanted. That was disturbing enough. But what if he meant literally, to kill me? "I want to go. I want you to take me to town tomorrow. I don't like this."

Even as I said it though my traitorous body hummed as he dipped a finger inside and drew back out to attentively swirl over my clit. My breath quickened and I felt that inevitable build towards blissful, powerful release. I stilled, frightened by my own reaction.

"Not yet," he murmured.

As I strained against his finger, against the ropes, against him, I wasn't sure if he was telling me not to orgasm or that we couldn't go to town yet. I pressed the issue. "Can we go to town tomorrow?" But my voice had no venom, no confidence. I was too distracted by the sensations he was drawing out of me, and I was afraid of him. Of all the things he could do to me. Of my own vulnerability.

The rope chafed, my calves strained. But everything in me felt centered on the core of my body, where he was coaxing me to release. To oblivion. It shouldn't have been that intense, but I was overly stimulated. On the edge for days.

His free arm lifted me up off the floor. "Wrap your legs around me," he commanded.

I realized he was going to give me his erection, finally, now of all times, here against the wall. So I did as he told me to, eagerly, forgetting why I wasn't supposed to be okay with any of this.

My weight resting on him, back scraping the raw wood, arms going numb from being raised up, I gave a cry of deep, guttural pleasure when he thrust into me. He paused, me pinned to the wall, his eyes trained on mine. It reminded me of the first time I'd seen him, just days earlier, when I'd opened my eyes and smelled blood. Those blue eyes had arrested me, frightened me.

They did both again now.

He paused, buried deep inside me. I could feel the throb of his cock and I swallowed hard, hovering on the edge of orgasm. One stroke and I'd be done. There would be no holding back this time.

"I'm not taking you to town," he said.

"What do you mean?" I whispered, sorry I'd brought it up. I didn't want to talk.

"I'm not taking you back ever." His voice was low, seductive, hypnotic. "I found you, Laney. So I get to keep you."

I stiffened. It was meant to be sexual, nothing more. Dominant pillow talk. Not literal. I tried to laugh, but it was breathless, weird, panicked. "You make it sound like I'm your prisoner."

"I guess technically you are."

CRASH

He started to move inside me, a slow deep rhythm that despite my confusion dragged a low groan from me. Gravity had me seated fully on him, and I couldn't have moved if I had tried.

I didn't. "You don't mean that." I felt lightheaded, confused, disoriented.

His grip on my hips tightened and he didn't break his steady pounding into me. "Yes. I do." Each of his words was punctuated by my back hitting the wall. "You're not leaving. Ever. I thought you understood that."

"I don't understand at all." He'd never said that. Anything like that. I had agreed to be submissive in bed, not stay with him forever, tied up. I felt crowded suddenly and my instinct was to wonder where my phone was. To call someone. To get the fuck out.

But I couldn't.

There was no way to call anyone.

Nowhere to go.

My back against the wall.

And yet, my body still opened for him, wet and welcoming, and my nipples were still taut because he didn't really mean I was literally a prisoner. He was just exerting his dominance and I could like it and it didn't mean anything.

When he gripped the back of my hair, and murmured in my ear, "You can come now," I did.

A big, sweeping, unnerving, appalling orgasm that shocked me in its intensity even as I thought I wanted nothing more than to go home and forget my stranger had ever existed. The game was too intense for me, and I didn't know the rules. And what if it wasn't actually a game? I cried out, agitated even as physical ecstasy and satisfaction rolled over me, body jerking.

It was both a heady and an awful combination, fear and pleasure. They didn't belong together, yet they collided within me like a pair of cymbals. Adrenaline and serotonin, a swirling cocktail that made my head spin.

He held me tightly. "You're going to be a very happy prisoner,

I promise you that. Unless you try to leave me."

His lips brushed mine and I shivered because I heard and accepted the truth. He meant it. I knew it in the core of my being. He wasn't going to let me go.

The touch of his mouth was soft, but his voice was rough. His grip in my hair tightened until my eyes started to water. "You won't try to leave me, will you?"

I shook my head, out of instinct, fear. Self-protection.

"Now close your eyes."

So I did.

PART
TWO

CHAPTER EIGHT

THE ROOM WAS DARK. THE ropes binding my wrists kept my arm extended painfully in the air, but I didn't dangle. The stranger held me tightly, my legs around his waist as he stroked in and out of me, not with violent stabs, but with passionate thrusts, his breathing hot on my neck.

I kept my eyes squeezed tight, black spots dancing behind my eyelids. I held my breath, too, hoping that I would pass out. Just fall right back into the oblivion I'd experienced after the plane crash. I'd wake up and none of this would have happened. No crash. No rescue. No strange stranger.

He wasn't taking me back to my life. He was keeping me with him, a prize. A prisoner. Like a pet. He couldn't be serious. But he had sounded serious, and I felt the press of panic. It was like an electrical current under my skin, making me skittish, jittery, breath ragged and uneven. Because I knew he was serious. Deep in my gut, where instinct roosted, I knew that this was what he had wanted all along. He had seen me, he had wanted me, he had been debating if he wanted to keep me. It was finders, keepers. To him, it had been like stumbling across an abandoned dog. You take it home, you feed it, then you decide if you want to take it to the shelter or let it lie on your floor every night as yours. I had passed the test and now I was a prisoner.

He'd made a spot for me on the rug at the foot of his bed.

I wanted to turn my head, escape his breath, his closeness, but I was afraid. Even as my body stayed damp and aroused, I was afraid, and that was what scared me more than anything. Why wasn't I screaming, fighting?

Because I was scared of his reaction? Or because I liked it?

The thought made my eyes pop open in defiance. I stared into his eyes, meeting his icy gaze head on. He didn't groan or moan or show any outward sign of enjoying what he was doing. Instead he looked like he was more excited by my reaction than the actual act of burying his cock in me. The only sound in the room was the wet give of my body with each invasion, and the sharp gasp of my breath that accompanied it.

We stared at one another, time standing still, my thoughts frozen. I was hypnotized by him, unable to break away, terrified that if I blinked, he would somehow own me. I would cease to be me and I'd be only his. I'd disappear into nothing, a puppet of skin and flesh, even my beating heart manipulated by him.

If I had words, they stayed locked in my throat. There was only the silence of night and the thump of my back into the wall, the tight release of air from my lungs.

He pulled out suddenly and there was the warmth of his ejaculate bursting over my inner thigh, though you'd never know if it felt good to him or not, given his blank face. But I didn't care. I just wanted him out of me. I couldn't handle the intensity of it, the unruly combination of anger and pleasure. The way I wanted to both hit him and wrap my arms around him. It scared me, made me feel fucked up, made me angry with him for doing this, angry with me for starting it. Because I had. Maybe he never would have done this if I hadn't asked him to.

But what kind of fucked up girl thinking was that? That it was my fault he wanted to hold me prisoner? It was exactly that.

Fucked up girl thinking. Because that's the message we always hear... that insidious implication of guilt and responsibility and it was wrong, all wrong. It was too many thoughts, too many emotions, too much blame and self-loathing, and unwillingness to just look at him and hate his face, like I should. I wanted to hate him. I swallowed hard and felt his cum sliding down my leg and I pictured kneeing him in the groin. Biting his lip off. Knocking my forehead into his.

Yet I couldn't. I wouldn't. I wasn't born with a gene for violence. I wouldn't hurt a fly. I thought about hooking the fish earlier. Or a fish. Confusion marred my thoughts and I concentrated on the sticky sensation between my legs.

I hadn't been taking my birth control pills. Pulling out must be his attempt to prevent pregnancy and it was a shitty, lame attempt. It was everywhere, his sperm pond, mere centimeters from my vagina, and I thought about having his child here in the middle of nowhere, like a kidnap victim, and I jerked against the restraints, finding that anger.

"No," I said, even though there hadn't been a question. I bucked and tried to shift away from him, wanting to go home to Seattle and take a week long shower. Put on soft fleece pajamas and watch hours of reality TV on my couch. I'd order Chinese food and pick up ice cream to spoon right out of the pint. I'd drink wine. Sweet, fruity pinot grigio. I would get drunk and blot out this moment. All these moments. All my feelings. I'd forget I had ever decided I could live in Alaska and I'd settle into the purely mundane and normal life I'd had before. Where I pretended that I knew what I was doing, and was good at the lies I told myself.

The stranger squatted down without speaking and shifted my legs to around his neck. I realized what he was going to do before I could react, and it wasn't until the first touch of his tongue was on my clit that I jerked, trying to move away. My shoulder hit the wall hard and I was off balance, wrists and forearms numb, totally at his mercy.

"Stop," I demanded.

But he didn't. Not even when I clamped my thighs around his head, squeezing in frustration, desperation. His fingers just gripped my ass tighter and his tongue did languid sweeps across my slit, and despite all my panic and anger, it felt good. Better than good. It felt like the answer. Like the knife that could cut through all the white noise and give me a solution. I didn't understand that. It didn't make any sense that I could be upset, want away from him, yet my body could greet his ministrations so enthusiastically. I let out a growl, irritated beyond reason that he could get his way and as always, like everything in my life, I had to just accept it.

I twisted and turned and made it difficult for him to hold me. His grip was so tight, I could feel the heat of his fingertips pressing deep into my legs and I knew I would be bruised. I didn't care. My wrists were chafed and raw and I thought irrationally maybe I should just yank my arms clear off in order to get away. Rip the constricting limbs right at the sockets and leave them dangling from the ropes while I tumbled to the floor, smacking my head and blacking out. With luck, I'd kick him on the way down.

But since that wasn't actually an option, in my frantic squirming and jerking I did manage to knee him in the cheekbone. I practically heard his teeth rattle. He yanked away from me and looked up, his eyes narrowed, nostrils flared. I went still instantly. I braced myself, expecting him to hit me. At the very least smack my ass hard or pinch me. He didn't.

Instead, he said in his slow, seductive, low voice, "Is this what you want? Me to stop and never do this ever again? Because I won't if you don't knock it off."

The moment dragged out, me staring down at him, him staring up. He was annoyed, but he was calm, in control. He was so ruggedly beautiful and that was so unfair. He also didn't let go of me, but just held me and waited for my response.

I moistened my lips, tension in my shoulders relaxing now that I felt reasonably sure he wasn't going to pop me across the face. "What do you mean?" I whispered.

"We can make this difficult or we can make this pleasant. Which would you like?" His fingers had eased up, but at the end of question he squeezed my cool flesh. Hard. A warning.

There could only be one answer, of course. Because I was the captive and he was the captor. Because while fear can make you do crazy things, I wasn't stupid. If he wanted the role of dominant, I would play the submissive. Even though my thoughts were wild and unfocused, bouncing around like a pinball, in everything I'd come across over the years about abduction cases, that's what the victim did. Placated their abductor. I read those stories with an odd fascination that had bothered my roommate. She wanted to ignore the idea that anyone could break into our apartment and snatch us for nefarious purposes. I had been the opposite, reading with fascination, pondering what I would do, how I would escape, an odd exercise that showed I always needed to follow through to the worst possible conclusion of every scenario, a sort of macabre fantasy.

But that had been the difference between Sammy and me. She'd been afraid because she had believed the possibility was real. I'd never thought I would have to use it. It had been an intellectual exercise for me.

Yet here I was. It was real.

So I had to be smart.

"I don't want it difficult," I murmured. I closed my eyes, swallowed hard. I couldn't show him what was in my eyes- fear, disgust, calculation. Maybe my own bit of crazy, though not as crazy as his variety.

It made sense now, why he was alone in the woods. He didn't play well with others. That much had been true. He wanted to make all the rules of the game.

"No? Good." He lowered his head and flicked his tongue over my swollen clit.

I shuddered, but whether it was from horror or arousal, I wasn't actually sure. Which then really horrified me. I couldn't still enjoy his sexual attention. I couldn't. That couldn't be normal.

Yet I did. It was clear that I did, even as I breathed in and out and tried to relax, to reassure him I wasn't going to fight him. Not now anyway. But as I stopped bucking against the restraints and him, as his tongue did intimate things to me, I felt the crescendo of desire again, despite everything. It was like my body knew he'd given me one orgasm, so why not two?

It was disturbing to me. I didn't want to give in. But he had skill and I couldn't shift away and if I had to be with him, he was right. Why make it difficult when I could at least enjoy certain aspects of it? This aspect. This wet, deep, vibrating guttural and sweeping pleasure, that could make me forget everything for two minutes. The sensation was overwhelming, dragging me away from the essence of myself, of all my thoughts and fears and anger. I bit my bottom lip to ground myself, to take my focus away from my clit, but it didn't help.

He knew it. He knew he had me.

The stranger ground his mouth between my thighs, plunging his tongue inside my depths, before sliding up in a long, luscious lick that had me coming hard. A tight, painful, annoying orgasm that I both enjoyed and regretted. I did succeed in preventing any moans from escaping, but he knew, of course. There was no mistaking or hiding it.

He shifted his head away from me. "See? That wasn't so hard. Do you want to be here, forever, without ever feeling that again? I don't think you do, Laney."

My name sounded different on his lips now. It seemed mocking. Less sweet and seductive. Maybe it never had. Maybe I had only wanted it to seem that way.

I swallowed excess bile. "It wasn't hard." It hadn't been.

What did that say about me? That I could separate the physical from the emotional so easily?

I knew exactly what it said but I wasn't willing to reflect too deeply on it at the moment.

"Thank you for being honest with me," I told him. "I'd rather know the truth." Sincerity rang in my voice, because I meant it. I didn't like the truth, but I appreciated knowing what reality was. Because if I didn't know it, I would create my own. A skill that I'd used more than once, with less than pleasant results in the end.

My inner thighs were sticky. My wrists, arms, shoulders all hurt. I felt like I was panting, though I hadn't really exerted myself.

"The truth? You'd like the truth?" he asked. His expression was fierce, his grip still firm on my thighs.

Maybe I didn't. The incongruity of the situation struck me. He was wearing me, so to speak. I wished I had more thigh strength, so that I could crush his skull, squeeze until his eyeballs filled with blood and his lips turned blue. The sudden and unexpected awful thought horrified me and I left my legs fall slack. Apart. I wasn't violent. I wouldn't hurt a fly. Or a fish.

"What truth?" I asked and my voice was hoarse.

He turned and licked my flesh. "The truth about why I live alone in the woods."

A shiver rolled over me, goose bumps rising in a wave down my arms, my nipples hardening. The roots of my hair tingled. "No. No, I don't." Because what if it was worse than anything I could imagine? What if he'd killed a woman? Dismembered her? Kept her head in his refrigerator?

Sammy was right- I watched too much fucking crime TV. It wasn't helpful. I knew nothing about how to protect myself, and far too much about how to scare myself.

"Smart girl." He rose, still holding me, so that my back arched and the tension on my wrists eased. With one hand he reached up and undid the rope.

My arms fell heavily down onto my chest, blood rushing into them so they burned and tingled. My fists clipped his face on the descent, but it was gravity and numbness, not my fault or intention. But he didn't react and it struck me as odd that I could perceive him as fair and thoughtful still. He was though. He knew it was an accident and he didn't get angry. I studied his face, afraid to stare at him too long or lock eyes, but wanting to understand him, what was happening. It wasn't the face of evil. Or so it seemed.

But what did evil look like?

And if we gave gradations to evil was that a delusion?

"Put your arms around me," he murmured.

I did. He still held me, wrapped around his waist. My nakedness felt obvious, awkward. I wasn't the triumphant seductress now, but the woman who couldn't leave, even if I wanted to. Yet when he kissed the swell of my breast, I oddly welcomed his touch. He was right. If I had to be here, it was better to have things easy between us than contentious.

The dark of my childhood apartment sprang to my mind, and the minutes crawling by with agonizing slowness while I waited. Waited for my mother to return.

Nothing was worse than loneliness. Not even captivity.

"How long has it been since you saw anyone else?" I asked him.

He carried me to the bed. "Not that long actually. Only four weeks. But in the winter I go almost six months without seeing anyone."

Oh, God. The thought of being that long without human touch made me shudder. I couldn't do it. We were approaching winter. If I didn't get out now I'd be stuck there all winter long and he'd be my only contact. The only skin I could touch. The only lips on mine. The only arms wrapping around me and the only masculine fingers skimming over my body.

"I think I would go crazy," I told him as he set me down on the bed. Was that what had happened to him? He came to the woods and went crazy? Or did he come to the woods *because* he was crazy?

"People shouldn't fear solitude so much. There's nothing wrong with silence."

If it was a choice, maybe not. But it wasn't my choice. It had never been my choice. "Is that your philosophy? Do you have a philosophy?"

"Yes. Don't ask questions."

I almost laughed, but I stopped myself. Everything had changed. I wasn't getting to know him. I couldn't help him or care about his opinion of me. He was an asshole to keep me from my family. A crazy, cruel asshole and every word he spoke, wrenched from him by me, every time he touched me, proved that.

"I guess you'd prefer me to be silent. You basically said as much." Not that I was holding to that, the irony being I was questioning him about silence.

He tucked my hair behind my ear and shook his head. "The more I hear you speak, the more I want you to continue. I like the sound of your voice. It's sweet and cautious and full of questions and awe at the world. It's as beautiful as you are."

Damn it. Fucking damn it. Why did he have to describe me in a way that I would have loved to hear from any other man? It was words that showed he understood me, on a certain level. From a guy I'd met online dating or at work, it would have been worthy of gushing over to my friends. But it didn't matter with him. It couldn't.

"I'll try not to make you change your mind about it." It felt strange to say that, because in truth, I meant it. But it sounded kinder, more seductive than I felt. The way I would have said it and meant it the day before. When I thought I could leave.

He leaned forward, caging me with his strong forearms and broad shoulders. "I don't ask a lot, you know. Really. You'll be happy."

As he invaded my space, I tried not to turn my head away from him. If I showed weakness, he wouldn't like it, I knew that instinctively. Submissive and weak were two totally different things. I widened my eyes as they welled with tears. I couldn't cry. That would be a huge mistake.

"I'm very easy to please," I whispered.

Something flickered in his eyes and he pulled back so quickly I jumped. He didn't say anything. He turned and went over to the kitchen area and turned the tap on. I watched him from the bed and surmised he was cleaning off his body. I swallowed hard, afraid to even contemplate getting pregnant. Nothing could be worse. So I refused to even think about it. I turned to the nightstand and picked up the pill pack he'd left there for me. I wasn't even sure what day it was anymore, so I just took two dry and sat there, waiting.

Waiting for him.

It occurred to me that maybe that was what I was going to despise the most. Having to wait for him to instruct me what to do. How to live. I wanted my freedom of movement back. I wanted my ankle healed and I wanted real clothes and I wanted to understand the world I was living in. I wanted to know my role.

He came back to the bed with a washcloth in his hand and I crossed my legs protectively. I didn't want him touching me with that. But he ignored my obvious discomfort and pried my legs apart, cleaning my inner thighs with the cold damp cloth. My cheeks burned and I looked down at the blanket, not at him.

"You're spotting," he said. "And I need to get condoms and some things for you in town. I'll go next week when the weather turns and I don't have as much winter prep to do." He tossed the washcloth on the nightstand and climbed in bed beside me with a grunt.

He was going to town. *He.* Not me. Just *he.*

I was sitting but he immediately lay down, his arm behind his head. "What do you need besides tampons?"

Hugging my knees to my chest, I wondered at how casual and normal he sounded. Like we were a couple, choosing to live in the woods together. My skin was itchy and I was cold, but loathe to just crawl under the blanket. He had excluded me in mentioning going to town, and I heard that loud and clear. I was going to be left at the cabin while he went to go and get supplies for my extended stay. If there was any question about his intention that sentence erased it.

It felt more restrictive than the ropes. More oppressive than his body crowding me. More painful than when he'd yanked my ankle from under the seat on the plane.

I thought about a million things I wanted yesterday. From cute clothes and a blow dryer to facial cleanser and a bottle of wine. Books. Music.

What I wanted today was the right to choose if I stayed or left.

I would leave of course.

But I couldn't have that. So what did creature comforts matter when I was a prisoner?

In the end, I asked, "Do you think maybe I could have some panties? I have money in my wallet. I can pay for them."

It was risky to ask, but I'd feel like I had more armor in place with underwear on. Besides, at some point presumably I would have my period. I was already spotting. Going without panties was a gross reality I didn't want to contend with long term. All of it was a gross reality I didn't want to contend with, but maybe I could handle it better wearing underwear.

"You don't have to pay for them. And yes, I will get you some." He stretched out his arm toward me. "Lay down with me."

Relieved that he hadn't gotten upset, I did as he asked, sliding in beside him. He pulled the blanket over us and I sighed at the protection from the cabin's frigid air. It felt like a damp cold had seeped inside my bones and taken up residence there. I felt frigid. Small. Brittle.

His arm around me was warm, strong. Comforting.

I told myself to think of him as Sam, as he'd instructed me to. If he was Sam, and we were a couple, then none of this was nearly as terrible as it well and truly was. If Laney and Sam lived in a love shack in the woods, then that was our choice. Because we loved each other and we loved Alaska.

I closed my eyes and tried to convince myself that my imagined truth was the real truth. I concentrated on his breathing, and my own. Mine was erratic, frantic. His was steady, even. If someone doesn't know they're crazy is that the actual definition of crazy? If he suspected he was insane did that mean therefore then he wasn't because he could recognize it?

What was I?

Who were we?

"You're so beautiful," he murmured, lips brushing over my temple.

I opened my eyes so I could see his expression. He did look content, loving. Boyfriend Sam to girlfriend Laney. There didn't seem to be any mystery there, any hidden depths or secrets.

After a second, I closed my eyes again. I couldn't sustain the fantasy.

All I could do was sleep.

Tomorrow I would plan my escape.

CHAPTER NINE

EXHAUSTION ALLOWED ME TO SLEEP dreamless, a welcome comforting void of nothing, and I woke up disoriented, not sure where I was for a minute. The air felt frigidly cold and I shivered, burrowing further under the covers. The blankets smelled like lavender, and when I reached to the left for my cell phone, I suddenly remembered where I was. Nowhere, Alaska.

A prisoner.

Heart rate kicking up a notch, I turned my head to the right, expecting to see him in bed with me. But his side was empty. There were no ropes attached to the headboard. His spot in the bed was straightened, like he'd never slept there. I sat up, looking around the cabin for him, the blanket falling away from my naked breasts. The stove wasn't emitting any heat that I could feel and I scanned the wall for his coat, his shotguns. I wasn't sure if any were gone or not. What I did know was he wasn't there.

A mix of relief and fear flooded me. I wasn't sure I could look at him, but at the same time I didn't want to be alone. Alone somewhere I didn't know how to survive. Forcing myself to swing my legs over the side of the bed, I shivered uncontrollably. The first thing I needed to do was get the stove going again. The floor was painfully cold and I found clothes to pull on, big slouchy pants and a sweatshirt and wool socks. I wasn't sure how he did his laundry, but I figured if I was forced to stay, I had a right to wear whatever of his I wanted.

Small defiance, but it was the only one I had.

Those feelings lasted as long as it took me to realize that there was no wood in the cabin. I was going to have to get some from the front porch. I was cold and tired and hungry. I was also very aware of my inner thighs and my wrists and how both had a lingering soreness deep inside. Shoving my feet into boots, I decided to forgo a coat and just go outside. It couldn't be any colder outside than in the cabin. Goddamn Alaska and its goddamn cold weather. I would take Seattle rain any day over cabins that didn't have heat that came on with a flip of the thermostat.

I stepped out onto the front porch and scanned the yard, looking for him. I didn't see him anywhere, though the dogs gave me a loud frantic greeting that may have been friendly or not, I couldn't tell. I blinked at the sunlight. I'd slept later than I'd realized, though I was losing sense of time. And place. The air was cold, but not brutally so. I breathed deep, filling my lungs with clean air. It tasted good, if air could have a flavor. My arms were sore from being strung up like a carcass. Or maybe from transferring fish. Or both. But they screamed in protest when I lifted a log off the tidy pile of wood stacked against the exterior porch wall. I had optimistically thought I could carry two at a time, but that wasn't possible. They weren't big logs. They were fireplace size logs and I was aware again of my physical limitations. I wouldn't last more than a day on my own in the wilderness.

He knew that. I knew that he knew. I went into the cabin and heaved the log into the stove, watching it smolder and catch on the still simmering ashes at the bottom. I repeated the process three times, leaving one log in reserve next to the stove. Then sweaty and tired already, I went to use the outhouse. Finally, I was ready for coffee and something that resembled breakfast. After I choked down dry crackers, unable to figure the stove out, I looked around me, wanting a strategy. Any strategy.

My best bet was to figure out where I was in relation to town. Also to have the stranger teach me everything he knew about survival. I needed to learn to use a gun. I needed to eat, a lot, to fatten up before a forty-mile walk. I needed to steal a compass, pack water to take with me. All of which seemed stupid and impossible. I couldn't walk five miles, let alone forty. He had said fall was swift and brief. The snow was due to fly in a few days and then what? I couldn't hike through snow, in subzero temperatures.

I sat on the bed, assessing the box I was in. Could I stay here, alone every day for months without going insane? Could I stay here with him at night, as he stripped my body repeatedly? At what point did he take my soul with my body? I leaped up, unable to sit still, agitated and antsy. I yanked open the drawer on his nightstand. There was a knife in it, matches, and a book. Praise the Lord an actual book. With words. It was a mystery, a creepy old house on the cover, shrouded in mist. I wondered why this book was special. Why it had made the cut. I had half-expected to see some sort of male manual on heading off on your own. Kerouac or *Catcher in the Rye*, or *Into the Wild*, about the guy who starved to death in Alaska. Not just a regular old who-done-it mystery that probably had no hidden message. No symbolism.

I ransacked his dresser again, though I found nothing of interest. I was afraid I would be tempted to open the ancient gift tucked behind his shirts, so I avoided that drawer altogether. I looked at flashlights, batteries, pots, canned goods, mouse traps, and gun grease all neatly lined up on his shelves and in his cupboards. He wasn't messy, but I already knew that. All it told me was that his mind wasn't cluttered. He had everything organized and easy to use. Like he had me.

I touched everything twice, going from one corner, down the

wall, to the next, and all the way around the perimeter of the cabin, looking for what, I had no idea. A manual on how to use the stove? A hidden cell phone or laptop? There wasn't anything. Nothing to connect me to the outside world. No access to the Internet or instant information. What had seemed like a mere annoying novelty in the days before now felt like as much of a prison as the four walls of the cabin. Isolation. My nemesis.

It was deafening, the silence. Even the dogs were quiet and I rushed to the window, wondering if somehow he had taken them with the sleigh without me noticing. But they were in the yard, half lying down, sleeping, though I thought a few were missing now that I was really inspecting the yard. I'd never counted the dogs, but there were more than the five I saw. So he had taken the sled, I just hadn't noticed it earlier. Maybe he'd gone back to the river. I wondered if I could find it again. The path couldn't be hard to follow. If I made it to the river, I could…

What? What the fuck could I do? Swim to safety?

"I don't know what to do," I said out loud, because the quiet was maddening and I needed to hear that I still had a voice, that I was still alive. That this wasn't a dream, a terrible, off-the-rails, crazy ass dream. My voice sounded small and pathetic and suddenly I heard the echoes of my mother, mocking me.

I had asked for a Barbie for my fifth birthday, but my voice was tentative and shaky, my desire and hope great enough to compel me to speak, but with zero confidence. And she shredded me, mocking my squeaky and trembling voice, before dismissing my request as an expense we couldn't afford. Later I found out that when she married Dean, she already had a hundred grand in credit card debt, and that all those days and nights she was gone from our apartment, she was gambling or shopping. Or sucking cocaine up her nose. She was fond of anything self-destructive and expensive and addictive.

She'd raised me in a way that I grew up meek, obscure. Never wanting to rock the boat. It was what it was. I knew why I was the way I was. I didn't even hate myself, or her, for that matter.

What she had done was her shit, and now what I did was my shit. Everyone has to carry their own bucket full of it. So while she carried hers in federal prison, I was carrying mine in Alaska.

Tired of being weak, I fought the urge to cry tears of frustration and fear. That would only confirm what I already knew- that I wasn't wily enough or strong enough or creative enough to solve my own problems.

But I had one thing going in my favor. I was a good actress. I could manipulate men. And I was the babydoll. The one everyone wanted to take care of. If I could figure out how to play on the stranger's heartstrings, he might feel sorry for me. He might trust me enough to take me to town with him.

Make him think I was scared of being alone. That I needed him with me at all times. That was what I needed to do.

But that would mean I'd have to be with him all the time. The thought made my stomach curl into a tight knot. But I could either do this and gain back my freedom or I could avoid him now to stay here forever.

Neither was an attractive option.

I paced and paced, my sore ankle complaining. The minutes, the hours ticked by. I tried to read the mystery novel. I couldn't get past page one because the words kept blurring. I would have loved to have read the entire thing. To lose four hours in the escape of someone else's world, a comfort I desperately wanted. But I couldn't focus. The loneliness I needed to present to him was gradually, with each passing second, becoming more and more reality.

What if he never came back? What if he died on the river or on a trail? What the fucking hell would I do then?

My anxiety kicked up a notch and I repeatedly walked to the window to glance out in search of any signs of his impending arrival. What would I do if he had just abandoned me? Gone to town without a word, never to return again? I would die here. I would die in the woods of exposure or starvation or flesh eating bacteria or a bear or the dogs or from childbirth.

CRASH

I was going to die. Alone.

———————◆———————

It was dark. I let the fire go down to embers, because I was afraid to go outside for more wood. I had started the day out wanting to exert my independence.

I was ending it curled up in a ball on the bed, huddled under the blankets.

Clutching my useless cell phone, I risked powering it on so I could look at the images on it. I still had twenty percent battery power but swiping through my pictures only made me feel worse. There was my little sister, mugging for me with exaggerated duck lips. There was my group of girlfriends in our hats, looking happy and carefree and slightly drunk. Was I ever that carefree as I looked? Had I been happy? Obviously not if I'd thought to seek answers in Alaska. Answers to questions I didn't even know.

I went way back, so far back that I found a picture of Trent on it and my nose twitched as I studied it. I didn't want to think about how quickly everything had gone so horribly wrong and how everything had gotten crazy and scary. I'd thought that was the worst thing I could go through.

But now there was this. I powered my phone down, plunging myself into darkness. The dogs whined outside and I listened, on high alert. Was there a bear out there? I should get up and shove something in front of the door in case bears were smart enough to turn doorknobs. But then he couldn't come in. He. I mentally scrolled through names for him. Each was an unsatisfactory attempt at labeling him. I didn't know how to label him. The stranger. The kidnapper. The lover.

Squeezing my eyes shut, I concentrated on my breathing. In. Out. But then the dark behind my lids scared me even more than the dark of the room and I whipped them back open.

When the door creaked and light flooded the entryway, I let out a startled shriek. "What are you doing in the dark?" he asked, his flashlight beam sweeping over me. "Are you sleeping? It's only eight-thirty."

The bright light blinded me briefly and I blinked. "I can't find a light switch." It sounded stupid. There was electricity from a generator, I knew that. I'd seen him turn on the light over the sink and there was a flashlight in the nightstand. I added, because I hated how pathetic I was, and wanting him to feel guilty for abandoning me without a word, "I didn't know where you were." It sounded accusatory and salty.

As I sat up, he shut the door behind him and turned on a light as he kicked off his boots. "I didn't know you needed my daily itinerary. I told you fall is short. I have work to do."

"But yesterday you took me with you."

He paused in taking his coat off and the corner of his mouth turned up. "Did you miss me?" he asked, his voice whiskey smooth and unrepentant.

"Yes." It was the truth. I couldn't stand to be alone. Not here, not anywhere, and his company wasn't offensive. He wasn't disgusting or vile or annoying. He was just... dominant. There were worse things. My rationalization made me swallow hard but I couldn't help it. *We could make this pleasant or unpleasant.* "I was worried about you."

That made him laugh, a genuine if somewhat rusty sound. "You're kidding, right? I know what I'm doing."

"But you were gone all day." I let the blanket fall down off my chest even though I was wearing a sweatshirt. It would draw his eyes and it did. "I thought something bad had happened."

His gaze flicked back to mine. "I can take care of myself. But it's been a long time since anyone worried about me."

I held my hand out, because I wanted him to trust me. And I wanted comfort. What an insane concept. Comfort from my captor. Yet I needed it. "I was. Come here and reassure me you're fine."

His head tilted. "Why do I feel like this is a trap?" he murmured. "Do you have a knife under that blanket?"

"Why would I do that?" I asked honestly, startled. I had thought he trusted me more than that. That I was coming off as sincere. "I can't survive without you. I'd have to be a total idiot to kill you, even if I was capable of stabbing someone. Which I'm not." I kicked the blanket down past my knees before peeling off the sweatshirt I was wearing so he could see my bare breasts, see I wasn't hiding anything. "Besides, we're making this easy, not difficult."

"Is that what we're doing?" He rubbed his jaw, like he wasn't convinced, but he did take a step towards the bed.

It seemed very important to win this victory, to get him to come to me. He needed to believe me or I would never gain the ground I needed. "Yes." I let my fingers drift down, like I was giving up. "I just wanted to feel your skin. I'm sorry." My left eye started twitching but I ignored it, concentrating on keeping my body relaxed, my lips slightly apart.

Reaching his hand behind his neck, he yanked off his flannel shirt, mussing his hair in the process. He was so goddamn good-looking. That was half the problem. I wouldn't have flirted if he wasn't, but then again, it made this all so much easier. I could want to yell and scream at him, hit him, but I could still effectively fake an attraction to him because it wasn't entirely fake. I focused on his bare chest, not his eyes, not those blue pools of intensity.

"You want to feel my skin?" he asked, moving towards the bed with graceful strides.

Nodding, I swallowed. I couldn't tell what he was going to do, couldn't read his expression. But then I never could. He wasn't totally unpredictable though. I anticipated him binding me. He didn't. Instead, he crawled across the bed to me and hovered in my space, hair falling forward, his eyes raking me, arms encasing me.

Then he kissed me. A sweet, simple kiss, his breath mingling with mine, his touch warm and reassuring. It shattered me. And I cried. It was so unfair, so fucking unfair.

He tucked my hair behind my ear. "I'm the one who is sorry," he murmured. "I didn't mean to scare you today."

Despising the fact that I was sniffling and watering, I took a shaky breath and reminded myself my own weakness could aid my purposes. He was being tender with me and that was an advantage I had to hold on to. "I know you didn't. But I'm out of my element here. I'd rather be with you so you can teach me what I need to know. Like how to chop wood and turn the stove on so I can cook."

Fire a gun.

In case I needed to shoot something.

Someone.

But I knew better than to say that now, when he still didn't trust me.

He nodded slowly. "Okay. Sure. Be with me. If that's what you want."

A shiver rolled over my bare arms and shoulders. "Yes. That's what I want."

"You know what I would like?"

My body stiffened. I forced myself to hold his gaze, to relax. My poker face sucked but my expression probably wasn't much different than it usually was with him- startled and unsure. "What?"

"For you to lie back so I can make love to you the way a man does when a woman cares about him."

His words confused me and I wasn't sure how to respond. What game were we playing? Was he parroting my behavior to show me it was ridiculous? He didn't actually *like* me. I was a plaything, a toy. A doll.

So I just lay back onto his bed. Reaching out I touched his chest, splaying my fingers over the hard, warm muscles. I had expected him to want to tie me up, to be rough, pull my hair. I'd been mentally prepared to hate him for that. But he threw me off balance with his softness. It was a con. It had to be.

He took my hand and raised it to his lips. He kissed each fingertip gently, before lacing his fingers through mine and bringing them both to the bed, clasped above my head, like we were lovers in the truest sense. Melancholy spilled over me, like warm honey, and I couldn't shake it off. An ache that had nothing to do with sex bloomed in my chest. This was what I wanted, in reality. Back in Seattle. I'd been on a dating hiatus prior to Michael because of what had happened, but I missed this. This connection. This understanding of who you were with someone, where you stood. That you were a we.

I could be touched a million times a day in the most casual sense by a boyfriend and never get tired of it. It sucked that I was being offered exactly what I wanted in false packaging. That was the definition of cruel irony.

But the impermanence of it, the deception, didn't make me turn away or reject it or hold myself aloof and removed from him. Oh, no. I opened. Physically and emotionally I sprawled myself apart for him to see, to touch, to taste, to take. I couldn't stop myself. The wall had crumpled and I wasn't strong enough to fortify it.

"I've seen many beautiful things," he said. "Sunsets and snowstorms and the fierce beauty of a rushing river. But I've never seen anything as stunning as you."

Goose bumps rose on my skin. I'd never been good at accepting a compliment. And I wasn't now. "You're just saying that because you haven't seen a woman in months."

He shook his head while hand covered my mouth, firm, but gentle. "Shh. No speaking. Let me feast on you."

I didn't have a choice. I had to let him. But I questioned if I would tell him no anyway. He had the strangest ability to hypnotize me, to relax me into doing his will, with his words and his touch. He constantly kept me uneasy, yet there was something addictive about that, about wanting to please him. I knew that there was something deeply unhealthy about that, but at the same time, so damn intoxicating. If I had to stay, I had to feel, and I'd rather feel something good and wonderful.

When he kissed my neck, hand still over my mouth, I flicked

my tongue over his finger, wanting to taste his salty flesh. His flavor was unique. It was like fresh air and wood chips and dirt, covered by a layer of hand soap. He was a man with an earthy scent, a masculine smell that appealed to me, and made me feel feminine. I liked the cage his arms created around me, the illusion of safety. And he would keep me safe, from everything outside. I believed that.

I just wasn't sure how safe I was from him.

His beard scratched the delicate flesh behind my ear before his mouth slid down, over my shoulder, down to my chest. He teased his tongue over my nipple.

"Luscious Laney," he murmured. "Soft and delicious."

I wasn't sure what to do with my hands, if I had permission to touch or not. They dangled at my sides even as I wanted to explore him, the angles and planes of his hard body. Then again, I wasn't sure I wanted to feel how much power was contained there, how much control he ultimately could and did have over me.

But the urge was too great, my curiosity too strong.

As he drew my nipple into his mouth, I tested the strength of his arms, squeezing his biceps, in awe at his taut ripped muscles. These were honed with nothing but manual labor. Hauling, chopping, lifting. That was sexy as hell. There were no supplements or protein shakes or expensive equipment to run on, machines to bulk his arms. It was just him and nature and survival. With nothing but his hands and his brains, he had carved out a life for himself and I found that fascinating. And sexy.

"What are you doing?" he murmured, pulling his head back slightly.

"Feeling your muscles." Using my fingertips, I lightly brushed back and forth over his skin, pleased when the motion called forth goose bumps. "I like how strong you are."

"You're a strange little creature, Laney." He cupped my cheek with his rough, worn hand, his thumb gliding over my bottom lip.

It was so hard to have him stare at me like that, his gaze intent, his body so overwhelming over mine. I felt the familiar uneasiness because I was both intrigued and afraid. Aroused and unnerved. "Why is that?"

"Because the things you do don't make sense."

I wasn't sure if that was good or bad, in my favor or against it. It did mean he couldn't predict me. "Do any of us make any sense?"

He pinched my bottom lip suddenly, hard. I winced involuntarily. "No. We don't." His nostrils flared. "I want you."

"You have me." I forced the words out. "Didn't you miss sex?" I asked, genuinely curious about that. I could feel the thick forceful erection against my thigh.

"I didn't miss sex. I missed *you*. I missed you before I even met you." He kissed the spot he had just pinched, tugging my lip into his mouth to gently suck. "And now you're here."

A shiver rolled over me. I closed my eyes, swallowing hard, the burn of tears at the back of my eyes again. He said the things I wanted him to say. He looked at me and it was the look I'd always wanted- one of rich desire, need. Here was a man who could love me with all the depth and intensity I had always craved. I could be his world, the way every fantasy I'd ever had as a child and teen had played out.

Yet he was my captor. I his captive.

There could never be love.

Only submission.

Without warning his cock thrust inside my body and my breath caught in my throat.

CHAPTER
TEN

A S HE MOVED IN ME, he took my hands and raised them over my head, in a tight grip so I couldn't touch him. Without the ability to hold on, I couldn't gain any purchase and with each thrust I shifted on the bed, restless, teased. Not my own motion or movements, but from the invasion of him inside him. Watching him, I left my legs slack, let him take me his way, then marveled at the irony of that. I wasn't letting him do anything. He did what he would. I took what he gave.

If I'd had a choice, I would have braced myself on the headboard so my body was still when he slid inside me, so I could feel the full force of his cock massaging my inner walls, tipping against my G spot. This was a frustrating squirm, a tickle that made you want to scratch for satisfaction, but you couldn't reach your itch. Shifting wouldn't make it better, so I actually went totally still. It seemed easier that way. Limp and still and let him do what he needed to do because I wasn't going to orgasm. I could feel that it would be elusive both because of my mood and because I couldn't grab his ass and force him to pound me consistently.

He didn't seem in any hurry though. He stroked leisurely, hair spilling over his eyes, changing his rhythm frequently enough to become maddening. There was no pattern. It was faster, slower, harder, deeper, softer, rounder, if there was such a thing. He was everywhere, he was full in, he was in retreat. I wanted to move so badly I felt it in every fiber of my being. I wanted to ask him what the hell was he doing because he was driving me insane. My body grew more and more damp, more and more desperate.

I broke my vow to be still and moved, searching for a way to brace myself, to dig in my heels so I could raise my hips and fuck him in return, force him to take me the way I wanted him to take me.

But there was no forcing him to do anything.

As I wiggled around he paused, drawing a soft cry from me. "Where are you going?" he asked, voice steady, smooth, enigmatic.

A trick question? "Nowhere." I raised my hips, testing. "I just… you are…"

"What am I?" His voice was low, smooth, just a hint of mocking behind it.

"You tell me." I stared up at him, memorizing his face, every line, every angle, making note of the exact dimensions of his scar. Marveling at how he was the only face I had seen for days, might be the only face I would see for months. What would he become to me? "What are you?"

I expected him to say my master. My survival. My food and heat source. Anything to exert his control, dominance.

But he didn't. Because he either knew how to play me like a maestro or he was the perfect peg for my hole. Maybe he was both.

"I'm your perfect fit." With one smooth move, his arm firmly around my lower back and ass, he rolled us over.

Had the thought been mine or his? Sometimes it was like he pried open my brain and scooped out what he needed to know and it was frightening, yet comforting. I wanted someone to know me, the real me. I was sprawled across his chest, legs splayed, his cock still embedded deep inside me. I tossed my hair out of my eyes, hands still pinned to the mattress by his firm grip. I no longer wanted to cry. I wanted to take him, take the madness he offered. I felt feverish and strange, out of control. My voice sounded like it belonged to someone else when I spoke.

Or maybe my true self.

"Can I fuck you?" I asked, excitement spilling out, startling me. I shouldn't want it so much, but I did.

"I think you can ask a little nicer than that." He cupped my breast and pinched my nipple, causing a jolt of desire to travel through me.

"May I please fuck you? Pretty please?"

"With a cherry on top?" The corner of his mouth turned up and the amusement looked genuine, pleased.

I nodded.

"You may."

Without hesitation I raised my hips up then dropped down onto him, enjoying the full seating of my body on his thick erection. It felt so damn good. Like he said- the perfect fit. I didn't care what message I was sending. I didn't care about why he was offering me control or if he might take it away. If it was a game we were playing, I would gladly lose for the pleasure and the power of sitting astride his cock and driving him deep into me. I sat up, pushing my hair back out of my eyes, moistening my bottom lip as I watched him, watching me. A smile teased at my lips, unbidden, because I suddenly felt like the girl with the juiciest, dirtiest secret. Him. No one else could have him, because I did.

He gripped my breasts, his hands large enough to completely cover me, rough skin on smooth, strength on tender flesh. I clasped my hands over his and used my hips to move my body up and down, an orgasm building inside me. I felt hot, alive, strange, both out of my body, and more in it than I ever had. Every pleasant sexual encounter in my past paled in comparison, a muted watercolor whereas this was the color red, splashed boldly in wild high arching splatters. It was arterial spray next to a paper cut. My nerves were strung out, my mind both empty of reason, and wild with insane and speculative thoughts.

I wondered, ever so briefly, in that two-minute ride of crazed abandonment, if I actually wanted to leave. If maybe I should just stay forever, to always have this. But even as the thought freaked me out, and I recoiled from it, renouncing it, I felt my body splinter, my orgasm sweeping me under, a hoarse cry leaving my mouth.

As it shattered me, I both grabbed it and tried to stop it, realizing I hadn't gotten permission to come. "I'm sorry," I breathed, even as I enjoyed every last inner quiver. "I didn't mean to."

"Oh, I think you definitely meant to," he said.

But he didn't stop me. He let me ride it out until I was pausing on him, panting, skin dewy and covered in goose bumps.

His grip on my breasts tightened. "I said I would make love to you," he murmured. "Yet all I want to do is turn you over and slap your ass. It's a good thing I've taught myself discipline."

Another convulsion ripped through me at his words, at the thought of him spanking me, my ass raised in the air for him. I wanted it. I wanted him to teach me a lesson, to not be passive and disinterested the way so many of my hipster sex partners had been. I shouldn't crave it, but I did. It would be less unnerving than a tender stranger, using the word love in any context. If he were nice to me, I'd get confused, more so than I already was. I might start to believe him, to trust him. To care about him.

So I shifted off of him and without a word I turned, going on to my knees. And I waited, saliva thick in my mouth, the cold air tingling across my heated flesh. My breasts felt heavy, nipples still tight, and I arched my back, tossing my hair from my eyes. For a moment, he did nothing. He lay there, casually, beside me, and I felt the searing stare of his blue eyes.

Then he moved, rising up so that he was on his knees behind me, hands threading into my hair. "I can't decide if you are being obedient or demanding. I just can't tell with you. Sometimes, you're so sweet, and other times... I see myself reflected in you."

Head tilted back because of the tight grip he had on my hair, I couldn't turn to see him. I wasn't sure I wanted to. I didn't know what he would see in my expression, or read there, regardless of what was actually there. Hell, I didn't even know what was actually there.

"Most people aren't all one thing or another," I said.

"True. So tell me, Laney, what part of you is your favorite part?"

A shiver rolled over me. Not from fear, but from the thrill I got at such an intriguing question. No one ever asked me what I liked about myself. They told me, without words, what I should like. What I should be. But not my stranger. He wanted to know what pleased me about myself. It was a heady sensation as his callused hand held my head still and his thighs brushed against my ass. He hadn't come so I knew what would be next, and I anticipated it with pleasure.

"I like the part of me that isn't afraid," I told him truthfully. "The me that is here, right now."

"Is that because you're not alone? Is that because you're with me?" His fingers loosened in my hair, trailed down to the ends, and abandoned the silken strands for the smooth skin of my back.

He traced my spine, one vertebra at a time, descending lower and lower until he reached the dip between my ass cheeks. The tip of his finger rested there for a minute and I shivered, expecting him to shift it lower still, but he didn't. I considered his words carefully and how I should answer. But then I realized there was no reason to weigh how I spoke, because he would like the truth. It didn't matter how I felt about the truth.

"Yes. I'm afraid when you're not here." I had been. The day had been long and miserable and lonely. I might not understand him and I might not want to stay, a prisoner, but the naked and brutal truth was I'd rather be with him than alone. "I'm not afraid with you."

His finger disappeared and I was disappointed. I had been expecting, hoping, he would fill me with his forefinger, and stroke my simmering desire back to a high flame. But then he shocked me by smacking my ass with the palm of his hand so hard I fell forward, elbows buckling. A cry shot out of my mouth. "What…"

"This is what you wanted, isn't it? It's why you're on your knees."

It was. But I didn't want him to be so harsh. I wanted a gentle smack. Fake spanking. Just enough to be arousing, not enough to hurt.

Wasn't that how I lived my entire life, with the exception of just one or two times? Just enough to fool myself in to thinking I was living, but never doing anything that was remotely uncomfortable. Never pushing physically or emotionally. Living a life of bored safety. Until Alaska.

I came to Alaska to be strong. Or to learn to be strong anyway.

So I lifted myself back off the bed, where I had tumbled forward. I reached out and wrapped my fingers around the headboard, gripping tightly. I spread my legs further, planting myself so I would hold steady. "Yes. It's what we both want."

"You don't understand how much I want you," he said. "How hard it is for me to hold back."

How far could I let him go? I didn't know. But I didn't want to hedge or hesitate either. Swallowing, I chanced a look at him over my shoulder, ignoring how the heavy weight of my hair obscured the view from my left eye as it tumbled forward. "If I was taken away from you, would you regret holding back?"

Unleashing the beast was a huge, huge risk. But it was the only way to gain his trust. Bringing up leaving was a shrewd tactic that my gut told me would be better than ignoring the elephant in the room. His eyes narrowed.

"Will you be taken away from me?"

I shook my head. "No. Who would take me away? There's no one who knows where I am. But it's a rhetorical question. Would you regret it?"

"If it's rhetorical it doesn't matter what the answer is." His nails scraped the soft skin of my ass cheek, drawing welts. "But the answer is yes, I would regret it."

"I'm glad," I said, voice hoarse. And I meant it. A part of me wanted to be missed, wanted to be wanted so much he couldn't let me go. Wanted him to want to lose all control over me. Simple, uninspiring me, who wasn't even sure who she was. Me, of the borrowed identity, floral hipster, modern hippie without the politics.

I had asked him who he was, but perhaps the better question was who was I?

A chameleon who changed with her environment? A shadow girl, who crept out only when the lights came on and she was called and coaxed? The mirror to everyone around me? Where was the true Laney? Stand up and be heard.

He caressed my backside, tenderly, lovingly, before giving me a firm swat. Less painful than the first, followed quickly by another and another. I let out a soft cry with each, turning to face the wall, concentrating on a knot in the board, focusing on it, forcing myself to relax. Each smack was a fresh jolt of pain, a sharp sting, my eyes filling with tears. Yet behind the pain was a razor sharp focus, a mental clarity, a rhythm to my breathing, to the sound of his hand colliding with my flesh, and an intimate connection between him and me that was indescribable. New. Enticing. I trusted that he wouldn't hurt me and he trusted that I knew it.

If there could be trust between a captive and her captor. I tried to remember that's what he was. That he was the man who was taking my future, my life, away from me. Yet I had never felt a greater sense of self. Of my skin, of my nerve endings, of the roots of my hair, and the depth of my womb. I felt alive, and strong, able to withstand his dominance. My ass went numb and my vagina went damp and my knuckles went white as I hung on to the bed.

CRASH

When he stopped finally, I stayed still, ears ringing with the sound of his slaps, while he caressed my hips, and pulled me back, murmuring, "Let go of the bed."

There was no hesitation. I fell into a child's pose, collapsing in a comfortable stretch, as he entered me from behind. I rested my cheek on the soft sheet, the tears trudging delicately down over my flesh, and dropping onto the fabric. My mind was empty and there was nothing but the ebb and flow of pleasure with each stroke. He had emptied me entirely and now, he was the one to fill me back up. I came once, then again, but I shuddered instead of crying out, my throat too tight to speak. He was silent as well, and it was like the stillness of a midnight sky, black and bright all at once. The absence of light but with the beauty of the twinkling stars.

Afterwards, he held me against him, spooning, stroking my hair, my hip, murmuring soft, wonderful things that were like whispers in a tunnel. I couldn't quite grasp them. Until he said, "You're right. Being apart isn't tolerable. I want you near me all the time. I want to see you and smell you and feel you. I want to wear you like a second skin."

I closed my eyes, but behind my lids all I saw was the dangling hunks of animal flesh in the yard and me, with a hook right through my gut.

Hands closed around my neck, squeezing, choking off my air, big strong hands that had tied me up and spanked me, hands that had covered my mouth and rendered me unconscious once before. Only now I knew the feel of him, I knew his scent. It was almost as familiar as my own after a week with the stranger, always with him, our bodies constantly brushing against each other, boundaries invisible.

Was it time for him to finally kill me? To cross the line from animal he toyed with to prey he killed? I fought to open my eyes, hands reaching out to claw at the air, finding nothing.

I jerked awake, only to find him sitting there, not touching me. Only watching. He always watched. It was like he was waiting to see when I might show the truth, reveal every single last thought, every muddy, twisted, convoluted ounce of insanity running through my brain as the days drew out and the nights went on. For days I had been with him every second, and while I liked not being left alone with my thoughts, it felt like I could no longer think. He was… absorbing me. Not because he was rude or cruel or harsh. But because he was simply him.

A man I was no match for.

I tried to remember what I was supposed to be learning, but then he smiled, and I couldn't make sense of how to betray him. No, not betray him. That wasn't it. I didn't care about that. Did I? How to survive without him. That's what I didn't know. Could I survive without him? In more than one sense.

"What's wrong?" I asked, voice hoarse. I sat up, sheet falling away to reveal my bare breasts. The cabin was cold. So cold I saw my breath. Shivering I reached out and touched his beard, rubbing my nails through it, like you would with a cat. I liked to imagine I could make him purr. "Are you okay?"

He shrugged, like he wasn't sure. "It snowed last night."

I had been with him while he completed his fall chores, chopping wood and hauling fish, cutting down trees, and greasing his traps. He had shown me a few things around the cabin, how to use the mysterious pump and how the stove worked. But mostly, I sat and watched. While he worked and watched me. We metaphorically circled each other all day, every day, then at night the gloves came off and we fought in bed, hard one on one contact, where he emerged victorious, breathless and covered in sweat. Me, skin red and covered in welts, body aching and sore, but satisfied in the deepest, darkest way. There was no fear, really, but a constant wariness that ironically only went away when I lost myself in submitting to him sexually. I didn't want to during the day. But at night, it was never in question. I would do anything he asked. Anything.

But he never did anything that I didn't like, and when the sun was out and we were walking, covered in clothes, doing day-to-day routine things, that unnerved me. Then night fell and I didn't care again. This morning as I raised my hand to his cheek I saw the raw flesh on my wrist, burned by the ropes he had tied me in the night before. I wanted to study the visual proof carefully. Revel in it. He must have seen it too, because he turned my hand and kissed the marks softly, all the way around, before kissing the palm of my hand.

"I should go to town," he said. "If not today, then tomorrow."

Without thought, I stiffened. I wasn't ready for him to leave. I had no plan. "Can I go with you?" I asked, before I could consider whether or not that was a smart move.

"Why?" he asked, as he idly teased my nipple before pulling the blanket back up. "You're going to freeze to death."

"Now? Or on the trip to town? I managed before and I didn't even have the right clothes on."

"I meant now." His gaze shifted from my chest to my eyes. "Why do you want to go with me?"

"Because I don't like being alone." Truth. It was easy to be convincing when I spoke the truth. But I also wanted to go with him, not because I thought I could escape him there, but because I wanted to both be seen by the people of the community, and to see how arduous the trek was. Surely someone would pause to wonder why the woodsman had a woman with him. Surely someone would say his name out loud. Maybe someone would even recognize me from the plane crash story that must have been on the local news. And I could see if the walk was impossible for me by myself, with no sense of the terrain or direction.

Of course, he knew all of that too. Which was why he said, "I'm sorry, Laney. You can't. You know that."

"I can stay in the sled. Under blankets. No one has to see me." My voice had risen, grown whiny. The bedding slipped again and I was shivering.

He grew stern, yanking the comforter back up and saying, "Get dressed. I'm not discussing this with you any further. You're staying here."

There was no brooking an argument with that tone. I knew him well enough now to know that. He wasn't a man who could be coaxed or wheedled. He despised whining. So I stood up and got dressed, walking gingerly across the floor both because it was ice cold and because my backside was still sore from a second round of punishment the night before after I had asked for it, quite literally. I enjoyed the way it shut my mind down completely and took me to a totally different sphere. There was comfort in the pain, in the tight focus. No whirling thoughts. Just a numb aftershock.

At the dresser I took out socks and put those on first, then some sweatpants. I was getting used to never wearing panties, but it only added to the effect of constantly keeping me aware of sex. As I started to pull a sweatshirt on he came up behind me and wrapped his arms around me.

"Don't be angry," he said.

He sounded melancholy, like it mattered to him, my happiness. Was he an Aaron? That seemed like the name of a man who would care.

"I'm not angry," I said. Again, I spoke the truth. My anger seemed to have leaked out gradually over the days, like helium from a balloon, until now, I was merely empty, slack. My emotions were numb, dulled, and I kept reaching backwards for the indignation I'd felt when I had first realized he wouldn't let me leave, but somehow it had been massaged into a more calm acceptance. I would leave. I was still planning to leave. But I could float through each day, the gentle bounce of the mostly deflated balloon.

I leaned back against his chest, because he was strong, and could hold me up. I closed my eyes and imagined that we were in Seattle, in a cute little apartment that I had decorated with flea market finds. It was Saturday morning and he was shirtless and barefoot and I was making coffee for us to share. In Seattle, he would just be considered a lumbersexual, a rough woodsy guy by choice, a design style. Our nighttime play would be a choice as well, a way we felt more alive in our love for each other. But during the day, we would simply be a couple, and he would cherish me, want no one but me, and he would miss me when I went to work. He'd bring home wine and send me cute texts and we'd ride our bikes along the trail in my neighborhood.

His fingers wrapped around a strand of my hair and he tugged my head back, so I was forced to look up and back at him. "Can I trust you here alone?" he asked.

So we weren't that couple in Seattle.

And I was numb but not stupid. "Of course you can. Why wouldn't you be able to?"

"Because sometimes in your eyes I can see that you want to leave." He pulled ever so slightly harder, his voice a low rumble. "And I don't like that."

You can't always get what you want. I could hear my mother, mocking me with that phrase. Rubbing it in. Enjoying my tears, because she was a mega bitch. Just a nasty, horrible, selfish sociopath who had no business having a child. As the phrase danced through my head, my breathing grew shallow. I had forgiven her. But that didn't mean she didn't influence my thoughts, and the words almost came out of my mouth, but I stopped them. I wasn't her. I wasn't someone who used words to hurt, and while maybe I didn't know what I was, I knew what I wasn't.

I wasn't her.

The way to get out of this cabin, get home, was not to default to her slash and burn behavior.

Turning in his arms, I kissed him. "I'm just not used to being isolated. I'm starting to feel like the woods are closing in on me. I need something to do. Put me to work."

"Your job is to do what I say."

A shiver drew goose bumps to the surface of my skin. "Okay,"

I said easily, marveling at my acting skills. Maybe when I got out, I'd start auditioning for roles. I could win a fucking Oscar.

Or maybe it wasn't so much acting skill as it was the blanket of numbness resting heavily on me. It was self-preservation and it served me well, but it was also why I had wanted him to spank me the night before, so I could feel. Pain was better than feeling nothing.

"What should I do today?" I asked him.

"Lay in bed and finger yourself. I want to think about that while I'm hauling supplies."

That was supposed to fill my entire day? I felt the panic starting to creep over me, that itchy irritating feeling of a mosquito that lands and flies, lands and flies, while you grow tense and wave your hand frantically, wanting it gone. I couldn't be alone all day, doing nothing. Just staring at the walls, cataloging his cabin for the third time, down to every last fork and ball of twine. I had never missed the mindless time suck of the internet more. That would have distracted me, made the day pass.

"How long will you be gone?"

"I'll be back tomorrow."

"Tomorrow?" I squeezed his arms, unable to hide the hysteria I was feeling. "But what am I supposed to do? What if something happens? Do I have to feed the dogs? What if a bear comes back?"

"Shh." He pushed my hair off my face. "It's okay. Just go outside to use the outhouse, but otherwise stay in with the door locked. The dogs are fine. If you're bored, do some baking or cleaning."

Because yay, that sounded like a blast. Not. "What do you do for fun?" I asked him, suddenly serious. I had asked him once before and I'd never gotten a true answer. Living with him haven't given me one either. He didn't seem to need or crave entertainment.

"I do you. That's my fun."

What did I expect, that he was going to suddenly open up?

Tell me who he was? Share how he had a stuffed dog at the age of five or had his first kiss at laser tag? He had no history. He had no hobbies. He was simply *him*. This man, right here, right now. My stranger. It made my skin crawl at the same time I wanted to bind him to me, the way he bound me. Hold him in the cabin all day so that I wouldn't be alone. It seemed sometimes like he wasn't real, like I had conjured a savior out of the wilderness. Yet then again, he was more real than me. He was flesh and blood and strong, rough hands that shot and cut and tied.

"Be careful." What else was there for me to say? He was going to leave whether I liked it or not. The only thing I could hope for was that he would buy something in town that raised a red flag for someone in the store. The panties, maybe, and definitely the tampons.

"Stay inside," he repeated.

"I will. Can I go to the outhouse now?"

His eyes narrowed. "Are you being a smartass?"

"No." I kept my voice even, expression blank. "I just have to pee."

"Okay. I'm going to pack a bag for myself while you do that."

I nodded and went to pull on the boots that had become mine. "How do you know how to get to town?" I asked.

"There is something of a trail for the first few miles. But then it's just follow the river. Not hard."

Not hard. That was good to hear. I could follow the river.

I opened the door and a piercing wind slapped me in the face. I shivered. I had gotten used to not pulling on a coat for the quick visits to the outhouse but it was much colder today. Too cold to even walk ten feet. I yanked the door back shut and went for a coat on the hooks hanging by the door. He looked amused as he padded around the cabin, barefoot, in nothing but boxer briefs. The cold never seemed to bother him. I didn't think I could ever get used to it.

"It's ten degrees," he said. "It's going to get a lot colder than this. It's a good reason to stay inside, isn't it?"

Again, I just nodded. His mood was a little edgy and I didn't want to irritate him with my chatter. He seemed speculative and maybe even secretive. Like while I was calculating, so was he. Our circling each other in the ring again.

When I returned from the outhouse, he was drinking a cup of coffee, dressed, a pack at his feet. He handed a second mug to me and I reached for it gratefully, taking a hot sip, and letting it slide down my throat, warming me from the inside out. I had never liked black coffee, but I was getting used to it. The bitterness was fading.

After a swallow, he took the mug back from me and set it on the counter. "I'll be back tomorrow. You'll be fine. There's plenty of wood." He tipped my chin up with his fist. "Be a good girl."

What did he mean by that? My nose twitched, just slightly, under his scrutiny. "I will."

I waited one hour, two, measuring time on the antiquated clock he had on a shelf above the kitchen. At first, I hadn't been sure it was accurate, but after days on end of staring at it, watching its hand make its rotation, I knew that it kept time if not one hundred percent accurately, at least close enough. Then I layered up my clothing, putting on two pairs of socks and three shirts. I pulled on snow pants and my coat and boots and cautiously ventured outside. The dogs that he had left behind all turned and looked at me. It seemed like their expressions were accusatory, or maybe that was just my fear.

Skirting them so they wouldn't start barking, I started counting my footsteps out loud. "One, two, three…" But then the sound of my voice was too loud, too startling in the still morning, so I retreated into my head with my count. I kept darting my gaze left and right, terrified a bear would just stroll out of the woods and charge me. The air smelled crisp, cold, and my breath was so frantic and foggy it rose in hysterical puffs above my eyes. At step twenty-four, I stumbled on a log, but I recovered without going down.

I had no idea how long it took to reach the river in terms of minutes, but it was eight hundred and twelve steps.

And when I took the last one at the edge of the frozen river, I saw him standing there.

Waiting for me.

CHAPTER ELEVEN

I LOOKED BACKWARDS, OUT OF INSTINCT, the urge to run almost overwhelming. But what point would there be in running? The only place I had to retreat to was his house.

Coming up short, I said, "Oh! Hi." A weird, nervous laugh flew out of my mouth. "You scared me."

He took a step towards me. "What are you doing? You're a long way from the outhouse."

"I wanted to see the river. I got bored." It sounded stupid. Totally illogical. But I had no better answer. My heart rate increased and inside my gloves my palms started to sweat, the perspiration my body pushed out tinged with anxiety. Fear sweat. "Where are the dogs?"

I could already hear them and see the sled out on the river. The treeline had blocked my view of them until I was right on the bank. The dogs were lying down so he had been waiting for a while. Waiting for me. I wasn't fooling him for one fucking minute. He knew I was going to try to leave, or at least look around. He wasn't stupid. If he were he wouldn't have survived life in the bush.

"Get in the sled," he told me.

I did, without hesitation, head down, unable to look at him. I didn't want him to see my fear. But when he stood on the platform, I did chance a look behind me. "I'm sorry," I said. "I wasn't trying to be disobedient."

"I think that's exactly what you were doing." He stared at me. "Do you not understand how dangerous it is for you out here? You have no fucking clue what you're doing. None. Now tell me the truth, Laney. Where. Were. You. Going."

Each word was spoken so shortly and deliberately that whatever I might have said caught in my throat. Nothing I could say would appease him. I knew that. So I kept my mouth shut and I faced the front, clasping my arms over my chest. I could already imagine what he might do to me back in the cabin. How he might punish me. How had he known I wouldn't stay put? Had the trip to town been a ruse just to test me?

The only way I would know was if he chose to tell me.

It was probably only my imagination but the ride to the house was rougher than it had been when we were fishing. Or maybe it was the snow and icy under layer. But it felt like he was driving the dogs faster, out of anger. I sat there on the sled, waiting for his direction when we arrived back at the cabin. It didn't take long. He yanked me up by the arm before reaching under my ass and just lifting me straight up into the air. Over his shoulder I went, a jarring disorienting bounce, my ribs knocking against his collarbone.

He was definitely angry.

I'd hung over his shoulder before, half unconscious that time. This time I was aware of every step, every clash of my teeth together.

In the cabin, he didn't bother to take off his boots. He just strode across the room and tossed me down with one arm, a giant heave ho. I hit the mattress painfully hard, bouncing, my hair falling in my eyes. Some innate sense of self-preservation had me crab walking backwards immediately, scrambling to get out of his reach.

"Stop moving."

I froze. I wanted to explain, cajole, but I kept my lips sealed. I knew him. I knew nothing about him, absolutely nothing about his past, what made him, yet I did know him. It was a bizarre thought. He reached down and tore my boots off and tossed them behind him. Then he took my coat off and two of my shirts. I expected him to take me down to nothing but skin, but he stopped there and instead, raised my arms over my head and tied me in the restraints on the headboard. My sore wrists were already rubbed raw, and I winced involuntarily. He didn't react at all, but just yanked my jeans down, scraping my skin with his fingernails in the process.

Then he brought a pitcher of water and a straw to the end table.

Wait a minute.

I suddenly realized what he was going to do. He was going to leave me. I fought the restraints. "No, don't go. Please. Don't. I'll be good. I swear."

He put a pot on the bed next to me. "I'll be back tomorrow. I'll lock the cabin when I leave. You'll be fine."

"Sweetheart," I said, because I needed a name for my plea and I didn't have one. "I just wanted to see the river but I've learned my lesson."

"You haven't learned anything yet." He took a breath and let it out, his shoulders tense. "My job is to protect you. Even from yourself. So show a little gratitude."

That stunned me. "I…" I was supposed to be grateful? For him keeping me prisoner, away from my life, my family and friends?

But then I thought about the fact that I would have died without him rescuing me. Hypothermia would have claimed me. Even here, in the cabin, I couldn't survive without his help and knowledge, that was undeniable. He had also made me orgasm more times than I could count.

I *should* be grateful. I owed him my life. How completely and utterly messed up was that? I had to be grateful to the man who had given me my life, but was simultaneously stealing it.

I stopped fighting the ropes. "I'm sorry. You're right. I am grateful. You saved my life."

He looked away, like he couldn't tolerate the sight of me. He took his hat off and tossed it aside. Then he peeled off his jacket. Then he unzipped his pants. I knew what was coming and I moved my legs apart. But instead of entering me he bent over and dropped his mouth onto my clit. Startled, I cried out, shifting restlessly at the unexpected heat, the flicker of his tongue. He gripped my thighs and worked me fast, furiously. I shot to the cusp of an orgasm almost immediately.

Which was when he pulled back and wiped at his mouth.

I gave a disappointed moan.

"I'm your *everything*," he said.

He was.

Savior, protector, lover. Jailer.

When he bent over and kissed my lips, I kissed him back eagerly, wanting to hold him to me. The hardness of his body was reassuring, every angle and plane of his face so familiar now, even twisted in stern irritation. He allowed me to wrap my legs around him, but he didn't take the bait. He didn't take me. After a hot and furious tongue tangle, he pulled back and shoved my legs down. I couldn't hold on to him with my arms bound.

"I should leave you here tied up until I get back. That would be a good lesson for you."

Was he waffling? I waited, holding my breath. A smile teased at the corner of my mouth because if he gave in, that meant I had even more influence over him than I'd realized.

"But I have a better lesson."

It should have been reassuring, but for some reason my blood chilled. It was the way he was looking at me, like he was disappointed in me. Slowly, he untied my hands. "What?" I asked.

"I need you to understand that if you try to leave you'll die.

Is that what you want, to die?"

"No. Of course not." Confused, I rubbed my wrists. "I wasn't trying to leave."

I hadn't been. I had just been scouting out the area to see if it was possible to leave.

"Get dressed, just the way you were before."

Not sure what was going on, I just stared at him.

"Do it!" He handed me my jeans.

I got dressed quickly, back into my layers, into my boots and coat and hat.

"Get outside." He pulled a gun off the rack and the backpack he'd been planning to carry in to town.

I stumbled backwards onto the porch, grabbing the doorframe. "Where are we going?"

He tossed the pack at my feet, into the drifting snow that had blown onto the porch. "You're going to survive out here without me. Since you don't seem to appreciate me and are perfectly fucking willing to risk your life to get away from me, the man who saved you, fed you. Fucked you. Since you think you can just stroll away without my help here's your chance." He held the gun out for me to take. "Good luck to you."

"I don't understand," I whispered. My teeth started to chatter, just as much from nerves as from cold.

"Take the gun and don't play stupid. I don't respect that."

So I took the gun. My arm fell slack. It was heavier than I expected. "I don't know how to use this."

"But you can survive, remember? You were going to walk forty miles to town on totally foreign terrain to escape me. So take the gun and show me what you're made of, Laney."

"Don't do this."

"You did this." He went back into the cabin and closed the door. I heard the latch close.

He was kicking me out. He was throwing me out into the cold. He was done with me. I was the prisoner who had pissed him off and now he was going to teach me the ultimate lesson-death. A surge of adrenalin sent me rushing to the door and I pounded on it, screaming.

"Let me in! Oh, my God, I wasn't trying to leave, I swear to you! Let me in." I didn't want to die. I knew that as surely as I had when I'd woken up in that plane, how many days ago, seven? Eight? Nine? I hadn't learned anything about survival in that time. I didn't know how to use the gun. I set it down on the porch so I could hit both my fists on the door.

He ignored me. I peered in the windows and he was sitting in the chair by the stove, just calmly putting wood into the belly. He looked warm. I felt cold, both from the sting of the wind and my fear. Should I break the window to get in? No. He'd kill me with his bare hands if I did something so destructive. It would piss him off. I could stand there, so he could feel the weight of my stare. Eventually he would have to turn around. Eventually he'd have to use the outhouse, too, right? If he left the cabin, maybe I would have a shot at convincing him to let me back inside.

I didn't want to die.

Freezing to death probably wasn't the worst way to go, but I would know it was arriving. With each minute, each shiver and teeth chatter and numbing extremity, I would know that death was approaching, like the sun casting a shadow. You couldn't stop its ascent, its encroaching creep, inch by inch. Hypothermia would be like that and I would die and then what? Would he bury me? Feed me to his dogs?

Frantic, I pounded again.

No response. I sank to my ass on the porch, needing a minute. I felt like I was going to throw up, my head spinning, vision blurred. I concentrated on breathing, drawing huge breaths into my lungs.

This was a pathetic ending to a rather lackluster life. I hadn't done anything yet. I hadn't proved anything. Achieved anything. I had floated and now I was going to float right into death. I sat there for at least a minute, maybe five, breathing in and out, trying to calm myself down. My ass got cold on the floorboards and my nose got numb. I brought my tears to a sniffle and put my hands on my knees, lifting my head to stare out into the yard. The dogs were moving restlessly around their houses, like I had unnerved them. Like they sensed hysteria and didn't like it.

That was what I did to him. I freaked out and he didn't like it. He wanted me to be strong. He would respect that more. I knew that without question. So maybe if I stood up and made myself a shelter and a fire, he would see that I wasn't worthless. I would see that I wasn't worthless. If I had made it this far, didn't I owe myself the chance at life? Shouldn't I fight for it?

I'd never fought for anything. My preferred method normally was to roll over and let life happen to me. To let sex happen. To let jobs happen. To let my mother happen. To let Trent happen. I was the passive voice in every story of my life. With one exception.

If some kind of inner strength wasn't going to lead me at the very least I should let fear run free and attempt to save me from death. So I did. I unleashed the terror that was coiling inside my gut, the dragon ready to spring. I let the fear thread throughout my body, invading every limb, every inch, every cell. It was like an influx of heat, hot molasses chugging through my veins. My cheeks and forehead flushed and my vision cleared. For a second, I thought again I might go down in a faint, but I hung on, and used my fear to goad me into action.

When I stood up, I didn't look into the cabin. I didn't want to see him. I didn't want to be stupidly hurt by him turning his back on me. I didn't want to cry, or wish I could have his arms wrapped around me, warming me. My lips were cold, as if he'd never kissed me. I was nothing to him. He was nothing to me.

Not that I believed that. But I needed to tell myself that.

Wiping the tears from my cheeks before they froze to my skin I sniffled and bent over to look inside the backpack. It was fully loaded and heavy as hell. There was a plastic tarp in there, along with water, granola bars, matches, a pocketknife, and a compass. Very basic survival. But if I stayed close to the house, maybe I could make it work. I did know where he kept the straw to make beds for the dogs in their houses. I had seen him get it from the outbuilding behind the cabin.

That's when it occurred to me that I could just move in to the outbuilding. If I had shelter from the wind and any new snow, I could wrap myself in the plastic tarp for warmth and build a fire on the floor. I could manage for a day or two at least. I wasn't sure what the end goal was, but it was a plan of sorts. There was no way I could get my ass to town and I knew that. I would rather hunker down and wait it out then die somewhere on a death march, because that's what it would be.

So I walked to the outbuilding and shoved open the creaking door, pulling it closed behind me. It was dark and still inside, the only light from the chinks in the wallboards. I dropped the pack on the floor and scrutinized. There was a chainsaw, straw bales, giant pots, tools hanging on the wall, a metal trap dangling from a hook, and a machete. Even in the case, that weapon made me shudder. It looked nothing but lethal.

I wondered if I could bring one of the dogs to live in the shed with me. Most likely that would annoy him, but I wasn't sure I cared. I wanted the comfort of a body next to mine. Something breathing. Maybe at night I would do that. I could stake his chain around something. But for now I needed to focus on gathering wood. That was the key to living in Alaska- fire.

Never had I missed Google more. I desperately wanted to do research on survival techniques. I also really wished I could hear the ding ding of an incoming text. Just the knowledge that someone out there in world was thinking about me. That's why we loved text messages so much. It meant someone took the time to communicate with us. That we were penetrating the membrane of their day in some way or another. Was he in the cabin thinking about me? I was thinking about him. I was picturing the way he looked at me, in his softer moments. The way he brushed my hair off my cheek, and ran his thumb over my bottom lip. Sometimes I thought that if a man like him could love me, I would be something really special. Because love didn't come easily for him, that was obvious.

In the yard, I kept my eyes averted from the cabin. I didn't want to make my longing increase to intolerable levels. I didn't want to beg again or break bones in my hands railing at the impenetrable door. There was enough snow to make everything an eyeball searing white, but not enough to bury the low growing foliage. I could still see random sticks and brush poking out and I started to gather it. I was pretty sure that damp wood wouldn't burn but I had the straw. I could use that as a quick flame to light the kindling to light the wood. In theory. I was going on common sense not any actual knowledge of how any of this worked. I hadn't even gone camping as a kid. My mother found all those clubs and organizations for kids irritating.

"I'm not a joiner," she would say. "I can't be tied down."

So no Girl Scouts for me. Not that I had cared. But I had wanted to do ballet. I had visions of myself as a ballerina on stage, performing *The Nutcracker*. I was Clara, twirling with my new party dress. In college I could have taken ballet. But by then, it felt too late. And I was lazy. That was the unmitigated truth. I was lazy, complacent. More skilled in complaining than changing.

But there was no point in complaining now. There was no one to listen.

I had no patience for my own whining.

I wondered then how he had even tolerated me. I was a whiny brat.

"What's worse than a whiner?" I asked myself out loud, my voice only a murmur as I yanked sticks out from under the snow, the powdery white fluff bursting up in a wet cloud. "Someone who talks trash about herself." Wasn't calling myself lazy just an excuse for pity?

Gathering an awkward armful of wood, I mused that maybe I was actually achieving what I had been trying to avoid by coming to Alaska. Self-awareness. Michael had after all been a huge avoidance tactic, a desperate move. If I could fall in love, get married, establish a household and a life somewhere new, then I could avoid facing why I was so malcontent in the very respectable life I had in Seattle. The busy details would keep me from wondering what would really make me happy. And who the hell I actually was.

Those had been uncomfortable thoughts I hadn't been willing to have. Yet I was perfectly willing to chase a fantasy into the Alaskan wilderness just to ignore them. That was the very definition of running scared.

I dumped my haul into the shed and went for more, this time for bigger logs. That proved harder because they were either too small to do more than burn quickly or they were too big for me to lift. Breathing heavily from yanking on a log that didn't budge I turned on my heel and went right up on to the porch, not looking in the window but keeping my eyes on what I wanted. The axe he kept by the door for his wood chopping. It was heavier than I expected and I cursed when I picked it up. I couldn't swing that over my head, there was no way in hell. But I could get it to waist level.

My first swing was pathetic. It barely grazed the wood. My second was better, but it took everything I had. The third was weak, my arms already aching. The fourth finally took a tiny chink out of the log. I kept my eyes on the target and I thought about spinning class, and how I'd given up halfway through. I thought about yoga and how I bullshitted my way through poses, hanging out in downward dog the majority of the class because it was the easiest. There was no consequence for bailing when my ass started to ache in spinning. If I didn't become flexible in yoga it was my own fault and it didn't matter in the slightest.

But here, it mattered. If I failed, I died.

He wasn't going to save me.

For the first time ever, I had to save myself.

So I lifted and I whacked and I lifted and I whacked over and over, until my shoulders were screaming and my nose was trickling snot that instantly froze down onto my lip. But after who the hell knew how long, I had a log that I could carry and burn.

My back was tense with pain but I huffed and grunted and got that motherfucking log back to the shed. I sat on it for a minute, breathing hard. I pulled one of the water bottles out of the pack and took a sip. I'd lost weight since the plane crash. I didn't need to eat as frequently and it was oddly liberating. So I ignored the granola bars and instead looked around for where I could build my fire. I couldn't just set it on the wood floor, obviously. I needed something like a trash can to put it in.

There wasn't one. The only metal thing I could see that might work was an old metal box filled with screws and nails. I dumped them out on a shelf and studied the box. It was small, but it was all I had. "Use your brainey, Laney," I said. Then I laughed, a hoarse croak that didn't have any real mirth. "Make it work."

It took me seven tries and six wasted matches to get my straw smoldering under my damp kindling. It sputtered out immediately. Maybe I just needed to let it dry out for a few hours. It was still covered in snow. I brushed everything off and sat and thought for a minute. I could use the time to go get more wood. That seemed wise. But my arms were protesting. I puttered around the shed, inspecting everything, wondering what could be useful. My breath was a misty plume in front of me.

There were probably all sorts of things in the shed that could be used to make my semi-outdoor camping less miserable, or at least allow me to live. But if there was, none of it was recognizable to me. It was just tools that I didn't know how to use. Machinery made by man to do things I had never learned. I sat down on a straw bale and assessed what I was good at in life. The list felt abysmally short.

I could dance. Not so useful in the bush.

I had good grammar skills. I could interpret Shakespeare with ease.

I could make myself invisible in a crowd.

I could survive being alone.

Pulling the plastic around me like a blanket, I leaned against the wall and closed my eyes. My shoulders relaxed. The urge to laugh suddenly washed over me but when I did, the sound was hollow, echoing around the shed. What was he doing in the cabin? Eating lunch? Taking a nap? Was he missing me? Did he jack off standing up or leisurely lying down, relaxed and sleepy. Why had I never put my mouth on him and sucked him? It seemed like something a dominant man would like... me on my knees before him. Bowing to his majesty.

His flesh would be warm. I would be able to feel the slight throb of his veins, the give of his cock as it bent slightly under my onslaught. His hard thighs would be right there, emanating heat, and his hands would hold my head steady.

My own hands felt numb. I had on gloves, but they weren't warming them, just shielding them. I put them between my thighs, hoping my crotch would heat them. The plastic crinkled as I shifted. I hummed a Taylor Swift song softly. I dozed off. Woke up. Dozed again. Woke up, worried that I was succumbing to hypothermia, ignored it and closed my eyes a third time.

It was a dream that jerked me so wide awake it snapped me out of the fog I was in. I stood up, panicked, stamping my boots on the floor to bring feeling back to my feet. "What the hell?" I asked myself, words shaky.

I couldn't believe I'd actually fallen asleep. Mouth dry, I went to the makeshift fire pit again and went at the kindling with renewed determination. I needed to start this damn fire or I was going to freeze to death, plain and simple. Methodically, slowly, I lit the straw, feeding more and more onto it to keep it smoldering while I held the tiny twigs over top, praying one would catch. It took a couple of failures, but I had a petite fire going a few minutes later, just enough to warm my hands. I decided I needed to use the tarp to create a barricade, making my area of the shed smaller so the fire would warm me. Using the bales of straw and a rake, I made a tarp tent over the fire. I realized I needed a vent for the smoke, so I used the knife to saw a jagged hole through the plastic. It was still smoky inside my dark half ass shelter, but it was warmer. Knees to my chin, I sat there and pondered my next move.

No answers came to me. Not for hours and hours. Not while I went for more wood. Not when I fed my fire. Not when I forced myself to quickly drop my pants and pee in a corner of the cold shed, steam rising from my urine. Not when I sipped more water and ate one tiny little corner of a granola bar.

I heard the door to the shed open but I was beyond being concerned. It wasn't a bear, I knew that much. So it had to be him. I just sat and waited. He'd tell me what he wanted. If I was allowed to return to him, or if he wanted to yell at me some more. I would know soon enough and there was no point in speculating, even for the sixty seconds it would take for him to reveal himself.

The tarp corner lifted and his face appeared. Those eyes. Those goddamn blue eyes. I raised an eyebrow at him but didn't speak.

"I'm just making sure you're okay," he said gruffly.

So he wasn't hoping to collect my corpse. It was mildly reassuring. "I'm okay," I said, but my voice was brittle. "Though I'm guessing if the temperature drops any more tonight, I will freeze to death." I didn't even have the desire or energy to add a bitter jab. This was his doing, but it was my actions that had brought me to this moment. To this frozen, miserable, damp, exhausting struggle to live, without a plan. I had nothing but naïve hope. Maybe that was all I'd ever had.

"If you would do what I say, like I asked you too, you wouldn't be out here."

My eyes burned from the smoke of my fire. But even as they watered, and possibly looked like tears to him, I felt no urge to cry. My days of crying were behind me. It never changed anything. It didn't make you feel better. It didn't release the sadness or the fear. All it did was make your face swollen and your eyes itch. I looked at him and I thought that for the first time ever, I could believe that everyone was capable of murder. Because I wanted to kill him. I wanted to reach out and choke him until he could no longer breathe and the light went out of his eyes.

But that would serve no purpose. I would be well and truly stranded then. Besides, I had no hand strength left. And even as I wanted to kill him, I still wanted to love him. I felt an irrational tenderness towards him, because on one level, I understood his anger. He was trying to protect me and I kept defying him. But at the same time, he was a monster, a man who kept a woman captive. He was the ultimate selfish boyfriend, in a twisted way, me the petulant girlfriend. No matter how we'd come to this point, we were both trapped in the ropes of the relationship we had forged. We were tied together, inexplicably, by our circumstances and our driving, primal need for each other.

By our loneliness.

"Is that why you're here, to rub it in? To remind me that I'm stupid and make poor choices?" I covered my icy nose with my glove. "I already know that, so save your breath."

His expression softened. He was squatting down and his knee poked through under the tarp as he crawled in beside me. "I'm impressed with your fire," he said after a moment's silence, as we just sat side by side. "You did a good job making a shelter for yourself."

"Thank you."

He pulled a ziploc bag out of his jacket. "Ash bark. Use it to start a fire if yours goes out. It catches even when it's wet." He set it down beside me.

"So I have to stay out here, indefinitely? Like one of the dogs on your sled team?" I knew I shouldn't push him, but anger that he wanted to blame me for everything pushed the words out.

"No."

That could mean either I was going to be allowed back in the house or he was going to drive me off his property. If that was his intention I just wanted him to get it over with so I could stumble off and die from exposure. So I told him that. "If you're going to kick me off your land, just do it now. We both know I won't survive so why drag it out?"

It was strange how optimism and pessimism could march in

harmony with each other. I felt the deepest hope and confidence that he wouldn't do that to me, that he couldn't. Yet at the same time, I was certain he was going to. It didn't make any sense. Maybe that was why even as I contemplated the prospect of death, I wasn't afraid anymore, because it didn't seem real. He wouldn't actually save me only to push me outside to die. This was just a punishment. A test of sorts.

It wasn't the moment that everyone faced in the seconds before their death. The total clarity and awareness that it was over, their life thread had snapped. I couldn't quite grasp that this was the end, because I still believed he had good inside of him. Down deep under the gruff exterior and the empty eyes. He could care about me. He wouldn't kill me, or condemn me to die.

Foolish, maybe, but also accurate.

"Laney." He took my chin, turning my head to face him. "The last thing I want is for you to die. I also don't want you to leave me. And I don't like it that you want to leave. It makes me angry and I act like an asshole. It hurts me, do you understand that?"

Just like that, the door opened wide. Beyond it was the warmth of the cabin, food, water, and his strong, arousing body…

I walked through the opening he'd given me. "Baby, I don't want to leave you." I reached up and touched his beard with my glove. "But I'm new at being obedient and I'm used to having my phone, the Internet, videos to watch, books to read. I get restless. I went for a walk. What else am I supposed to do when you're not home?"

Even as I spoke the words, I marveled at how sincere they sounded. They floated out of me, like musical notes, hitting just the right pitch. Always the chameleon, that was me. When his troubled expression eased a little, I felt a certain sort of pride, an odd pleasure that I'd eased his emotional discomfort. I pressed my lips to his with all the confidence of a lover, a woman who is assured of her reception. "You're right, you know. You're my everything."

He was.

Yet I was amazed at myself. I really could use the label survivor, because what was the definition but someone who stays alive under adverse circumstances, using whatever means necessary. Not only had I built a fire, I'd put out the flames of his anger.

"I'm used to the quiet," he said. "But I can see how you wouldn't be. But you have to understand, if you defy me, I will punish you."

I fought the urge to break eye contact, my heart rate increasing. He looked so calm, so confident in the fact that he was right.

"And the punishments are going to get worse if you put yourself in danger again. So don't say that I didn't warn you."

There was nothing I could say to that other than, "I understand." But then a calm equal to his fell over me and I added, because I couldn't resist, a phrase from the depths of my memory. "Does it hurt you more than it hurts me to punish me?"

If he had said yes, then I might have screamed. I might have run, straight down into the river, drowned myself in the frigid water and been done with it. But he didn't. He smiled and kissed my lips softly.

"Of course not. It hurts you much, much more. But you like pain, don't you?"

I did. There was no denying it. Or the fact that my body started to wake up even now at the mere thought. "I do. But I don't want you angry with me."

"Come back into the house with me and prove it."

"I can do that."

I stood up, ready and willing to walk back into his house, watching him put out the fire I'd made. I had the sense that we were more equals than before. I had earned his respect.

Next I wanted his trust.

And a part of me even wanted his love.

So I went with eyes wide open to receive the punishment that would hurt me more than it would hurt him.

CHAPTER TWELVE

I DIDN'T REALIZE HOW STIFF AND weak I was until I tried to push open the door to the shed and every muscle in my body protested. I barely made it budge. His arm came up over me and he gave the door a shove, opening it for me.

"I chopped wood," I told him. "My arms are sore, but I did it. I chopped wood." I was proud of that fact. I wanted him to know.

"I'm impressed. I really mean that." He put his hand on the small of my back. "Are you tired? I can carry you. You haven't eaten anything and you must be frozen."

The intriguing paradox of my stranger, showing concern for me after shutting me out in the cold for at least eight hours by the look of the sun, maybe more. Suddenly now he was worried that I might be frozen? It was hard to wrap my head around on the surface but I knew that to him it made total sense. He had proven his point that I couldn't survive outside. He wanted me to understand the danger. I did. I always had, but he was right. I really, really grasped how perilous human life was in the bush and how easy it would be to die now. If the bear hadn't done it, this had.

He cared about me, in his own maddening and twisted way.

What I found fascinating, more so than I should, was that he did. I wondered if he saw me as a whole human being, or as an injured creature he'd taken in. Was he interested in me because I was Laney, or because I needed him to survive? I didn't know. So I decided to ask him. After I tested the boundaries, and how interested in honesty he was.

"I don't need you to carry me. But I would like you to carry me. But at the same time, I want to do it myself because I need to know that I can."

For some reason, that amused him. He smiled. "My Laney, always thinking out loud."

If only he knew the thoughts I had.

"Some might call that stubbornness," he said. "I like to think it's because you're determined. Determined to come into your own. Is that right?"

"It is." As we walked, the wind cut through me, and I marveled that on some level I could actually get used to the subzero temperatures. That I could withstand what was as much a mental challenge as a physical one. "I guess that's why I thought I was coming to Alaska."

"Thought you were?"

My steps were slow, methodical, but I climbed onto the porch, cheeks feeling like they might crack. Just split in half, frozen, exposing raw meat and muscle. Like a lean cut at the butcher counter. "I thought I was coming to find some inner strength, to be independent. But I was really coming here to run away from the fact that I didn't know what I wanted to do with my life back in Seattle."

He held his hand out to me to help me walk and I took it, needing to lean on him just a little. "At least you're honest with yourself."

"Why did you come here?" I asked.

"I was born and raised in Alaska."

It was a non-answer. Information he'd already told me. "Were you honest with yourself?"

"Always. So why were you traveling from Fairbanks up north? What was the final destination?"

"I was meeting a friend. It was going to be an adventure." The more I walked, the more my body hurt, but at the same time, my mental fog started to multiply. I'd gone into a bizarre blank space in that shed, a sort of self-preservation where I wasn't thinking about much. When I had thought, it had all been so clear. It seemed like heightened awareness, where everything made sense and I had all the answers to life, if not to how to survive the frozen Alaskan night. But now, it was cloudy again, a mist hovering over mud, thoughts that came to me than drifted away.

"I suppose your friend is looking for you," he said, pausing at the front door to study me. "There are probably a lot of people looking for you if she is the type to really push for answers."

"I don't know if he is or not," I said, putting a slight emphasis on the pronoun. "I haven't seen him since we were kids."

He opened the door and stepped back for me to enter first. "So he's not a lover then?"

"No." It was the truth, if not the whole truth. "Does your family miss you?" I asked. "Do you ever go and see them?" I shuddered with relief as the warm air of the cabin crossed over my face. My tense shoulders fell.

The corner of his mouth lifted up as he followed me inside and shut the door. "Is this where we share? Where I tell you who I am by cute little stories of my childhood? How would you even know I was telling the truth? Everyone remembers the past incorrectly, intentional or not."

"Maybe it's a stall tactic. So you won't punish me." I sat heavily in a chair by the table, unable to even consider divesting myself of clothes. I didn't have the energy left and I felt frozen straight through the middle. It was going to take an hour to warm up.

"You don't look afraid to be punished. You also don't look angry. I would have expected a woman to want to smack and slap at me out of anger. I was prepared for you to claw my eyes out."

"Then you don't know me any more than I know you." I pressed my cheeks, just to make sure they were intact. "I am not a violent person." I also wasn't stupid enough to attack a man who could easily overpower me, hurt me. More than he already had, that is. The thought confused me. I should be angry, he was right, but I felt less angry than triumphant, albeit weary. "Did you want me to claw your eyes out? I can try if you'd like."

He studied me. "You sound so strange…. I think you need food and a nap. You don't sound like yourself." His brows furrowed. "Maybe I left you out too long."

That brought a rusty laugh from my mouth. It was safe to say he had, yes. Twenty minutes would have been sufficient. "Like mayonnaise? You left me out too long and I started to spoil? A nap would be nice but I thought you needed to punish me still." I wanted to get it over with then sleep.

"No. That was your punishment. I think you learned your lesson."

"I did." I learned that I was never getting away from him unless he wanted me to go. And even that didn't ensure he'd escort me to safety. I had to be whatever he wanted me to be in order to get out alive. Eventually, someone would find me. They had to.

After removing his boots and coat, he squatted down between my legs and gently peeled my wet gloves off my hands. They were an angry red and I couldn't bend my fingers. "They need to acclimate to room temperature gradually. We'll just leave them uncovered for a few minutes."

I didn't care, particularly. They could pop off one by one and I wasn't sure it would matter much to me. I wasn't ever going to text again.

"I don't want you to think I'm a cruel man." He bent over, undoing the laces on my boots. "That's not what this is about."

I said nothing. I wasn't even curious what he was going to say. It didn't matter what it was about. It only mattered that it was.

He unzipped my jacket after taking off my boots, then went and made me tea. He held it to my lips while I sipped, the steam making my nose itch, my cracked lips awkward and slow to grip the mug. I burned my tongue. "Motherfucker," I said.

"Such language from such a sweet girl."

I was a sweet girl. I was also loving. Malleable. And more than a little willing to take a detour into crazy when the moon was full...

"Sometimes nothing says what you feel like a curse."

"I used to feel like a curse all the time."

I watched him blowing the tea for me, and moving the cup so it would swirl off some of its heat. "Yeah?"

His eyes lifted and met mine. "Yeah." He put the cup to my lips. "Try it now."

I did. It was perfect. Sometimes you just needed to wait a second and it would be exactly what you needed.

"Lie down. I'll get you out of these cold clothes."

He was gentle with me. More so than my mother had been. She'd always been brisk in her dressing of me, shampooing, shoelace tying. Irritated that she had to hit pause on her life and care for me. I'd learned to be clean early on so she wouldn't have to pick up after me. It was not a surprise that my apartment now was an explosion of clothes and kitsch, a floral chaos. It was the freedom of living without her rules.

Lying back, I let him take me out of his clothes I'd been wearing. I was still cold, the deep to the bone painful cold. "Do you have kids?" I asked.

That seemed to actually shock him. He jerked a little pulling my shirt up. "Do I look like a father?"

"What does a father look like? But you do know how to take care of me."

"My feelings for you aren't paternal."

A shiver rolled over me. "What are they?"

He smiled and it was intensely sexy and more than a little disturbing. "They're distracting. They're hot and dirty and alive.

They're possessive." His hand covered my breast and he rubbed his palm over my nipple. "To answer your question, because I'm feeling generous, no, I don't have kids. I've never met a woman who was enough of a match for me."

It was sick and twisted, but I wanted him to say that he had now. That I was the match for him. It would be, in a sense, the ultimate acceptance, to be loved by the solitary man in the woods. I already had a bizarre sense of pride that he didn't want me to leave. That he was holding me captive. Not every woman would be kept by him, I was sure of it.

Yet at the same time I wanted him to be forced out into the cold the way I had been. I wanted him to understand that he couldn't just keep me against his will. That he couldn't break me that way. But then I wondered if he even needed or wanted to break me. I had no idea what his ultimate goal was.

"What do you see happening between us? Like in six months?" I asked, genuinely curious. Did he want to keep me forever? Or just for the winter? If he tired of me, I wanted to know that he would take me to town and I could regain my life. I needed that reassurance.

Seeking reassurance from the man holding you hostage is stupid. I should have known that.

He made a face. "Oh, my God. Is this where we discuss our relationship and where is this going and what exactly we mean to each other? Blah, blah, fucking blah. This is what is happening between us- you obey me. That's it. The whole story."

I nodded. "Okay. When you go to town can you get me a book please? I need something to do."

"You're relentless. And not at all afraid of me, are you?"

"Is that what you want, me afraid of you?" I was sleepy, head still foggy. I put my hand over his, stroking the back of his knuckles.

"No. That's not what I want."

I stopped asking questions, but I did know what he wanted. He was clear about it and he was right- it wasn't complicated. He wanted me obedient. A companion on his terms. I would give him what he wanted, and maybe, when the time was right, he would give me what I wanted.

Or I could take what I wanted.

The plan was forming in the back of my frozen brain. It was a very cracked out idea, one that I never would have considered a month ago. Yet, it all suddenly made perfect sense. I could have what I wanted.

Most of my life, I'd been passive, reacting to what others did. Never initiating action. But when I chose to be manipulative, I was good at it. It was the innocent eyes. That's what Dean had told me, anyway.

"Can you show me how to use the chainsaw?" I asked. "I can cut wood while you're out hunting. I want to be useful."

"Sure." He wasn't listening that closely to me. He was already stripping my pants down and starting to tease between my thighs with his fingers. Then he stopped. "Let me get you warm clothes."

I rolled onto my side as he moved away from the bed, so I could watch him. I should feel afraid of him. He was strong and volatile and hiding from the world. He had tied me up. Strung me up. Locked me out. But I wasn't anymore. It was like surviving a day in the shed had shown me that I was made of sterner stuff than I'd ever given myself credit for before. Than anyone had given me credit for.

The babydoll could be dropped and she wouldn't break.

It made me smile, even as my body felt pummeled, bruised and tired, cold and weary.

He turned and caught me. "Why are you smiling? Are you going to kill me with the chainsaw after I show you how to use it?"

That was for me to know and him to find out. "Don't be silly. I don't like the sight of blood, you know that."

"I like the sight of you. In my bed." He stood there, clothes in hand, watching me. "Forever."

"I'm clearly not going anywhere." I held out my hand. "Come

and teach me a lesson about my place."

I was being too flippant. I couldn't help it. I felt a certain sense of giddiness. I wasn't going to die today. And the stranger cared about me.

His eyes narrowed. "I would have thought you would be cowed by being out in the bush all day. Or in the shed, anyway. You don't seem like you learned a goddamn thing."

But he liked me more for it. I could see it in his blue eyes. My sassiness was arousing him. Unleashing the beast. He tossed the clothes down on the foot of the bed and peeled off his own shirt.

"Are we taking a nap?" I asked.

"Naps are for babies. We're going to fuck."

Without warning, he reached out and grabbed me by the hair. I winced at the sudden sharp pain. He rolled me onto my stomach, but when I started to rise up onto my knees for him, he shoved me back down. "Stay on your stomach."

I twisted my head to see him, trying to gauge what he wanted to do, my body responding to him like it always did- eagerly and with instant moisture. I expected him to bind me, but he didn't. He just leaned in next to my ear and said, "Don't move. Save your energy."

That alarmed me. I started to rise instinctively. Save my energy for what? But he pushed me down again, harder. I went still.

Then he hauled my ass up and lowered his head. His tongue teased around the sensitive flesh between my cheeks and I jerked, shocked. I didn't expect that. It didn't seem like a dominant move. Then again, he was no trained Dom. He was just a man who took whatever he wanted. I gave a cry as he delved deeper, feeling way too exposed, too awkward. It wasn't a comfortable position, the angle of my head cutting off some of my air, back arching too tautly. Besides, I'd never been one for this type of play. Not sober anyway.

Then I thought about how good it actually felt when I stopped being self-conscious, how boneless and liquid the position had me, and how truly sensual it was to be exploring sex without alcohol. I could never go back to drunken hook-ups, half-numb bumblings in the dark. I could never go back.

The thought had me giving in, offering myself up fully to him, moaning my approval. He stroked in my damp sex, the rhythm of his fingers matching his tongue and I tensed up all over again. Not from discomfort but from the need to hold off an orgasm. The sheer forbidden, at least to me, quality of what he did to me, always took me to the edge faster than I expected. It was like arriving too soon for a party and catching the host off guard. You never knew what to do and say. My body was flushed, the chill finally beaten off by his hot breath, his arms enveloping me, the steady pace of his plunges into me generating friction.

Without warning, he pulled away and I heard his jeans unzip and the fabric rustle as he removed them. I lay there, cheek smashed into the mattress and tried to breath, my mind empty, clear. He took me to a place I didn't even understand, but where I wanted to stay indefinitely. A beautiful, serene, yet frantic state of existing wholly in my body, in that very moment. No past, no future. Just now. It was completely grounding, and freeing, and when he shifted me so that he could ease into my ass, I shuddered in awe at the agonizing pleasure of it.

His hand slipped underneath me and he teased my clitoris. I raised my hips to give him better access to both front and back, the easy, gentle plunge lulling me into that nothingness I craved. That place where it was only him and me and a connection so real, so raw, the world disappeared. The place where not only did he have no name, I didn't either. I was skin, I was bone. I was blood. I was an undulating amoeba-like sexual creature, just nerve endings and breathing, overwhelmed by pleasure.

"You know the rules," he told me, pushing a little deeper.

"Yes," I murmured. "I know the rules."

"Not until I say."

"Only when you say." I was starting to pant, inner muscles tight, the onslaught of his fingers and cock simultaneously driving me crazy. I wanted release. I needed it. But I wouldn't ask for it. Never. He had to give it to me. It made me feel strong to hold on, to prove that I was obedient. Going to the river had raised suspicion, made him question my intentions. He was right to question them. But here, in his bed, there was no question. He was totally in charge and I would willingly submit to him. It had nothing to do with wanting to leave.

He paused and it was agony. Glorious agony. It was hell to stay still, to not push myself back onto him, but I did. When he moved again, I bit my lip hard, eyes cast back over my shoulder to have something to focus on. He slipped two fingers inside me and said, "Come now. You have sixty seconds or your chance is over."

That was new. I'd never had a time limit before. It made me anxious, but it was for nothing. Before he was even finished speaking I was crying out from my orgasm, letting it roll over me like a fire backdraft, all flash heat and oxygen robbing. Before it was done, he was moving again. I lay there, overwhelmed, blinking, clitoris still tingling, and he went on and on. It was slow, easy, methodical. Infinite. He took me for what felt like forever, with a control that was insane.

I was used to him coming with a barely detectable grunt under his breath. He never yelled out. Maybe he thought it was too revealing. Maybe he was still just holding on to his control. Whatever it was, at times, I found it sexy, masculine. Other times I wished he would show me that he really enjoyed me. That I overwhelmed him.

He wasn't going to give it to me. Instead, he pulled out and without a sound came on the curve of my ass, the hot fluid still giving me a sense of satisfaction even without his verbal approval. I laughed softly, amused at the oddity of sex. I could never get enough of him.

Could I leave him and give it up? What if sex was never the same? What if the intensity of my situation took it to a different level and I could never find that kind of connection again? It was possible. The thought made my stomach tighten.

But for now, I let him turn me over onto my back so he could stare down at me. He shook his head.

"What?"

"Nothing."

I smiled. "Oh, come on. You can tell me."

His finger trailed down my jaw. "If I ever decided to fall in love, it would be with you."

That was unexpected. Goose bumps rose on my flesh. "What's holding you back?" I whispered.

"I'm waiting for you to fall in love with me first."

I had been turning my head, rubbing my chin against his palm, craving his touch. But that gave me pause. It was a trap. I could only gain his love by giving mine. Which left me in the vulnerable position of wanting more first. I couldn't do that. I wouldn't do that. I'd be a fool to do that. Though everything inside me shuddered with longing to feel the full depth of his affection. His love. It would be a powerful, amazing triumph. It would be a loyal and intense love. His eyes would never stray to other women or to a cell phone screen. He would be all in, more so than most women could handle.

It was all I had ever wanted. I could handle it. I would grab and hold it and relish in it. I would fucking wrap my hands around it and squeeze it so it could never escape and we would drown in happy solitude, our relationship our mutual obsession.

First though, I'd have to hand him my heart on a plate and I couldn't do that.

"I already do love you," I said. It was a lie.

Yet it came off my tongue very easily.

CHAPTER THIRTEEN

THERE WAS NO RESPONSE FROM him. But I had learned to read his enigmatic eyes. He was pleased. Slightly skeptical. But pleased. He pushed back off the bed and padded across the cabin naked. I would never get tired of that view. Instead of cleaning up at the sink, he pulled his clothes right on and went into his boots. He plucked his coat off the hook.

I was still sprawled out, damp and dewy, sticky at the curve of my backside. "Where are you going?"

"You'll see."

That alarmed me. "How long will you be gone?" Panic rose and I sat straight up.

"Relax. I'm just going in the yard. I've been thinking about doing something and now is the time."

That could mean anything. So I would just wait. I wasn't getting any better at it, but I was getting accustomed to it. When the door slammed behind him, I gingerly stood up, pulling on my sweatshirt and socks, but nothing else. The shirt fell below my butt and covered me well enough. I just didn't want to put on pants when I felt so sore and sticky. All my muscles were tired and aching. I finished drinking the tea he had brought for me, even though it was cold now. It still tasted good.

Rummaging around, I found some banana chips and I munched on them. I was hungry. Ravenous, actually. There had to be something I could cook for myself but all I could find was canned vegetables and beans. Deciding it was better than nothing, I opened a can of corn and dumped it into a pot. As I was stirring it, he came back in, barely visible behind a giant metal something he was hauling in. When he set it down by the stove, I realized what it was. A bathtub. Oh, my God, a bathtub. The idea of soaking, and getting clean, totally squeaky clean, made me shiver in anticipation.

I hesitated to ask him what he was doing, in case I was wrong, or if my question would irritate him. I just fished out a spoonful of corn kernels to test how hot it was and ignored him. He disappeared again and returned with an armful of stones, which he put directly into the stove. Then he left again. When he returned a third time with a drum of water, rolling it through the door, I was eating corn on a cracker. Not exactly gourmet, but it filled my stomach.

When I bent over to access more crackers from the pantry, he made a sound in the back of his throat. I realized I had given him a flash of ass. I straightened and smiled at him. "Are you hungry?"

He shook his head. "You are so beautiful it hurts."

There was no way I looked good. I was lacking in hygiene and a hairbrush. I hadn't looked in a mirror in almost two weeks. But I could see his attraction to me and I preened a little. I couldn't help it. I was a girl who liked pretty things and it had been hard to be without my lotions and scrubs and tweezers and perfumes. "Thank you."

"How about a bath?" he asked. "I can put some bath salts in it for you and you can soak for awhile."

Yes. Yes, yes, and a million times yes. "I would love that. Thank you, that's really sweet of you."

"You've had a rough day." He turned and started to fill the tub using a hose connected to the drum.

"It wasn't all rough. Or at least not a bad rough." I ate another cracker. Funny that I could say that and genuinely mean it.

He shook his head slightly, scoffing a little. "You're asking for it, you know that?"

"Yes."

He laughed. "You like to push back, don't you?"

Maybe I did. "I like to think of it as flirting."

"No one ever accused me of being a flirt." He draped the hose over the side, then went and got a bottle of bath gel. He squirted some into the tub. Then with tongs, he started retrieving the stones from the fire and dropping them into the bottom of the tub. Bubbles rose enticingly.

I could smell the lavender scent of the gel and I wandered in closer. "Why do you have a bath tub outside but not inside?" I'd never seen it before. It must have been in his other shed.

"Because in the summer I use it outside. In the winter it's too much of a pain in the ass to fill it and it wastes water, so I didn't bother to put it in the house."

"Thank you for filling it for me."

"You're welcome. I never meant to buy a tub. It's kind of a funny story, actually, how I got it." He went to the cupboard and got me a bath towel. He pulled the chair up next to the tub and set it there.

I waited, but that was all he said. "So what's the funny story?" I asked.

He shrugged. "It's funnier in my head than if I tell it out loud. Get in the tub."

Frustrated that he couldn't even share a stupid story about a bathtub I lifted my sweatshirt off and tossed it angrily on the bed. At the edge of the tub I peeled off one sock then the other. I was using the edge of the tub to climb in but he forced me to use his hand for stability instead. Except his arm moved and holding on to him was far more unstable than a solid metal tub. For a second

I thought I was going to slip when one foot hit the bottom, but he held me with an iron grip. The water wasn't hot, but the tepid liquid still felt fantastic on my sore muscles and itchy, dirty skin. My bathing had been sponging off and nothing could compare to the sensation of sinking into the floral scented water and washing away the stink of sweat and sex.

I sank down and leaned against the back. It wasn't a bathtub for a house in the lower 48, but more of an oversized wash bin. But it might as well have been the most glamorous tub in the world's most luxurious spa the way it felt right then. I sighed, closing my eyes.

"Does that feel good?" he murmured.

Eyes popping open again, I saw that he had sat down in the chair. He was going to just sit there and watch me. "It feels amazing."

"Better than sex?"

That was a trick question. "No. Nothing feels better than sex with you does." There was truth in that, though I wouldn't have turned down a piece of chocolate cake and a glass of red wine. But every time I thought about him, how he touched me, his firm hand coming down hard on my ass or his cock thrusting into me, I wanted him again. I wanted more. I wanted him to push me as far as I could go.

"Good. Because I'm not finished with you yet."

I studied his face, not sure what he meant by that. Whether he meant right now, or if there was a general as yet undetermined expiration date for our sexual relationship. Arms resting on the side of the tub, I said, "Do whatever you need to do to me."

Take the pleasure, milk it from me. Nourish us both in ecstasy. The warm honey of desire laced with pain.

He reached out and yanked my hair, pulling me away from the walls of the tub. I winced, tears forming at the assault on my roots. But I kept my hands down by sheer will power. I had to. I couldn't risk letting my instincts take over, where I would try to block him or defend myself or shield my body from him. I had to take it, even as my weight dragged me further under the water and I wanted desperately to brace myself.

"Do you like it when I spank you?" he asked.

I nodded.

"And when I tie you up?"

I nodded.

His mood had shifted. His cock was hard beneath his jeans, just inches from my head. I had no idea what he was thinking or wanted to do, his expression telling me only that he was aroused.

Without warning he yanked my head down, submerging me completely under the water. I got a mouthful of bubbles before I tightly clamped my lips and eyes shut, holding my breath. I was about to start panicking, fighting him, when he pulled me back up.

"Your hair was dirty," he said. As if that were an explanation.

I was coughing a little, blinking to get the water off my eyelashes. Sucking in a lungful of air made it worse, though it felt good to know that I could breathe. He used his free hand to scrub my hair, a rough and futile shampooing. This time I was ready when he took me under, clamping my mouth shut on the way down. He held me under even longer, seconds ticking by slowly, me fighting to stay loose, relaxed. Compliant.

When he brought me up, he wiped my eyes for me, and my mouth. He was clearly pleased, his grip loosening. He kissed my damp lips softly. "I do love you," he murmured. "I never want to be without you."

I wasn't expecting him to say that.

Nor was I prepared for the emotion that overwhelmed me at his words. My heart swelled. My goddamn motherfucking heart actually swelled in my chest and I was giddy. Pleased. Triumphant. Bashful. Awed. None of which I should be feeling. Yet I was. The corner of my mouth lifted before I was even aware I was going to smile.

"Yeah?" I whispered. "Why do you love me?"

"Fishing for compliments?"

"I just want to know if it's me or just the fact that no other women are available to you." I did want to know that. Would he keep any woman? Or just me?

"I can have other women. I can go get a woman. But I want you. I love *you*. Because you're smart and sexy and sweet and trusting. You're the perfect combination of all those things. You're perfect."

It meant more than it should. Everything in me softened and I felt my eyes widen with unshed tears. My whole life I had wanted a man to look at me the way he was right now and it was all wrong. All wrong but so painfully right. "I love you too."

I did. I could deny it or call it something else, but I loved him for loving me. For choosing me.

His hair fell forward as he bent and I thought he was going to kiss me again. But he held me there, keeping all my weight on his arm as he brought my face to his so he could stare into my eyes. I raised a hand to touch the softness of his beard stubble, to trace his jawline with one finger.

"Tell me something I don't know," I whispered to him. "Share something with me."

"I'm sharing my house. My life. What else could you want?"

"Just a little something. Anything. A story, a picture of you. Something that makes you sad, or makes you laugh."

"Funny story? Okay, here's something funny. The last person who used this tub drowned in it."

As his words sank in, fear gripped me as tightly as he did. "Was it an accident or did someone do it on purpose?"

"What difference does it make? The end result is the same. She's dead."

We stared at each other, my breathing shallow, heart racing. He smiled, and it was evil. The smile of a man who knows he has the upper hand. There was no way to pull myself out of his hold, with his fingers wrapped around my hair, locking my head in his grip. How easy it would be for him to drown me. He wouldn't even have to break a sweat or strain. Just lower his arm and hold.

I could flail and kick but it wouldn't get me out of the water or out of his control.

"Who was she?"

"Nobody." He let go of me so quickly I slipped down and got a mouthful of tepid water. "Sit up for a second. I'm going to join you."

I sat up, lip trembling a little, teeth chattering. It wasn't from the cold. I scooted forward, hugging my knees to my chest in an illusion of protection. But nothing could protect me.

He shucked off his jeans and stepped into the tub. Once seated, he pulled me back so I was resting on his chest, floating between his legs. He kissed the back of my head and I sighed, relaxing back in to his arms. I would take comfort from the man I feared. It was better than nothing.

And it wouldn't be the first time.

I raised my leg and stared at my toes. I needed to clip the nails and buff the calluses off. I needed some peach scented lotion to massage between my toes and into my heels. Toes were so odd. I wondered if they were really necessary. Like truly necessary. Or were they more of an add on, a frivolous accessory to the skeletal outfit. Trent was massaging my arms gently, his lips brushing over my hair, back and forth, back and forth.

"You're right. This feels amazing," he said, with a deep sigh.

"It feels even better now that you're in it with me." It did. He was warm and strong and he loved me. I bet he loved even my toes. It was a freeing feeling. That I could just be me, and Trent would still love me.

I started to hum, a Taylor Swift song. I felt very pop song happy. There was a fear clawing at the back of my mind, but it only served to heighten my nerve endings, to make me feel more totally in the moment. "What are you doing tomorrow?" I asked, pausing in my song. "I'd like to help you if I can."

He kissed the top of my head. "I'm not used to having a partner. But I like it. I like that you're willing to pitch in."

"I want to help. You work so hard." It was sexy, how he

survived by his intelligence and his physical strength without help from anyone. He was a man in the truest sense of the word. The hunter and gatherer. Who protected his home and his family. Me. He protected me.

From everything else. I wasn't sure who was supposed to protect me from him. Me, apparently.

"I want to get a caribou before they're gone. That's meat for six months."

Fruit would be nice too but I wasn't going to complain. "It seems like you have enough already to me." There were carcasses dangling all over the yard.

"It goes faster than you think." He idly stroked my nipples.

I closed my eyes and wondered if he tried to kill me, would I fight him? Or would I just go, quietly, without a sound? Accepting my fate. At the moment I wasn't sure.

I was tired. Tired of living on edge. Tired of fighting. Tired of bracing myself.

For now, in the tub where someone had drowned, I just wanted to relax, and be a woman with her man.

He pinched the bud of my nipple hard and I let a whisper of a groan slip out in total hot, wet, boneless pleasure.

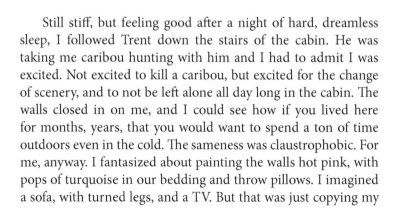

Still stiff, but feeling good after a night of hard, dreamless sleep, I followed Trent down the stairs of the cabin. He was taking me caribou hunting with him and I had to admit I was excited. Not excited to kill a caribou, but excited for the change of scenery, and to not be left alone all day long in the cabin. The walls closed in on me, and I could see how if you lived here for months, years, that you would want to spend a ton of time outdoors even in the cold. The sameness was claustrophobic. For me, anyway. I fantasized about painting the walls hot pink, with pops of turquoise in our bedding and throw pillows. I imagined a sofa, with turned legs, and a TV. But that was just copying my apartment in Seattle.

Here it was wood and snow. Snow and wood. Dirt and trees. Wildlife and blood. So I should decorate in red, white, green, brown. Maybe then the cabin wouldn't feel so cell-like. So stark.

I breathed in the fresh air, even though it was cold. Sometimes the cabin got stuffy, and I eagerly left it, shutting the door behind me. This hunting venture would also give me a chance to see where I was. I'd never ventured past the riverbank on my own, and only once had I gone on the river with him when we'd retrieved the salmon. Alaska was huge and I had seen a microscopic pinhead of space in the vastness. I wanted to get my bearings and figure out where the next dropped pin settlement was.

Because despite all my daydreams on decorating, I didn't want to stay forever. Not as a prisoner. I wanted to be able to leave if I decided to. Before he drowned me.

We walked for a long time. My breath was short and my nose went numb. We followed a trail along the river and I was amazed at how huge it was, even though it was covered in a layer of snow. I wanted to see it in summer, with the water rushing, the trees around it green, wildflowers blooming.

"What temperature do you think it is right now?" I asked him when he paused for a second, eyes scanning the horizon.

"Shh." He held a finger up to his mouth, not looking at me. "I see tracks," he murmured under his breath. "Moving north. Be quiet or you'll spook the bull."

I nodded, heart starting to race, though I wasn't sure why. I wasn't going to shoot a caribou. There was no reason for me to be nervous.

He lifted his binoculars and scanned across the river. "There." His binoculars went into his coat and he raised his gun.

Not even seeing it, I took a step forward, scanning left and right. It bothered me that I couldn't see the animal.

"Get back, Laney," he murmured.

But I had seen a flash of something downriver. A glint of sun on metal. "What is that?" I asked, taking three more steps.

Trent swore and jerked me back by the arm. "What the fuck are you doing? The bull just ran off, he saw you moving."

"But there are people down there." I pointed left, in awe. This was the first sign of life from any one other than the stranger in two weeks. I was stunned, and not even sure how I felt. "Who is that?" I started walking even faster, curious. My ankle turned, but I still kept going.

It was two men, walking on the other side of the river, guns in hand.

"I don't know who that is. I don't get much traffic around here." Trent raised his binoculars again and looked. When he did, they paused in their walk and looked over at us.

"I think they see us," I said, excited. I waved.

He yanked my arm back down by my side. "Go back to the house. I don't know who that is. It could be anybody. Bush people aren't always sane, you know. Those guys could see you and have nothing but raping you on their minds. Though I could protect you. I just don't want to get into it with anyone."

Oh, the irony. I almost laughed. Not that he had raped me, because I had been willing, but he had manipulated me, kept me prisoner. Tied me up and left me naked in his bed for hours. Locked me outside in the cold. So he was right in that bush people weren't always sane, but the question was, did I stay where I was with what I knew, or risk a scenario that was worse? With him, I knew that I could take the pain, and revel in the pleasure. I knew him, and his brand of insanity. I loved parts of him and how he loved me. Betraying him was ungrateful.

Yet freedom was tantalizingly close, a temptation that was virtually impossible to resist.

I couldn't have both.

So I took off running.

Trent was yelling my name with ferocious anger.

It occurred to me as my pathetic not-at-all-athletic legs strained to get a rhythm going, feet skittering on the slippery snow, that he could just shoot me. But that would be my answer-

CRASH

I had gone out fighting.

But no shot rang out.

Instead there was the ominous crack of thin ice, my legs going out from under me, and a cold so shocking, it felt like my body had been electrified. A thousand volts of pain burst through me in an explosion and all I could see was white. Blinding white, everywhere. Over me, around me.

I thought I heard my name ringing out again, but maybe I was imagining it. Maybe I was yelling it myself in my own head.

My legs were sucked down and I scratched at the ice, but I couldn't get a grip.

Then everything went dark and silent and murky and this time, my stepfather couldn't save me.

Not when he was as trapped as I was.

Prisoners, all of us. Mom, Dean, and me.

And all of it was my fault.

PART
THREE

CHAPTER FOURTEEN

FOR AN ENDLESS MINUTE I sank into the silent cold of the Yukon, body too shocked to protest, mind empty of all save one thought. I was going to die in Alaska. It seemed in that moment poetic, really. A rather remarkable death for an unremarkable woman. My lungs burned and my ears popped and I watched the hole grow smaller above me.

Then he pulled me out.

Using his bare hands, he hauled me heavy and limp, choking on the water, out of the hole, out of the river, and it was like being born, being ripped from a mother's warm womb and exposed to the searing light and icy air. I lay sprawled across the powdery glass surface, yanking in air, teeth chattering. I hadn't died, but he was going to kill me, and maybe that was an even more deserving death. Even without looking at his face, I could feel the waves of fury radiating off of him. There were voices, growing louder.

"Holy shit! Is she all right? What happened?"

"My wife isn't a native," Trent said. "She doesn't always realize when the ice isn't safe."

"Oh, man, that was scary as hell," a higher-pitched voice than the first said. "Do you need help getting her home? How far are you from camp?"

I stared at the glittering crystals of the ice surface and tried to control my shivering. I couldn't seem to speak. Here was my chance for freedom. Here was what I had run for- the opportunity to tell someone I wasn't with him of my own free will. But nothing came out of my mouth. I didn't speak. I didn't even look up at them. I didn't correct his lie that I was his wife. I just lay on the ice, catatonic, relieved to be alive. There was still the urge to live, to breathe, to love. To right the wrongs of my life.

Without him, I would be dead.

Yet, without him, I would have been found, taken to Michael. Back in Seattle by now, or marrying Michael and settling into life as an Alaskan wife.

I could still have that anyway.

"I've got her," he said. "Though if you can just watch a second and make sure we get off the ice okay, I'd appreciate it."

"Sure, sure, no problem."

Trent lifted me and my hair crackled as it tore off the ice, where it had already started to freeze. "Wrap your arms around my neck, doll," he murmured.

"Why did you save me?" I asked, staring up at him. It took a great deal of effort but I managed to lift my arms and secure them around his neck.

"Because I don't want you to die. Were you trying to die?"

I shook my head. "No. I don't want to die." With a sigh, I closed my eyes and relaxed against his chest.

As he carried me across the ice and I felt my soaked clothes stiffen on my skin, my hair brittle and frozen, I realized that his arms were always there to hold me. In my whole life, only Dean had saved me before the stranger. And that wasn't even the same thing. My life had never been at risk. Dean had saved me from my mother, from loneliness. But the stranger had saved me from death. Not once. Not twice. But three times.

His chest was solid. He was solid.

While he might require obedience, he was never, ever going to let anything happen to me.

Wasn't that the devotion and love I'd been seeking my entire life?

Hauling me out of the river could have pulled him down into it as well. He hadn't had rope, or anything to brace him. Saving me he'd risked his own life, getting sucked down into that black ice hell, where our lungs would have slowly filled with water, our eyes locked, as we drifted away from each other into oblivion. But he hadn't hesitated. He'd been right there, using his vast strength to haul my sorry ass out of the hole. Even after I'd run away from him.

There were voices again and he yelled loudly, "All clear! Thanks for your help."

We must be on the bank then. He was walking faster, putting the two men behind us in the distance. I wondered if he cared that they knew where he lived now, or if they'd seen me. Not that they'd gotten a good view of me before I'd fallen into a hole like a complete idiot. But it would be noteworthy. A story they would tell to friends, people at the store, wherever they would go.

Saw a girl fall in the ice. Scary as fucking hell, man. Her husband hauled her out like it was nothing.

At the house, I tried to help him take my clothes off, but my fingers wouldn't bend. Far too many times, he had been forced to undress me, defrost me. I vowed I wouldn't let it happen again. I wasn't helpless. I wasn't stupid. I couldn't stand the thought that he would think of me that way.

"What were you doing?" he asked me, once I was stripped and wrapped in a blanket.

"I'm not sure," I answered truthfully. "But I just wanted to talk to someone else for a second."

That was a lie, and I knew it the minute the words passed my lips.

"Are you lonely here?" he murmured, using a washcloth to attempt to dry off my hair. "I don't mean for you to be lonely."

"I'm used to a lot of people being around me." I leaned against the wall, raising my knees to my chest and pulling the blanket tighter around me.

"You were running, Laney. Running across the ice." He was sitting on the edge of the bed, studying me. "I know what you were doing. You were trying to escape. Like any prisoner, you were trying to escape."

My heart rate increased and I just watched him, waited. I couldn't answer, because he already knew the answer and saying it out loud wasn't going to make it more palatable for either of us. But he didn't speak either. We were locked on each other, everything left unsaid, but everything so obvious. He knew the truth and I knew the truth. What did it mean? That, I didn't know, and as each second passed, each breath expelled from my lungs, and each finger dug harder into my blanket, I felt him slipping away from me. Losing interest. No longer seeing me as special. It was there in the way his shoulders relaxed, the way his head tilted ever so slightly, as if he were viewing me differently. It was in the fact that he didn't touch me at all. He sat back, removed from me, and he might even be falling out of love with me.

That couldn't be. It would destroy me. I needed to count on his obsession with me, his desire for me. If I didn't have that, I truly had nothing.

"I'll let you go," he said, finally, after the pause grew so great I thought I might scream or start confessing to things I wasn't even guilty of. Beg him for forgiveness. "I'll take you to town if that's what you want, no strings attached. You can go see your friend or go home or do whatever you want."

"You don't want me anymore?" I asked, voice small, hoarse. My chest felt tight and I willed him to fight for me.

"Of course I want you. But I was wrong about keeping you when it isn't what you want. I'm... disappointed. But I want what's best for you."

His dismissing me, dumping me off, returning me, was not what was best for me. I knew then, without a doubt, what was.

It was him.

I couldn't lose his desire. His affection. His obsession.

I needed his need, his deep, dark, driving need to claim me, take me, possess me.

"I don't want to go home. I want to stay here with you." I reached for the headboard with shaky fingers, to where he kept the ropes. I looped them over my wrists and held them out to him to tighten. "I'm yours. Not a prisoner, but captured by you. Totally. For as long as you want me."

He didn't question it. Or try to talk me out of it. Instead, he yanked the ropes tightly, his air expelling from his nostrils in a short burst. He was aroused and pleased. The desire, his interest were back, better than before. He looked like he wanted to whip me, flaying the flesh from my body, and consume me. Piece by piece. That was how much he wanted me and my skin flushed from excitement. He was going to take me because he owned me and I fucking loved it. I loved him.

Pushing up at my elbows, he moved the ropes behind my head, so my wrists rested on the back of my neck. The position was a vulnerable one, my breasts thrust out, my arms straining. He could easily pop out my shoulders this way, or crack a bone. But that was the exciting part. He yanked me right up to his face and I refused to look away, our breath mingling.

"I want you forever," he said. "You're mine. And if you stay now, if you agree to belong to me, there is no leaving."

My cheeks felt feverish, my body prickling with desire. "I don't want to leave."

Without warning, he pulled the ropes, flipping me around and pushing me down into the mattress. I shifted my head to the right so I could breathe, but otherwise stayed loose. My shoulders drew back tightly, uncomfortable, but not painful.

"I'm really pleased," he murmured behind my ear. "And really fucking turned on by you. I'm not sure how much control I have right now."

His lips tickled my ear and I shivered. "Do what you want."

I was afraid, but the fear was sensual, the anticipation titillating. This was going to hurt and I was going to enjoy it. I was alive and I had found a greater plane of existence here with him. Gone was the vanilla day-to-day of the retail employee who sleepwalked through life.

"I need to ground myself, get myself under control."

That meant he was probably going to step away from the bed. I was disappointed, but I didn't really mind. I would just wait for him. I would wait indefinitely for him.

His weight pulled back and I saw out of the corner of my eye him going over to where he kept his weapons. He pulled a knife down off the rack and tossed his hair back out of his eyes. I stiffened, not sure what his intention was. But I would have to accept whatever he gave. That was the decision I'd made. That was the relationship we had.

By giving over total control to him, I felt like I had more freedom than ever before. I had to lose myself to find me.

It was a truth as blinding as the sun dappled snow outside the cabin.

He wouldn't hurt me in a way I couldn't handle. His intention was not to kill me with the knife and I had to fully trust in that. I had to. He had held my life in his hands from the minute the plane had hit the ground and he had never failed me. My life had value to him, and whatever the knife was for, it wasn't to murder me.

Trent returned to the bed and tied my ankles together. Every rough slide of the rope chafed my skin and made my nerve endings tingle. It felt like my skin was alive. Everywhere the rope touched, he followed with a soft brushing of his fingertips, soothing my flesh, soothing me. Goosebumps rose, a trail in his wake. Before he tightened the ropes, he raised my feet, knees bent, and shifted my legs apart with a soft lover's touch, cupping the curve of my backside briefly. He was such an intriguing mix of soft and hard, tender and rough. He had a body filled with physical power, muscle and strength, and callused, scarred skin.

There was no hesitation on his part to use his strength, yet he always tempered it with a feathery touch or a sweet word or a gentle kiss.

It was an intriguing combination I couldn't resist, nor did I want to. So while he was in check now, I knew at any second he could shift and I would feel the sting of a slap on my ass or the hard twist of my nipple between his fingers. Or the blade of his knife.

"You feel in control to me," I said, giving him a smile over my shoulder.

"I'm getting there," he murmured.

It was then I felt the cool glide of steel over my bare ass as he ran his knife where his fingers had just been. I swallowed hard, caught off guard. I'd seen the knife. It was big, lethal. I felt panic pluck at my arousal, and I fought the restraints without meaning to.

"Shh. I'm not going to hurt you, Laney. I'm not going to cut you. Not unless you ask me to. And you might ask me to before we're through."

He had no idea the effect his words could have on me. "I won't ask you for anything. I'll beg."

With a short laugh, he moved the knife up my back, along the ridges of my spine. I pictured him driving the tip through my vertebrae, to the hilt, pining me to the bed. My blood would spill down my sides and soak the mattress and I wouldn't even be able to jerk and convulse and fight to get away because I'd be paralyzed. That was the irony of course. He wouldn't do that to me because he didn't need to use violence to keep me still and at his mercy. Not really. The domination was an agreement, a consensual concession to his control, and while I hadn't always obeyed, I was learning. Getting more skilled at it.

So I concentrated on relaxing the tension in my body, letting him move the blade over me without wincing or struggling. He used the knife to shift my hair off of my neck and teased the tip over the delicate flesh at the back of my ear. He traced my jaw, never applying any pressure, so it felt as smooth as a melting ice cube. Across my lips. I involuntarily sucked in a breath. I wasn't scared. I was turned on. I wanted to bite the knife, to pull it between my teeth.

He didn't react and just moved on to my opposite shoulder, down my bicep, past my elbow and over my wrist. The blade traced each of my fingers and I shivered. It almost tickled. But in the way of a spider crawling over you, implying danger. I didn't shake it off. The cool steel disappeared though and I waited for its return.

It didn't. I heard him exhale sharply, but I couldn't see him. A few seconds later, something warm dripped onto my back. I jerked at the unexpected sensation and I wondered what it was. Candle wax? It didn't harden though. It rolled.

"What is that?" I asked.

"My blood."

I tensed. "What? Why, are you hurt?" It was a stupid question but I didn't know a different one to ask. It was just incomprehensible. His casual tone. The drip, drip. Like the blood on the plane. That was an uncomfortable thought.

"No. I cut myself so I could do this." His fingertip dipped into a droplet and smeared it.

"Do what?"

He didn't answer immediately but instead dragged the blood across my skin, curving up and down in a series of swirls.

"Are you drawing me a picture?" It was a disturbing thought, yet not one I recoiled from. He had bled for me, for whatever reason. He'd taken steel to skin and sliced through it.

"No. I'm giving you my name."

The words settled over me and I processed them slowly. His name. He was writing his name on my back in his blood. He was claiming me, and giving me what I had always asked for. The truth of who he was. Letters that would tell me what to call him. Yet I already knew I had his name just as surely as he had mine. Tied together, forever. But I reveled in the gesture. It was sexy, and romantic. When he took me from behind, he'd see his name drying, staining me. Becoming visible on the outside the way it was already seared on my soul.

"I accept it."

"Good." His touch left my back and he shifted his arm to where I could see it. He'd sliced up his forearm, not a deep wound, but a straight two inch cut, the blood flow slowing now to a sluggish stream.

"Didn't that hurt?" I asked, wishing I could touch him, soothe him. I didn't get to touch him enough. He held me at bay with the ropes too often.

"Your pain is the breaking of the shell that encloses your understanding," he murmured.

I shivered, the scent of his blood filling my nostrils. "Who said that?"

"Khalil Gibran. He's a writer."

So the man who had no books save one was well-read. The enigmatic quality of him now felt like something to look forward to, a peeling of his layers, rather than a frustration. We had endless days and nights and if he could give me his name, eventually, he would give me all of him.

"I've never read him."

"Taste my blood, Laney." He teased the cut over my bottom lip.

It didn't bother me. In fact, I flicked my tongue out to taste, curious. I wanted to take whatever he would give me. "What did your pain allow you to understand?" I asked.

"That I belong here, in the bush."

"With me?"

I could see him nod out of the corner of my eye.

"Yes. With you."

Kissing the tip of his finger, I descended on it, wanting to capture his essence, his scent. His blood. Wanting to be as intimate with him as it was possible to be.

"What does your pain teach you, doll?"

"That I'm not as weak as I thought. That I'm strong." I sucked his finger, drawing it deep into my mouth. I had never tasted his cock, never wrapped my mouth around his thickness. I craved that, wanting to tease him the way he teased me. But I wouldn't unless he wanted me to. Unless he told me.

"You are strong. It's your greatest asset."

"What's my biggest weakness?"

"Self-doubt. And a tendency to be petulant."

I made a sound of protest. But I couldn't really deny either. He was right.

"But you're learning. Growing." He pulled his finger out of my mouth and wiped the moisture down the curve of my breast. "I am too. I'm learning patience."

That amused me. I wouldn't have classified him as patient. But I thought about how I would react to someone completely invading my space and decided he was an impatient sort of patient, impossible though that was.

I closed my eyes as he reached up and undid the knots holding my wrists tightly behind my neck. My shoulders relaxed, the pain easing. He didn't touch my ankle bonds, but instead just rolled me fully onto my side, then onto my back.

"Don't you want to see my back?" I asked. "See your name on me?" In blood.

I did. I wished I had a full-length mirror so I could stand up and gaze over my shoulder. I had always been content with my body, not in love with it, but not hating it or desiring to change it the way so many woman were. I always thought it looked fine, but nothing extraordinary. It had only been since I'd been here, with him, that I had felt the full force of my sexual essence. The seductive qualities of my body. How every inch was erogenous, valuable, tempting to him. I felt sexy, in a tangible way, whereas before it had just been an awareness that certain men, in certain circumstances found me attractive.

Now I understood there was a whole new level. Beyond the pain, was the ultimate awareness and we overwhelmed each other in the best way possible. It was so intense to be with him that I wanted him to rein me in, so I didn't tear off chunks of my flesh and hand them to him to covet.

Thoughts like that scared me.

I scared myself far more than he scared me.

He shook his head. "Now I want to see your blood."

"You're going to cut me?" Fear and excitement overlapped each other, in an erotic embrace. "Where?"

His finger rolled across my neck and I shivered. "I'd like to here, but it's far too dangerous. I can't risk actually hurting you, not when we're so far from town. I don't want to hurt you." He cupped my cheek. "I want to keep you forever."

Turning my head, I kissed the palm of his hand. "I want that too."

The knife lowered, shifting down, down. I sucked in a breath, the anticipation of pain huge. As he passed each body part I thought he might cut and it remained unscathed, I felt relief. Yet disappointment. I'd thought he would tease the tip into my breast, or give me a matching slice on my forearm to his. But instead, he eased it over the mass of curls I now had between my legs and I swallowed hard, desire making me damp, nipples tight. It would be the worst kind of pain I was sure and I opened my mouth, ready to protest. I couldn't. He wouldn't.

It was just a whisper of steel over dewy curls then it was gone. He didn't want to hurt me. He'd said so himself.

Instead, his tongue flicked over my clit and I jerked at the unexpected pleasure. But immediately following, there was a sharp pain on my inner thigh. I sucked in a breath, tears forming in eyes. He distracted me from it by using his tongue on me again, as I felt both the pain and the pleasure. The wet trickle of my warm blood felt strange, like an itch, something that needed to be wiped and blended with my damp arousal. It was a confusing thought, everything was confusing.

I went down into some unknown head space, a weird sort of vacancy of thought, of strumming nerves and high pleasure, of intense pain and muddled consciousness. All I knew was him. And all he knew was me. I could hear the tenor of his breathing change as he reached down, flicked his tongue over my blood, then back to my clit. We were elemental, at our darkest origin, blending into one mysterious and off-balance creature.

"Come for me," he urged. "Without my mouth on you. Without me touching you. Come for me just by the sound of my voice."

I shifted restlessly, not sure how to achieve that. Wanting to.

"Look at me," he commanded.

I did. His cool eyes were fiery, intense. "Imagine my tongue on you, imagine me sucking your clit. Can you feel it?"

"Yes." It was as if he were touching me through a gossamer shield, obscured, distant, but still very real. It wasn't, of course.

Nothing could be real. None of this seemed real.

Yet this moment, this life with him, was more real than anything that had happened to me in all the other millions of seconds I had existed before this.

"Now come, Laney."

So I did. Our gazes held, his grip on my thighs tightening, his thumb slipping across my blood. My body seized and let go and I achieved perfect obedience.

The corner of his mouth turned up and I knew the purest bliss I'd ever experienced.

Both Alaska and the stranger had taken my life and plunged it into an icy river and made me feel when I hadn't even known I'd been numb.

I smiled back, proud of myself.

CHAPTER FIFTEEN

"**D**RESS WARMLY."

Yawning, I slipped out of bed naked and stretched in a way that would make his eyebrows lift. It did. I smiled as I watched his eyes rake over my breasts. "What are we doing today?" I asked as I went over to the sink fully naked to start brewing some coffee.

I rubbed absently at my inner thigh, where my cut was starting to heal, itching as it scabbed and pulled. I had shown him something that night inside of me and he had changed in the days since, loosening up, talking more. I had changed too, reveling in my body, in him, in my role as mistress of the cabin. I had become more domestic, learning how to feed him. Learning how to please him.

Nudity was liberating, made the mundane tasks of cooking and cleaning more interesting, plus he had been right. I was starting to get used to the cold. There was something elemental about having it cool my flesh. It kept me limber, moving quickly. Aware of all my joints and how much effort was required to do my daily tasks. I had been to Mexico a few times, where the heat robbed me of ambition, made me lazy, complacent, relaxed to the point of not caring about anything other than the sun on my face and the drink in my hand. But here, I was embracing the cold, because it got my heart pumping faster and forced my step quicker.

"We're going to town."

I glanced over my shoulder, surprised. "We?" It had been days. I thought he'd abandoned the trip. Certainly I wasn't expecting him to take me with him.

"Yes, we."

He was already in his jeans but his chest was bare. He wasn't the only one whose gaze could wander. I lowered my eyes, taking in the length of him. He was the hottest thing in the cabin, by far. "I didn't think you wanted me to go with you." I poured the grounds in the coffeemaker.

Why was I debating it with him? I should keep my mouth shut and just take advantage. But I was suspicious. I couldn't help it. I didn't want to get my hopes up and then be disappointed. I didn't want to escape him, not now, not ever, but I did want a razor and tampons and maybe some sugar for my coffee. Panties. He had promised me panties. Mostly though, what I wanted wasn't stuff, it was to see other people, even if I didn't speak to them. Maybe eat a slice of pizza. Hear the news on the TV at a bar. Sip wine. See something other than these four walls. I wasn't totally acclimated. It would take a long time to get used to the lack of variation in my scenery, but I knew I would eventually. It was just an adjustment period.

In the meantime, I might be able to satisfy all those cravings with an afternoon in town.

"I always wanted you to go. I just didn't trust you."

I turned the coffeepot on and turned around. Leaning back on the counter, I asked, "And you do now?"

"Yes." He had moved in front of me and he tipped my chin up and gave me a soft kiss. "I do. You've earned it."

A shiver rolled through me and it wasn't from the frigid

temperature. It was because it made me giddy to please him. In only three days, I had fully brought that look back- the one that made it clear that he wouldn't be done with me for a very long time, if ever. That was the look I wanted. One of fierce need, desire, attraction, obsession. Love.

"Thank you," I murmured. "I'll be good, I promise."

"I know you will be. Just keep your hat on and your head down."

"I can do that." I put my arms around his neck and kissed him fully, opening my mouth for him. "Mmm. What do you want for breakfast?"

"Tongue."

"Coming right up." He wasn't being flirty. He didn't mean a French kiss from me. He meant caribou tongue from the animal he'd taken down the day before when he'd gone hunting. "Can you get it from the shed for me?"

"Of course." He pulled on his boots and opened the door.

Immediately, he brought back the tray of ice he'd set out the night before. It didn't seem like someone who lived in the Alaskan bush would want to make ice cubes but he did faithfully. He put them in his coffee, two per each cup, to cool the scalding liquid down. It was a curious habit but it had become endearing to me. But now he broke routine.

As I bent over and pulled out a saucepan to cook the tongue, his hand slid between my ass cheeks and settled right where he could cup my sex. I went still. "Well, hello," I said, flirtatious. He wasn't usually a morning sex kind of man but I wasn't going to object.

His hand disappeared briefly and he commanded, "Don't move. Stay bent over."

"Yes, sir." I waited, anticipating his cock thrust hard into me. My body went damp for him at the thought.

But instead of the warm skin of his erection, the cool wetness of an ice cube slid between my cheeks and deep into the heat of my vagina. He followed it with a second one and I sucked in my breath, startled by the sensation.

"How does that feel?" he asked, sounding curious, but sleepy still. Like he wasn't really fully awake and was just playing. Like when men tugged at their balls as they emerged from sleep.

"Interesting."

"Let me know when they melt. I'll go get the tongue."

"Should I stay still like this?" They already were melting a little, and slipping downward, gravity too strong.

"No, keep doing what you were doing. But don't let them fall out."

"I don't think they'll stay in."

His hand cracked my ass, hard. "Then squeeze. Don't question me, babydoll. I'm in a really good mood."

When he asked things that were illogical, I wondered. In the back of my mind, I questioned if staying with Trent was the right thing to do, and if somehow I was losing track of what was right and wrong. What was my choice and what was still imprisonment. But then I squashed those traitorous little thoughts. They didn't make me feel as good as he did.

So I stood up and poured his coffee while I held the ice inside me, the urge to reach down and tease my fingers over myself a huge temptation. By the time two mugs were filled with coffee the ice was gone and I was disappointed. When he returned with the tongue I told him.

"More?" he asked.

Maybe if I went numb from the inside out I wouldn't be so aching. In all sense of the word. I nodded. "Yes." Leaning on the counter, I arched my ass out, shifting my legs apart.

He pushed one, two, three cubes this time, and it felt different. Not as shockingly cold on my hot insides, but more clinical. I was disappointed. When I stood, he could see it on my face. "Too cold?"

"I can't feel it as much."

With one finger, he hooked one back out, raised it to his lips, and sucked it. Then he dropped it into his coffee with a wink at me.

Such a strange thing, me and him.

Maybe neither of us was entirely sane.

But I wasn't sure I wanted to return to sanity.

Though for some reason, I did reach into the nightstand when he went outside to use the outhouse, and palmed my cell phone. I hid it in the interior of my jacket. Not because I wanted to call anyone, but because I wanted to look at my pictures in the camera roll and the battery had been dead for a while. Maybe I could recharge it.

Guilt made my cheeks heat. That I was lying to him.

And guilt because of Victoria. Innocent, sweet, Victoria, left behind in Seattle in the mess her parents had created.

All alone with only Grandma Jean, who spent her days deadheading her perennials, her hair tightly permed, expression perpetually pleasant. The human labradoodle, all naiveté and misplaced trust.

I missed Grandma Jean.

And Victoria.

Not my mother.

And for once, not Dean.

I rode in to town on the back of his snow machine, hugging his waist with my arms. It was windy and hard to see anything, even wearing the face mask he gave me. My eyelashes felt frozen, but I took in the majesty of the area as we drove. Trees, trees, and more trees, jutting towards the sky with confidence, their branches coated thick with early snow. At places he didn't feel the river was safe enough for the weight of us on the snow machine, but it was hard to believe just a few weeks earlier the river had been running and we'd been fishing.

That I'd fallen through when I was stupid enough to run.

There was no point in running when you don't know where

you're going.

Eventually I closed my eyes and leaned my head against his back, feeling jostled and unused to the motion. I had only been on his dog sled since the crash. No cars, no buses, no bicycle. It was odd to be zipping along at such a high speed.

I hadn't given a lot of thought to what town meant or even what it was called. But in my mind, I was picturing something picturesque. Cute and colorful. The Norway of the bush, with chateau-like houses and quaint little shops. The reality was it was a mishmash of buildings, garages, sheds, and trailers. There was no order to the layout, no design, just something here, something there, a woodpile in a yard, a broken down truck on blocks, dingy, weather-beaten wooden houses sagging against the backdrop of the mountains in the distance. A sign in front of one gray building, no bigger than a garden shed, read, "United States Postal Service, Rush, Alaska."

There weren't more than two dozen buildings all together, including outbuildings. It wasn't impressive. It wasn't a place to find a good night out with drinks and a band playing a set. I doubted there even was a restaurant, and my hopes for pizza evaporated.

He pulled into the post office and parked. "I have a package I need to pick up."

"Can I come in with you?"

The look he gave me indicated he thought that was a stupid question. "Of course."

How would I know that? I would have thought that he didn't want anyone to see me close up. There was no real explanation for who and what I was. But he held his hand out and lifted me off the snow machine and I wasn't going to turn down the offer. I was eager to see other people. There was only one clerk and one customer inside. The clerk was a middle aged woman with black hair, the customer a grizzled old man. They glanced at us but neither smiled or looked particularly curious.

When we approached the counter the old man turned to leave

and he simply nodded at us, nothing more. Trent said, "How's it going?" on his way to the counter. The clerk didn't acknowledge him but went into the back and returned with a package that she pushed across the wooden surface.

"Sign here."

I could have shifted so that I could see the name written on the package, but I didn't bother. I was still wearing my mask but I gave a smile anyway to the clerk.

"You new around here?" she asked.

"Yes."

"She's my mail order bride," he said. "Came up from Fairbanks last spring."

The clerk's weathered face registered zero surprise. "Well. Congrats then."

"Thank you."

My skin prickled beneath my layers and I wanted to ask her why she didn't think that statement was odd. Why none of it seemed odd to her. Shouldn't a total stranger in a small town be noteworthy?

Apparently not.

The same thing happened in the general store. We filled a basket with feminine toiletries and batteries and matches and kerosene and a toothbrush and condoms and no one even glanced at us. There were at least six people in the store and not a single soul gave us more than a cursory nod. We approached the counter and Trent started unloading our basket.

"Hi," I said to the clerk in a voice that sounded ludicrously loud in the hushed store. Everyone moved so silently doing their business. It was unnerving. I wanted to hear people, see smiles and listen to laughter.

This clerk was a guy in his twenties and he looked at me like he thought I was a freak. "Hi."

"Damn it, I forgot you wanted sugar," Trent said. "Wait here, I'll go get it."

"Thanks," I told him. I watched him walk away, curious

to see his movements here, in a store, versus at home, the way he normally was. He didn't look uncomfortable in town. Just efficient. I had a thought.

Turning back to the clerk, I asked, "Do cell phones work here?"

Now he really stared at me in doubt. "Uh, yeah. Of course. We're not like off the grid here. Fuck that."

"Do you know where I can charge my phone? I don't have the charger."

"Like without a charger you can't do a whole lot." He was scanning our items one by one and dropping them into a bag. "I don't know what to tell you." He looked up and his eyes narrowed. Curiosity crept into his voice, the first person to exhibit any. "Where are you from?"

Trent moved in beside me right then. "Why do you ask?" he said smoothly.

My palms went damp and I hoped he wouldn't ask the clerk what we had been talking about. He wouldn't approve.

The clerk just shrugged. "Just figured she's not from around here since I've never seen her before."

"No one is from here," Trent said. "She's from Fairbanks."

As he scanned at the register, the clerk paused briefly, his hand on the box of condoms. He glanced at me, with lascivious interest. He couldn't even really see much of my face or my body but it didn't seem to matter. It must suck to be single in a place like that. Not many options.

"Hurry it up, kid," Trent told him. "We need to get home and fuck."

The clerk dropped the box guiltily and I watched his cheeks burn. Mine were too, under the fabric of my hat. Sometimes the stranger was too crude for me. He made me feel… kept. Like a prisoner.

The thought made me wince. I didn't like reality forcing its way in. And for the first time witnessing his world and the real world colliding, I paused to wonder. To ponder my choice.

CRASH

My hand slid into my pocket and fingered my cell phone before I even realized what I was doing. I stood very still, eyes trained on the clerk. When he glanced at me again, his eyes widened slightly at whatever he saw in my expression. Maybe he saw me pleading. Maybe he saw my fear. Maybe he saw that something inside me had gone feral from my captivity and I needed a heavy dose of normal.

Whatever it was, after Trent paid and we gathered up our bags and started to leave, the clerk called me back. "Miss, you forgot a bag." It was still in his hand, behind the counter. I doubled back and when I took it, his eyes darted to the bag, then back to me. I followed his gaze and saw he had put a cell phone charger inside. My mouth dropped open and he nodded ever so slightly.

"Thanks," I murmured, using my fingers to discreetly shift a bag of dried fruit over it.

"You're welcome. Take care."

"Come on," Trent called from the doorway, sounding impatient.

I hurried to follow him, heart racing. The restroom. I would find a restroom.

"I think I just started my period," I blurted, the second we were outside. "Is there somewhere I can use the restroom?"

"Just now you started it?" he asked, sounding skeptical. He stared at me, long and hard.

"I think so. I feel something wet."

He looked like he was about to say something but then stopped himself. "Fine. Let's go eat lunch and you can go there."

"We can eat lunch? I didn't think there would be a restaurant here." There was something off in my voice- a sort of high-pitched manic quality- and I fought to rein it back in. I was acting guilty when in reality I had nothing to feel guilty for. I was allowed to use my phone if I wanted to.

Being around other people, especially several people who had seemed so disinterested, had me on edge. I had thought that somehow we would stroll into town and I would have to make up a fake name and manufacture a story as to who I was and what I was doing there, and that all of it would put Trent into a foul mood. But he seemed perfectly at ease. It was me who felt caught off-guard, by initial ambivalence, and then the caring subterfuge of the general store clerk, who clearly thought I was being abused or something. Nothing felt like it was going in a way I had assumed and I realized I wanted something more. Drama. I wanted drama, and something to have impact. This trip to town was my big excitement for months to come and this couldn't be it. Not just picking up supplies and being ignored by the locals.

It just seemed like it should be bigger.

But I would happily settle for some French fries. The restaurant was in combination with a laundromat and a bar. It seemed like an odd combination but at the same time, there were only three patrons in the whole place, so it made sense to offer multiple services. We sat down at a cafeteria style table and after ordering a soft drink I excused myself to go to the restroom, grabbing the bag with the tampons and the phone charger. It was a single stall and I locked it behind me, immediately searching for an outlet. There was one under the sink and I plugged my phone in, relieved the cord fit, and pulled my ski mask off my face.

Then I opened the box of tampons, pulled one out, then shoved it back in, like it had been a false alarm. I did use the restroom, marveling in the flush of the toilet, before going to the sink to wash my hands. It was then I looked myself in the eye for the first time in three weeks.

The change was dramatic. My hair was wild and unkempt, dull from lack of shampooing. My cheekbones were more pronounced, my lips pale and chapped from the wind. There were shadows under my eyes and a scratch on my neck I hadn't even realized I had. But it was my eyes themselves that stared back at me, so familiar, yet so strange. They looked feverish, edgy, excited. This Laney hadn't come out to play in a long, long time, and even then, when she had been so nervous and bold and determined as she had stepped into Dean's room that night, she hadn't been this crazed looking.

It was my true inner self, staring back at me, let free from the chains of the mundane, free from having to fly under the radar, to be ordinary. Normal. No one could know. No one could ever know. That's all I ever heard and I believed it.

But here, in Alaska, under the very firm hand of the stranger, I had come back to me, and taken me to the next level.

"Hello, Gorgeous," I murmured, with a cocky grin. Because I was gorgeous. Maybe my hair could stand a good brushing and my lips some balm, but whereas before I had been cute, attractive, now I was intriguing, mysterious. Sexy. I was fucking sexy.

Leaning against the countertop, I slipped my hand down my pants and played, just a little. Just to remember what it felt like to pleasure myself, to see that change it wrought to my face, to give myself a little pat on the back for being so hot. But I didn't want to waste time so after just a few seconds I gave my clit a little squeeze and abandoned my pants, tasting my finger briefly before washing my hands again.

I turned on my phone, and saw it was only at eight percent, but good enough. I indulged in a couple of seconds of scrolling through images, pausing on Sammy and me doing a duck lip, studying the way I looked. I agreed with my earlier assessment. Cute then, sexy now. Muted before, fluorescent now.

Once I had everything tucked into the interior pocket of my jacket, I left the bathroom. There was a soft drink waiting for me and as he watched me intently I picked it up and drank half of it with one sip.

"Oh, my God, that tastes so good," I sighed.

"It's liquid cancer."

"I have to die of something."

"That's true."

I paused, setting the glass carefully down again. Everything he said always seemed to have double, triple meaning. "What are you ordering for lunch?" I lifted the menu the waitress had slapped down in front of me and studied the plastic sheet.

"You took your hat off," he said.

My eyes shifted off the sandwich selections and up to him. "Yes. It would look really strange if I wore a ski mask inside a restaurant."

"I know. But I feel like you're naked. It makes me want to cover you."

Sometimes I needed to be exposed.

"You know what they say? It's better to hide in the open." I reached across the table and put my hand over his, stroking his knuckles. I noticed how wretched my nails looked, all different lengths, some broken, some chewed, one pinky still mysteriously painted. The polish while not pristine, was mostly intact, just grown out. Ballet Slipper was the name of the color. Soft and delicate. Just a tiny bit of me was still Ballet Slipper. The rest of me was like a ballerina really was. Sinewy and resilient, callused and feminine. A hungry, spinning, wild-eyed creature with scars.

"I suppose they say a lot of things."

He hadn't trimmed his beard in a few weeks and he too looked especially wild in the vibrant light of the restaurant. It was weird to see him somewhere other than the cabin or the yard, to watch him interact with other people. The scar on his forehead looked glaringly white and his cheekbones were ruddy, probably from the wind. The love I felt for him was a living thing; it breathed, it grew hungry, it was strong yet vulnerable. So strange to love someone whose life was a blank, but maybe that was why I could love him. Maybe when relationships started with two people pouring out their histories, verbal dossiers, they were given a clear directive on who each other was. They were led, false or true, to a conclusion based on what each chose to reveal.

When nothing was revealed, only the present is relevant. What they say, what they do. Nothing else.

Yet I liked the illusion that I could get to know him, that some day, I would read a menu and be able to guess with ninety percent accuracy what he was going to order. As it was, I had no clue. I also didn't know what I was going to order, because the idea of anything with cheese was making my mouth water. I also decided I didn't want any meat because that was primarily our diet. So when the waitress returned, I asked for the spaghetti with parmesan cheese. And garlic toast.

He ordered a burger, which seemed weird, given how much caribou we had been eating. But it came with fries, which I was hoping to steal. Though when my pasta arrived I was too busy shoveling it into my mouth to even reach for a fry.

The waitress eyed me when she came to refill my soft drink. "Don't you feed her?" she joked to him.

"Of course I feed her," he said, his tone angry. "She's not starving," he added defensively.

My cheeks burned. But the waitress just rolled her eyes. "I was kidding, asshole," she said. "Fucking relax."

I paused, fork midway to my mouth. Calling him an asshole was not going to make him happy.

But to my surprise the tension in his shoulder eased. "Sorry. You know we get defensive when we're subsistence living."

"You also all get weird," she told him flatly. "Living alone is not what God intended. Glad you found yourself a wife." She turned back to me, my empty glass in her hand. "I'm Rhonda, by the way."

"La-" I started to say, automatically. But then I felt his foot come down on mine, grinding in. "Laura." It was a lame finish. Laura was way too similar to Laney. But there was no other recovery so I had to own it. "It's nice to meet you, Rhonda."

"Likewise. Where are you from?"

Rhonda was in her fifties if I had to guess, tall, wearing full make-up. She was wearing jeans and a sweatshirt, but her shoulder-length hair was curled. I wondered what brought her to Rush and why she had stayed.

"I'm from Wisconsin." It was the first state I thought of that wasn't anywhere near Washington. But then I realized I didn't know a whole hell of a lot about it, other than the whole cheese factor. Maybe that's why I chose it. I had dairy on my mind.

"I'm from Sioux City," she said. "Came up here fishing and met my husband and that was it. I never looked back."

"We met in Fairbanks," Trent said. "Last spring. I finally talked her into visiting and she decided to stay."

As the conversation continued I felt less afraid of being caught in a lie and more intrigued by what Rhonda might say. She knew the stranger. They were acquaintances, anyway. What would she reveal to me about him? A past wife? His name? A personality trait?

But Rhonda disappointed me. All she said to me was, "Make sure you wear sunglasses. You don't want to get crow's feet like me."

That was it. I gave an awkward laugh. "Will do, thanks."

That was the reality of it, wasn't it? She didn't look at me and wonder who I was or where I came from or why I was with him, not really. After her mild curiosity was appeased with very ordinary answers that required no thought, she immediately looked at me and thought of herself. My youthful face reminded her of her aging one. She coveted my collagen and the past, while most likely enjoying the present.

It wasn't about me.

Which summed up so many aspects of my reality back in Seattle. It wasn't about me. Yet here, with him, it was. Sure, it was about him, but he was about me. I was his focus. It was a good reminder that while I had lost a lot, what I had gained was actually something I'd craved my entire life.

So I opened my mouth and confessed the second Rhonda went back into the kitchen.

"I brought my phone," I blurted.

He had been dragging his fry through a puddle of ketchup and he paused. "What do you mean?"

"I brought my phone with me because I wanted to look at the pictures on it." I pulled it out of my pocket and held it up for him to see. "I turned it on in the bathroom but it only has five percent battery so I turned it back off." I couldn't read his expression. "I just wanted you to know because… I don't keep secrets from you."

"Your secrets are yours to keep. Though how long was your phone on?"

"Two minutes tops." I frowned. That wasn't the response I was expecting.

"You better hope it wasn't long enough to ping off a cell phone tower. Or whoever might be looking for you will know exactly where you are. Is that what you want? Someone to find you?"

"No one is going to look for me," I said. The only person who would was my stepfather and he was in prison.

"What about your friend?"

"I'm sure he thinks I'm dead. I'm sure everyone thinks I'm dead." It was a bizarre thought. But even if Michael didn't think I was dead, would he really look for me?

The door to the laundromat and restaurant pushed open, the bell jingling the arrival of a customer and I had my answer.

Michael walked through the door.

CHAPTER SIXTEEN

I WAS SO SHOCKED I JUST stared at him. I hadn't seen Michael in person in a dozen years but I was very familiar with his adult face from pictures. Besides, he stood out from the other people I had seen in Rush. He looked fresh. New to the bush. His jacket was still crisp, his boots stained from snow, but still unbroken. He was clean-shaven and good looking, a walking advertisement for LL Bean. He stomped his boots in the doorway and then looked up.

Our eyes met.

He started. Then he shook his head, clearly exasperated, before breaking into a huge smile. "Laney!"

"Michael. Hi." I wanted to stand up, go to him, but I looked at the stranger. He was assessing Michael and then turned to watch me. His eyebrows rose in question.

"I'm so glad you're okay, Jesus Christ, Laney. I thought you were dead." He came towards us with huge strides.

Now I did stand up because I had the overwhelming urge to stave him off. Keep him over there. I had heard people use the phrase 'two worlds colliding' but holy shit, this was that in spades. It felt like a woman must feel when her husband and her lover end up in the same room. The cocktail party that overlaps two men she fucks. The awkward attempt to behave normally, the meaningful glances with the lover, or the even more obvious attempts to completely ignore him. The ignorant husband, laughing and joking with friends while she stands there and aches for the lover, her panties growing damp with her dirty little secret.

It felt like that. Or the way I'd felt with my mother and Dean. Panicky, nervous, yet kind of excited.

"I'm not dead," I said. "Though no one else survived the crash. This is the first time I've been able to get to town. What are you doing here?"

My voice sounded high-pitched. Manic.

"I'm looking for you." Michael reached out and pulled me into a giant bear hug. He squeezed me. Hard. "I'm so glad you're okay." He kissed the top of my head. "Oh my God, I can't believe you're alive. I was here to find your body, honestly. I didn't think there could be any way you'd be alive."

"It's me, in the flesh." I hugged him back, because he was Michael, and I had intended to marry him, but at the same time, I felt the stranger's eyes on me, watching. So I carefully disengaged from him. "The pilot and the other passenger died. It was terrible, Michael. I feel so bad for their families."

"Yeah, I know. The plane was found. The assumption was that you were injured, wandered off, and died of exposure." He took a step back and swept his eyes over me, still holding both my arms. "Where have you been? You look like hell."

I frowned. I didn't look like hell. I looked *alive*. I opened my mouth to say something, anything, but the stranger spoke first.

"She's been with me." He slid his chair out and stood up too, rising with an easy possession, but a caged intensity that I recognized. "She was injured, but she's recovered now. We had to wait for the river to freeze over before we could travel. I live a few miles from the crash point and I found her."

Michael took it all in and didn't register any suspicion on his face. He put his hand out. "Well, then, thank you for saving her life. I'm Michael St. Clair."

My muscles tensed and I waited, not sure what the response would be.

"I'm Trent," the stranger said, an easy smile about his lips. "Laney said you're childhood friends?"

Always so smooth, my stranger. Nothing rattled him. Unlike me, everything sending my nerves jangling, my words tumbling out of my mouth in panic. At least, before anyway. I was stronger now. Here. With him. I'd grown.

"Sit down, Michael," I said, gesturing to the table. Rhonda was back and she was watching us with interest. Besides, I wanted a chair to hold my weight. My legs felt like matchsticks, ready to snap. "I can't believe this."

I couldn't believe he'd come all this way to look for my body. To retrieve me. Maybe he did love me. Maybe everyone had been wrong in suggesting I was an idiot to pin my hopes on him. Even a nice guy wouldn't poke all over the bush looking for a corpse. What would be the point? Only someone who genuinely cared about me would do that. I pushed my fingernails into my palms to ground myself.

"I can't believer it either." Michael sat heavily into a chair. "I need a beer." He glanced around. "Do they serve alcohol here? It doesn't look like a happening town."

"They have beer," Trent said. "So why did you think you could find Laney if the authorities couldn't?"

It sounded rude. Michael unzipped his jacket and gave Trent a long look. "The authorities weren't looking for her. It was a closed case when they found the plane and her next of kin was notified. I was also notified because they found my address in her purse. They assumed I was her destination." Michael gave me a long look. "I assume I was her destination as well."

I stared back, defiantly. Silent. So I hadn't told him. It was supposed to be a surprise. *Surprise, Michael.*

"I didn't really expect to find your body," he told me. "I just wanted confirmation that no one had seen or heard from you. It seemed odd to me that your cell was gone but your body wasn't found immediately around the plane. I didn't think you could get far without help. I guess I was right."

"They notified my mother?" I asked Michael. "Did you talk to her?"

He nodded. "Yes, but I haven't talked to her. I don't really remember your mother all that well. I wasn't sure what to say to her."

Of course he didn't remember my mother. That was during her spa phase, when Michael and I were spending all that time together. She kept taking spa vacations on Dean's dime, which were actually more like hotel rooms in warm places where she could easily buy drugs, but regardless, she hadn't been home much. I hadn't cared.

"I understand."

What I also understood was that you can't escape the past, even when you crash into a forest and are rescued. It was there, sitting across from me, in the flesh. The past, the present, and the future were rubbing up on each other, getting awkwardly acquainted.

"Would you like some lunch?" Trent asked Michael. "We're about finished eating, but I could go for a beer myself."

He sounded so strange. So casual. So friendly and polite. I hated it. I wanted to wrest him from this restaurant and have him be normal again. I wanted him to grab me by the hair and murmur seductively in my ear while I felt sure of myself.

"Thanks, I think I will order something." Michael lifted his hand for Rhonda to come over. He asked for a menu. When she left to retrieve one he bent closer to me. He was seated next to Trent, so at a diagonal from me. "I did call Dean," he murmured. "He was extremely upset."

My blood felt hot and sluggish, stuck in my veins, building up until I exploded. My skin splitting and all of my insides bursting out for everyone to see. "I'm sorry to hear that," I said. Because what else could I say?

I still had Dean's last email to me. I had read it a million times.

I've met someone.

He'd met someone.

I'd met someone.

We'd all met someone.

For the first time since the crash I felt as if I'd left my body. That I was in that weird space where I was saying the right things and doing the right things, but I wasn't really truly present. It was a skill I was good at. I had floated away to that hazy place where passive Laney liked to twirl her hair and daydream about nothing in particular. Seeing Michael and hearing him speak out loud about my life had sent me into retreat and I didn't like it.

"So what have you been doing?" Michael asked. "I have a hard time picturing you hunting and fishing."

"I have been. I know it's hard to believe, but sometimes I surprise myself." That was certainly true.

He turned to Trent. "I've only ever seen her in floral dresses. Laney has always been such a girly-girl. Everyone always thought she was so cute."

They had. Until they hadn't.

But fuck cute. They could keep it.

The stranger thought I was sexy.

"She is cute," he said. "But she's a lot more than that."

My cheeks heated. The way he said that... there was no question we had been intimate. It sounded so obvious to me, but maybe it wasn't to anyone else.

Rhonda returned and said, "What can I get you?" to Michael after Trent ordered himself a Budweiser.

"I'll take a burger, medium rare. And whatever beer you have in a bottle."

"None," she said flatly. "Just cans."

"Okay, that's fine. Whatever you have."

Her lips pursed but she just nodded. "Busy day today. All kinds of folks in town. Huh."

We had finally caught the interest of a local, but only in so much that we were all noteworthy. I didn't think Rhonda was going to press. I was no longer worried about the clerk in the general store blabbing that I was an abused wife either. He was the least of my problems compared to Michael sitting at the table with us.

"How is Victoria?" I asked.

"Dean said she's fine. He hasn't told her about you yet. Which is good actually, because now he doesn't need to."

"That's good. I worry about her." I did. She wasn't fragile, not like I had been at that age. But she had been disappointed so many times by people who should know better, her life's foundation quicksand. She wasn't good at putting down roots, or sticking to one thing, instead flitting like a butterfly between activities and friends and loyalties. She cared about everyone, she cared about no one.

"So where are you from?" Michael asked Trent.

"Alaska. You?"

"Seattle, like Laney."

Rhonda had arrived with the beers and two glasses and she paused in setting them down. "I thought your name was Laura."

And so the house of cards started to shake. "It is," I said.

Michael looked at me, his mouth open in astonishment. His eyes shifted to Trent, as if seeing him for the first time. "What kind of injuries did you say she had?"

"Sprained ankle, some lacerations. Mild concussion. A little exposure."

He nodded, slowly. He reached across the table, touched my hand. "Are you okay? I know things have been hard lately and now all this… are you holding up okay?"

"Yes." I was, and I resented the question, the sympathy I saw in his eyes, because it was dangerously close to pity. I wanted to flick his hand off of mine. It felt cold and heavy and damp, the touch of someone who knows what is best for me, who thinks I need advice. But I didn't. "I have to say that this has actually been good for me. I've had time to reflect on my life."

Could I sound any more ridiculous? Any more trite? This had been more than zen-like reflecting. What had happened had been empowering and life-changing.

"That's good. I'm impressed with how well you're handling this. But you've always been a survivor."

I suppose he was right. I had. If hiding in the dark corners of my life was survival. "Thanks. That means a lot to me."

He squeezed my fingers again before releasing them. "You have a great heart, Laney."

There it was again. He was being so caring that it confused me. Made me believe maybe he had wanted our relationship as much as I had. The thought warmed me. Pleased me.

"I'm going to go wash my hands, excuse me." He stood up and went to the restroom.

I watched him go, taking in his confident walk. He was a good man, Michael. Truly.

"Just friends?" he asked. "I thought you told me you were just friends."

"We are." That wasn't the whole truth though and he clearly knew it.

"I don't give a shit if you rubbed your knees raw sucking him off for seventy-two hours straight, just don't lie to me. Ever."

"I'm not lying." His tone should have frightened me, but I enjoyed the jealous undertone. It made me shift on my chair. "We've never had sex, real or virtual."

"Do you want to?"

I thought about that. I remembered the feel of his hand on mine. "No. I don't."

"He's going to assume that you'll leave with him. You know that, right?"

"Yes." What I didn't know was the stranger's feelings on that. He didn't look like he gave a shit whether I did leave or I didn't.

"What do you think I should do?"

That was a pathetic sort of request for affection. I despised myself for saying it.

"I think you should go to Ft. Yukon with Michael and convince him that neither one of you belongs in the bush. You should move to Fairbanks, to a nice suburban split level and you should have nice sex and push out nice pale babies and have a nice life."

"That's really what you think?" I asked, angry. He couldn't possibly see that as my future. He was just mocking me, his pale blue eyes hypnotic.

"Yes, that's what I really think." He reached out and slid his finger lightly up and down the length of my forearm. "But before you go I'm going to carve my name in your skin so you never forget where you truly belong."

I shivered. "You could just take me right now while he's in the restroom. Kidnap me and take me back to the cabin." That's what I wanted him to do.

"I don't think so. That's too easy. You have a choice, Laney, and I want you to make it. Not me. I know you can be obedient, but I also know you can think for yourself." He didn't need to lean closer for me to feel his presence. I already felt invaded by him, in every sense of the word. "You can do anything you set your mind to. I believe that."

He believed it more than I did. I sat there, troubled, uncertain as Michael returned and ate his food and made small talk. He talked about the salmon run and dog teams and the price of fuel in Ft. Yukon. They sounded so normal. But nothing was normal.

"So how do you feel about heading back with me?" Michael asked softly at one point. "I feel like I should take you to Fairbanks, have a doctor check you out."

The thought nauseated me. My pasta sat heavy and hard in my gut. "I don't think I need a doctor."

"Why don't you come back to the cabin with us, spend the night?" Trent said. "Laney can get her stuff and then tomorrow you can leave at first light. The days are getting short. We should be heading back soon today."

I wasn't sure what stuff he was referring to as mine. The only thing I owned was my cell phone in my pocket. Everything else was his, including the panties and razors and toothbrush he had bought me in the grocery bags at his feet.

"I would like the chance to say goodbye to Laney," he added. "She's been good company."

There was a world of innuendo in that sentence and Michael was smart enough to pick up on it. "Right. Of course. I don't want to just yank you out of a safe place, Laney. Does that sound good to you, leave tomorrow?"

"Yes," I said, because I was hurt that he didn't say he wanted me to stay. That he merely wanted a chance to say goodbye. Him. Not Michael. Him. My everything. Yet he was going to let me go without any sort of protest or fight.

No one ever stopped me when I left.

Was it wrong to want someone to stop me when I tried to leave?

I would have rather had him yank me by the arm, throw me over his shoulder, and haul me off.

Then, at least, I would know he wanted me.

———————•◆•———————

He picked up the tab for Michael's lunch along with ours and gave Michael instructions to follow us. For a minute, I wondered if he planned to lead Michael into danger. Like over a soft spot on the river or off trail where he might hit a tree. But that was ridiculous. I was paranoid.

I smiled and went along with the plan because I wasn't sure what else to do. Seattle felt so far away. We rode back to the cabin, me aware of Michael's eyes on my back, my arms uncomfortably wrapped around the stranger. He wasn't Trent. I couldn't think of him as Trent any more.

Though he was as rotten as Trent, betraying me. Turning me over.

I had loved him. *Loved* him. And he was letting me leave with Michael. It made my chest tighten and my eyes sting. I wanted to be thrilled at the prospect that Michael cared about me, but it fell flat. There was no excitement there. He was a good, kind man, but he wasn't right for me. I wasn't suited for the life the stranger had outlined for me. The suburbs, the babies, the minivan and the PTA and the handsome, ordinary husband in golf shirts and khakis. That was for women who hadn't been abandoned by their mothers.

Who hadn't had sex with their stepfathers.

Not for women like me.

That night, back at the cabin, with the moon high and the stove piled with logs, Michael produced cigars from his pocket and invited the stranger out onto the front porch to smoke them. It didn't take a genius to figure out they would be talking about me, so I sat on the floor by the door and listened. I didn't even have to press my ear to wood. The sound carried easily.

"What has Laney told you about herself?" Michael asked.

I heard the flick of a lighter.

"Nothing." His voice was further away, muffled, like he'd moved down the porch.

"She's had a hard life, you know. Her mother was a mess. Running around, doing drugs, leaving Laney alone."

It was so strange to hear my past spoken about out loud. So casually, really. I squeezed my nails into my thighs, through the cotton of my sweat pants.

"She's a very sweet girl. Too sweet. She's been... taken advantage of more than once. Most notably by her stepfather."

Is that what Michael thought? Funny then, that he'd called Dean to tell him I was missing. Such a polite phrasing too, taken advantage of, as if he had been present at the time he would have stopped it. Oh, the beautiful patriarchy of men thinking they knew what was best for me. For the first time it occurred to me

Dean had kept his mouth shut about what had happened between us not to protect me, but to protect himself. What a weak man he would seem to be if he admitted that I had seduced him, in all my virginal guile, at the age of sixteen. If he told people how I had crept into his room and climbed onto his bed, and stroked him in his sleep until he was hard as a rock. And that how once he had woken up, he had all of two seconds of hesitation and one brief, spineless protest before he rolled me on my back and broke my hymen.

I had never regretted that night, or the many nights that came after it. I loved my stepfather. I still loved my stepfather, or I had until he had betrayed me with that email from prison where he admitted he'd been one of those men who had hooked one of those pathetic women who write to prisoners. Such a cliché.

I've met someone.

As if that changed everything. As if I was supposed to forget and move on.

I tried that once, when Dean had first gone to prison for statutory rape, and look at how that had turned out. Trent and the restraining order. So much legal mess in my family. We were the law firm's wet dream.

"Laney is sweet but she'd also tough," my stranger said. "Though I'm not sure why you're sharing this with me."

Good question.

"Did you sleep with her?"

"Yes. Every night. There's only one bed."

Michael made an impatient sound. "You know what I mean. Sex. I'm assuming you had sex with her, but you have to understand, Laney attaches. She fixates on men."

"Why are you telling me this? She's going back with you. If anything, I should be asking you what exactly you plan to do with her."

"I'm going to do the right thing. I'm going to take her back to her family."

"To the family that took advantage of her? Why would you

do that?"

Good point. I did love that blunt honesty the stranger had.

"Because she's unstable. And she has a daughter who should be her focus, not me. Or any other man."

My nose itched. I scratched it. He was sounding an awful lot like a fucking shrink. He didn't know jack shit about Victoria and what she needed. I did. What she needed was for everyone to keep their big fat ugly mouths shut about where she came from and let her live her happy little ignorant life with Grandma Jean. It was the least I could do for her. I'd given her up so she would have that safety, that freedom from people's opinions, that stain of scandal.

It was my gift to her.

My own personal heartbreak. So if I attached to men, excuse the fuck out of me, because I had a hole in my heart from where my child had been ripped away from me, for her own good.

"I didn't know she had a daughter."

Nor should Michael. It was a secret, allegedly. So who had told him? My mother, most likely. She couldn't keep a secret to save her life. But when would she have talked to Michael? Or maybe Michael was just smart enough to put it together. It wasn't a secret why Dean was in prison, just that Victoria came from my uterus, so maybe he was just guessing.

"Does that change anything?"

"No. I want the best for Laney."

"She doesn't have custody of her. She was only seventeen when she was born."

"Why are you telling me this? I think this is Laney's story to share, not yours."

Thank you.

"I just wanted you to know that if she tries to talk you in to letting her stay, you can't let her. She needs to go back with me, but she's probably attached to you. This was a traumatic experience."

Of sorts.

The floorboards creaked. "Thanks for the warning." He yanked the door open suddenly, just a crack.

I knew he was going to. I could sense his movement, feel him shifting toward me. But I didn't hide or scramble away. I wanted him to see that I knew. That I knew he knew. He obviously wanted me to know he knew as well because he locked eyes with me and gave me a brief smile. The door shut again.

"Wait, was she listening?" Michael asked.

"No."

"Okay, good."

"So what are you going to do with her?" the stranger asked.

"I'm going to marry her. Once she feels secure, she'll be a great wife. She's a sweet woman."

Well, that was unexpected. Michael thought I was a victim, clearly. He wanted to save me. What a do-gooder. But I had to admit, I was flattered. Even a little bit charmed, though he was something of a prick to be spilling my dirty laundry out of the basket for the stranger to see.

"Are you engaged?"

"Not yet."

My scab was tugging again so I reached into my sweat pants and yanked it off, pressing my finger down to stem the bleeding.

Then I stood up and went over to the bed, no longer interested in their conversation. I'd heard all I needed to. I picked up the mystery novel off the nightstand and started to read it. I actually made it through two chapters, getting engrossed in the story, when they came back in the house. I ignored them.

"You can share the bed with Laney," the stranger said to Michael.

My nose twitched again. I didn't want that. I wanted one last night close to him before I left. Because clearly I had to leave. Michael wanted me and the stranger did not. It didn't seem to matter that here, I had figured out who and what I was. That I had found a place. No, they together had decided that I was going to have to return to the confines of my life in Seattle, my boring, passive, ordinary life where I went through every day pretending I was just another twenty-something trying to find herself.

"You sure, man? I don't want to kick you out of your own bed."

"It's just one night." He sat down and pulled off his boots.

Annoyed, I just set my book down and flicked off the lamp on the end table. The kitchen light was still on, but I resolutely closed my eyes. After a minute I felt Michael's weight climb onto the bed. It was a violation, having him there, in the bed I shared with the stranger. Michael's scent was like cologne and peaches. It should have been pleasant, and under other circumstances I would have welcomed his embrace, opened myself for him to pump away for a few minutes. But not here. Not in this bed.

By sheer force of will, I didn't scream when he brushed my hair off my face. "It's going to be okay. I promise. I'll take care of you."

"Okay," I said, because if the stranger didn't want me, then Michael was a reasonable alternative. It didn't matter that my heart felt like it was shattering into a thousand tiny pieces. It didn't matter that I had worn his blood on my skin, that I had been strung up for him, that I had bared my body and soul for him to see. That the intensity of our love at times felt so sharp it was like he could flay the flesh from my bones with one look.

No one seemed to care that despite what Michael said about my attaching, which was true and I could own it, I didn't fall in love easily. But I had. I had fallen in love with the stranger and taking me from him was not going to 'be okay.' I had looked in his eyes and seen my own reflected back and that was special. That fucking mattered.

But I would go back to Seattle and I would marry Michael and I would have more children, and someday I would see the stranger again. I would return back to this cabin when I was old and a widow and find him here, grizzled and hunched and rougher than he was today and I would stay.

Because once taken, you can't be given back. You can never

fully go back.

So while my body would be in Seattle, the rest of me, the messy insides, would be here.

"Thank you," I said.

"You're welcome." Michael shifted away and fell asleep promptly. I heard him snoring in the dark.

The light went out but I didn't hear him lie down on the floor on his sleeping bag. He stayed in the chair and I stayed awake, listening to him sit.

Then, in a tone so low I thought maybe I had imagined it, "Laney."

"Yes?" I whispered, well aware of Michael's snoring next to me.

"Come here."

I climbed out of bed and went to him. He pulled me onto his lap, yanking my pants down simultaneously. I felt the nudge of his erection and I gripped his shoulders so he could guide me down onto him. I gave an involuntary gasp and his hand clamped over my mouth.

"Shh. Let's not wake our houseguest. Your rescuer."

"You're my rescuer," I said through his fingers.

The corner of his mouth turned up. "And you're mine."

Before I could ask what that meant, he thrust up into me, gripping me hard at the waist. I threw my head back and closed my eyes, wanting to feel. I couldn't see his eyes well in the dark, so I just embraced the shadows, and let go. I already knew every line of his face, every curve of his scar, every nuance and subtle detail of the landscape that made him who he was. Briefly, I brought my head down, so I could take in his scent, fill my nostrils with musk and sulfur and cool air, and erase Michael from my nose.

With my mouth buried in his hair, I took the opportunity to whisper, "I love you."

For a second I didn't think he was going to answer. But then he said gruffly, "I love you too."

"Do you?" I asked, intently. I tried to see into his eyes but it was too dark.

He buried his hand into my hair and pulled my head back. "Don't ever doubt it. You're my perfect fit. If a man like me could be happy, I've come the closest to it with you."

I waited for him to bite me or yank my hair hard or squeeze my nipple. But he just buried his nose in my neck and kissed me softly. "I do love you, with all the corners of my very black heart, I absolutely love you."

I wanted to cry.

"You can come now," he said.

I could come. And then I would go.

I did, with tears in my eyes.

CHAPTER SEVENTEEN

MICHAEL WAS IN A GOOD mood. He woke me up with a gentle shake and a kiss on the back of my head. I would have expected to wake up disoriented, jerking when he touched me. But I had barely slept, hovering always on the edge of full consciousness, and there was no question about where I was or who I was with the second my eyes opened.

Before I even acknowledged him, I sought out the stranger. But he wasn't in the cabin. Most likely he was outside gathering wood. It was dark out still, but the days were getting shorter and I didn't have a good sense of time in Alaska. The lack of light messed with my sense of time. Since I was alone with Michael, I figured it was a good opportunity to question him.

"Are you really going back to Seattle with me?"

"Yes." He was a very cute man, and post-sleep he was all smiles and floppy hair.

I felt guilty for involving him. For contacting him and dragging him into my life when I found out that Dean had abandoned me and I had needed a focus, a little bit of hope. Someone to love me.

CRASH

"Why? I'm not your problem, Michael." I was no one's problem. Just my own.

"It's not a problem. I want to do this."

I didn't get it. But then again, I remembered Michael taking rocks and using them on the playground to encircle a bunch of worms after a storm so no one would step on them and squish them. I had helped him, but only because I wanted Michael to like me. Not because I particularly cared about the worms and their slimy tubular bodies.

I wondered if Michael knew all my secrets. Or if he would feel the same way if he did.

"I'm not sure I want to leave Alaska," I said. But my voice sounded tentative, questioning, without my meaning it to.

It was enough doubt to have him firm in his conviction.

"Laney. You know you don't belong here. We only talked about this as a vacation, not a permanent move. You belong back home. Now don't argue with me." He smiled and touched the tip of my nose. "Though you look cute when you're pouting."

Cute, cute, cute. So cute. That was me, according to everyone.

Everyone but me. And him. The stranger.

"I'm going to use the outhouse," I said, because his expression made me uneasy. I knew that a man like Michael would take care of me. It was probably ultimately what I needed, if I had any common sense.

But Michael couldn't make me feel alive. He couldn't make me feel consumed, make me feel like I was the center of his universe, the blood that flowed hot through his veins. Outside, I found the stranger feeding the dogs. I was wearing panties for the first time in weeks, a protective layer between me and Michael in bed and I didn't like it. They were constricting as I walked.

"I don't want to go back with him," I said, not bothering with a greeting.

"You should." He poured slop into the dogs' bowls. "I kept you here against your will, remember. You should go back and you should tell the police and you should have me arrested for kidnapping."

"Is that what you want?"

"It's the right thing. The moral thing."

He was confusing me. "Don't you want me to stay?"

"We already had this conversation. If you want to stay, then you stay, on your own. But it's not my job to get rid of Michael. It's your job. He's your boyfriend."

I frowned. "He's not my boyfriend."

The stranger didn't respond. He bent over and rubbed one of the dogs' flank and spoke soft words to her. Finally he looked up at me. "You know what to do."

Did I? Turning on my heel, I went to the outhouse, throat tight.

I did. I would leave with Michael. I would go back to my daughter, pretend to be her sister, like I always had. Like I was, in a way. I would help Grandma Jean as best I could and I would forgive Dean. If Michael wanted to marry me, I would.

So I smiled at him as he chattered on with me and the stranger, drinking coffee, catching me up on all the world news. I even laughed, even though it sounded hollow to me. In time, once I left, I would lose the sense of why it had mattered so much, of how beautiful and painful and arousing and intense it had been to be bound on that bed, gloriously naked. I would forget that with one look he could make me orgasm and that for the first time, I could be truly, wholly myself in someone's presence.

On the porch as we were leaving, I squinted against the snow glare. The sunlight was so precious it seemed such a shame that our eyes couldn't handle the intensity of it against the snow.

Turning, I took in the yard, the dogs, the woods, the outhouse, the woodpile, the axe, the cabin itself.

Him.

"Let's roll," Michael said cheerfully. "As soon as we get back to Rush, I'll let everyone know you're alive."

I was alive. Truly, madly alive. I froze on the porch. I looked to the stranger, then to Michael. "I don't want to go."

Michael frowned. "Laney, we talked about this. Now come on."

Everyone always thought they knew what was best for me. Michael didn't know me. He knew nothing. Less than nothing. "No. I'm staying."

Michael gripped my arm suddenly, without warning, and the look he gave me was firm. "If you don't go with me," he said, in a low voice, leaning in close, "I'm going to tell the authorities the truth."

"What truth is that, Michael?" There were so many truths.

"About you. The hospital."

That made me scoff. I didn't care about that. Well, I did. But it wasn't a threat.

"I see the bruises on you, the cuts. The look in your eye. I could tell them that. About him. About how Trent isn't his real name and that maybe something isn't right here and that maybe you shouldn't be given a choice to stay." Michael's voice was low. Soothing, some would say.

But my need to be soothed was long gone, left in that old apartment we lived in, before Dean.

Michael wanted to control me, to command me with a veneer of charm. The Nice Guy. I didn't want his coddling control, where he convinced me I was stupid, less than him. That I needed him to decide for me. That wasn't so very nice at all, was it? He wanted to take care of me under false pretense, which made him a liar.

"I'm not a victim," I said, because I wasn't. I was done being the victim, the girl people felt sorry for. I was a woman, and I wasn't going to let him put the stranger behind bars for keeping me when I wanted to be kept.

"Come on, sweetheart, let's go." Like he was coaxing a feral stray out from under the porch. He took my hand, tugged gently, and when I followed him, he let go. "I'm calling the police."

He pulled his cell phone out of his pocket. It wouldn't work, but it would in town, and then the beautiful crystal glass of my life here, with *him*, would shatter and there wouldn't be any way to glue the pieces back together.

Not only would it cut and slice me when it broke, it would fall through my fingers, tumbling down, disappearing into the earth, and I would never have it again. I would never have the electric thrill of being loved for me, and of loving the stranger.

I heard Dean's voice in my head.

Under the right circumstances, everyone is capable of murder.

As Michael turned his back to me, I picked up the axe, wrenching it from the wood.

It only took one swing. It connected with a hard, wet smack, blood arching up like confetti, Michael falling forward down the stairs.

I turned to the stranger. "I've gotten strong," I said. Because I had. And some secrets needed to be left alone, in the bush, where they'd been hidden.

"Good girl," he said, reaching his hand out to me, a smile teasing over his lips.

I took it, using my sleeve to wipe blood off of my face.

Because the greatest love stories don't end in marriage.

They end in death.

ABOUT THE AUTHOR

Drew Jordan has always liked the dark, mysterious, and sexy, and she wrote CRASH after a writer friend challenged her to "write without rules." She lives in Miami Beach, the opposite of snowy Alaska, a fact she is grateful for every day in January.

Connect with me online at
www.facebook.com/DrewJordanBooks
Sign up for my newsletter here: eepurl.com/bDQwcv
Email: authordrewjordan@gmail.com
www.drewjordanbooks.com

If you enjoyed reading CRASH, I would appreciate it if you would share that with others readers. Please recommend CRASH to friends, readers' discussion groups, and discussion boards, and let others know what you liked about the book by leaving reviews.

Want to read more about Laney and the stranger?
Watch for the sequel to CRASH in 2016!

Made in the USA
Middletown, DE
22 May 2020